Hard I...

Sabina never thought it would come to this. But her head had won the struggle with her heart. Common sense had triumphed over romantic scruples. She told Captain Ashton she would be his bride in order to inherit her fortune—in what, of course, would be a marriage in name only.

She was even willing to make a concession when he displayed reluctance to accept her proposition.

"If you worry about the appearance of such an unusual arrangement," she told him, "the house I will inherit is large. We will be able to live under the same roof."

"You may not have any pride," the infuriating captain responded, "but I do. I will not marry you unless it is a marriage of love."

He moved closer to her. She tried to back away, but his arms went around her and held her fast. "You remember love, don't you, Sabina? It tastes like this."

Captain Ashton had kissed her before through an act of deception. But he masked nothing now. . . .

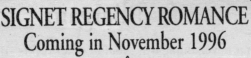

The Rival Earls

by

Elisabeth Kidd

A SIGNET BOOK

SIGNET
Published by the Penguin Group
Penguin Books USA Inc., 375 Hudson Street,
New York, New York 10014, U.S.A.
Penguin Books Ltd, 27 Wrights Lane,
London W8 5TZ, England
Penguin Books Australia Ltd, Ringwood,
Victoria, Australia
Penguin Books Canada Ltd, 10 Alcorn Avenue,
Toronto, Ontario, Canada M4V 3B2
Penguin Books (N.Z.) Ltd, 182–190 Wairau Road,
Auckland 10, New Zealand

Penguin Books Ltd, Registered Offices:
Harmondsworth, Middlesex, England

First published by Signet, an imprint of Dutton Signet,
a division of Penguin Books USA Inc.

First Printing, October, 1996
10 9 8 7 6 5 4 3 2 1

This book is dedicated to
the members of the
Connecticut Chapter of RWA
for generous support over many years.

Thanks, guys!

Chapter 1

Four tall, black-clad figures stood stiffly distant from one another in the library of Bromleigh Hall, exchanging inconsequential conversation in unnaturally hushed voices with a decided undertone of irritation. The three gentlemen and one lady were well enough acquainted, being siblings, to overcome any conversational restraints in ordinary situations, but this was not—as Henry Bromley reminded himself—an ordinary family gathering.

"I do not doubt," began his eldest brother, Fletcher, the new Earl Bromleigh, "that the sorrow of the occasion which calls us here today, an occasion which I suppose we must be thankful has been rare in the family since we were children . . . that is, I mean to say, let us not allow the strain to cause us to be less civil to one another than . . . er, ordinarily."

Fletcher, Henry reflected, had been something of a prig as a boy despite his brothers' efforts to pummel humility into him, and had grown increasingly pompous with age and the expectation of the position to which, at thirty-eight, he had at last succeeded. He stood now, rather like a marble statue of some Caesar, with one hand resting on a fragile-looking Sheraton table and the other on his waistcoat, looking the picture of dignity—and spoiling it the moment he opened his mouth.

"Don't be any more toplofty than you must, Fletcher," Randolph remarked, voicing Henry's thought in less discreet terms. "We know you too well."

The Honorable Randolph Reginald Bromley, the next in age to the earl, wore his habitual expression of detached, slightly sardonic amusement at the follies of the world in general and his own family in particular. Good-looking and dressed, even in mourning, with exquisite care, Randolph was presently in a testy mood that Henry suspected was due less to the lugubrious occasion than to his being obliged to go hatless and thereby expose the prematurely bare spot on the top of his head to people inclined to remark on such things merely to annoy him.

"And for heaven's sake, Sabina, do stop pacing and sit down so that we may do so as well."

And then there was the Lady Sabina. Only daughter of the late earl and the youngest of his five children, she had survived an undeniably trying childhood as both the bane and the delight of her four brothers' existence to grow into a stunning beauty with rich chestnut hair, large brown eyes, and a generous mouth now set in determined lines. Her expression was due, Henry supposed, to Fletcher's unthinking remark earlier that Sabina, freed from her father's restraining influence, would no doubt now be happy to set up house at Carling and have nothing further to do with the family she obviously considered an obstacle to her freedom to behave as notoriously as she pleased.

Since Henry knew this to be precisely what Sabina intended—although he also knew she did not wish to be rid of quite *all* her siblings—he was uncertain why she had taken offense at Fletcher's bringing it up, however untactfully. Not that she had said anything to that effect—she had, indeed, maintained an ominous silence—but Henry was certain now that Sabina had deliberately remained standing so that her brothers would be obliged to do the same. She pretended now not to have heard Randolph's impatient request and wordlessly picked up a Caithness glass paperweight. She smoothed her hand over it as if caressing a dear friend, and Henry remembered that it had been a gift to her from her father on his return from a journey to Scotland years before.

Doubtless only such reminiscences kept Sabina from taking her usual lead in keeping the conversation going, but she was thereby forcing the rest of them to maintain the civilities by themselves with considerably less skill. Sabina could be stubborn in the most awkward ways. Henry could only hope that Mr. Quigley, the representative of the family firm of solicitors, would arrive shortly so that they could all sit down to hear the will read.

"What in blazes can be keeping them?" Randolph asked querulously, again voicing Henry's thoughts. He extracted a cigar from the lacquered box on the table, looked at it, thought better of the idea, and put it away again. "Surely there can be no mystery about the disposition of the estate. Fletcher is Earl Bromleigh now, and given that he has been attending to Father's affairs for the last year, he must be well aware of how they stand at present."

"There is the small matter of Sabina's portion," the new Lord Bromleigh punctiliously pointed out.

"Bosh. We all know Sabina was Father's pet. She may as well have begun spending it weeks ago."

Sabina leveled a look as black as her bombazine mourning costume at her next-to-eldest brother. Although she and Randolph were separated by almost a dozen years in age, they were too much alike in temperament not to come to drawn daggers within ten minutes of entering the same room together.

"For a man so famed as you are for his polished address, Randolph, you can be quite astonishingly tactless," she said finally, drawing herself up to her full five feet, ten inches, which—Randolph being the shortest male in a family tending to resemble a miniature forest when all planted in the same ground—brought her fulminating gaze more nearly on a level with his light green eyes, which gleamed with amusement—or pique, only Sabina ever knew which. "I would not dream of speaking so disrespectfully to Papa's memory."

This platitude was so unlike Sabina's usual mode of expressing herself that Randolph gave a hoot of laughter and conceded the contest to her. Henry shot a concerned glance at his sister, but she had laid down the paperweight and turned her stiff back on Randolph and was now gazing with unconvincing intentness out the window at the leafy summer green of the home wood, so that he could not read what she was really thinking in her face.

Randolph, still chuckling, helped himself to a cigar after all. Fletcher clasped his hands together behind his back, sighed, and fixed his gaze on the pattern in the Axminster carpet at his feet. Henry shrugged and hoped that Sabina would confide in him, or in her sister-in-law, Dulcie, which would do as well, when she felt less emotionally volatile.

Sabina, unnoticed by her brothers, blinked her eyes rapidly to stop the tears that welled up only too readily of late. She was not ashamed of her tears, but long years of hiding her deepest emotions from the sometimes unthinking comments of her family prohibited her now from confiding in them as she would have liked to do—and indeed had done countless times over matters of less moment.

None of them knew how bitterly she had already wept over their father's death the week before. For however long the family had been expecting the event, Sabina had indeed been closer to the old earl than any of them, and she felt his death too deeply to confide her feelings to anyone—at least, not just yet, while the memories were so fresh.

It was her father who had held her close when she was a child and told her how beautiful she was after her brothers had teased her about her thin legs and coltish stride, despite her determination to run just as fast and play just as hard as any of them. Later, it was the old earl who, when Sabina's adolescent experiments at transforming herself into a demure schoolroom miss had ended in a brawl with Randolph on the nursery floor, had convinced her that it was her quick mind that mattered, not how quickly she filled it with French phrases and geometrical equations. And, still later, it was her dear papa who, when Sabina had turned down the season in London which her Aunt Sybil had declared was her only hope of finding a husband tall enough for her, had assured her that he was in no hurry to lose her to another man, however, tall, handsome, or eligible.

Sabina loved her brothers too, but they would never understand the special bond between their father and his youngest child and only daughter. She could never explain it, nor ever describe the special sense of loss she now felt, which was perhaps no less deep than theirs, but not the same. She would certainly never let Randolph, or even Henry, see tears in her eyes, however much provoked she might be. That pride, too, was ingrained in her too long ago.

Becoming aware of the continued silence behind her, Sabina unclenched the hands hidden in the folds of her black skirt and schooled her carriage to one of supreme dignity. She raised her head high, and when she turned around again, there was no lingering sign of redness in her eyes.

"Sabina has never shown any resemblance to either a spendthrift or a recluse," Henry observed mildly, "and I do not imagine she intends to change now."

Sabina smiled gratefully at him, and Henry winked back. Randolph made a sardonic noise in his throat, but Fletcher forestalled any response Sabina might have made to this provocation by remarking that they would none of them be uncomfortable and, in any case, Sabina's portion would doubtless be managed by the same firm of solicitors which had served the family for years.

It was, as usual, the wrong thing to say. "Are you insinuating that I cannot manage my own affairs, Fletcher?" Sabina said, turning on him.

"Eh? No, certainly not!" Fletcher hastened to assure her, uncertain how he had drawn her wrath.

Fortunately, the library door opened just then to admit Sabina's sisters-in-law, Alicia, Countess Bromleigh, and Dulcie, Henry's wife, who propelled her husband's twin, Lewis, in his wheeled chair. The end of this little procession was brought up by the solicitor, Mr. Quigley.

Lewis had been an invalid for the eight years since he fell into a nearby stretch of the Grand Union Canal and contracted a severe chill that left him with no feeling in his legs. He had come to accept his affliction stoically, if with growing signs of Randolph's mordant turn of humor, but thus far only his twin had been privy to any serious expression of it. Now Lewis glanced up from his chair at each of his siblings in turn, seeming to gather from that comprehensive glance an accurate impression of precisely what each of them was thinking.

Henry quirked one eyebrow questioningly at his twin when Lewis's gaze came around to him and received an answering grin which told him there was something afoot that would raise the kind of family dust-up that Lewis took perverse pleasure in observing, if not actually instigating.

Having retained much of his boyish lankiness, Lewis gave the impression of youthful sunniness of disposition and no great intellect, but although Fletcher, and even Randolph, did so, Henry knew better than to fall into the trap of believing either of these characteristics to be all there was to Lewis.

"I do apologize for having kept you all waiting," Alicia said, smiling graciously and drawing everyone's attention immediately to her.

Henry could not help reflecting that had Fletcher deliberately chosen Alicia as a bride with a view to her becoming a countess one day, he could not have done better for himself. Alicia was not only handsome—severe black became her and somehow brought out the full beauty of her dark eyes and hair, which was parted in the center and gathered in a coiled braid at the back of her head—but she was possessed of a great sense of what was due her position that did not prevent her from being well loved and respected on the estate and throughout the district.

"You are all acquainted with Mr. Quigley, I fancy," Alicia went on, indicating to the solicitor that he should come in and take the chair arranged for him at the massive oak desk at one end of the room. Alicia then deposited herself gracefully on the sofa, signaling the other ladies to join her. Dulcie did so, but Sabina sat down on the window seat instead and turned her face outward again. The gentlemen sank gratefully into the remaining chairs.

Dulcie, who had thus far said nothing, glanced toward her husband, who sent her the same questioning look he had to Lewis; Dulcie only shrugged her slim shoulders and turned her lovely blue eyes to the front of the room.

Mr. Quigley cleared his throat, rustled the sheaf of papers in front of him, and glanced up to see if he had everyone's attention. Sabina continued to stare silently out the window, but the others focused their attention on the solicitor.

Interest quickly waned, however, in the contents of the Last Will and Testament of George Fletcher Bromley, Fourth Earl Bromleigh, when after five minutes nothing more was revealed than what all the company already knew and which gained no further interest through being couched in dry legal phraseology.

Fletcher, still freshly conscious of the dignities conferred on him, stared straight ahead as if to demonstrate that such a great weight of responsibility neither awed nor unduly alarmed him, and he left it to his countess to make note of the disposition of the household linens, plate, pictures, and porcelain. Randolph stifled a yawn and shifted his attention to his sister-in-law Dulcie's profile, finding it infinitely more admirable than Mr. Quigley's.

Sabina looked uncomfortable to be indoors and draped in black on such a fine summer day, and Henry could almost see her mind take flight over the familiar fields and woods of her childhood home. He wondered for the first time if she would have preferred to remain there. Fletcher would, naturally, give her Carling, the one of their father's many residences of which she was most fond, but it would not be the same as living at home. Not that living at home would be the same now, but he could not think it right that his sister should live alone. Perhaps, Henry thought, he would suggest to Dulcie that they invite Sabina to move in with them.

Mr. Quigley thus arrived scarcely noticed in his dry, monotoned reading to the various small bequests to family friends and retainers, most of which were already known to the family, or at least not unexpected. When, however, the solicitor intoned the words, "to my gentle and much beloved daughter-in-law Dulcie Jerome Bromley, I leave the choice of any of the works in my personal library, and in especial of the first edition of the *Songs and Sonnets of John Donne,* which she alone of my children has read and appreciated," Henry smiled at his wife in recognition of this particularly appropriate bequest.

Dulcie looked straight ahead and did not meet her husband's eyes. Henry knew that she had been a witness to the signing of the will and thus privy to its contents, but it was a moment before the significance of the bequest was suddenly borne in on him. That particular first edition had been purchased at auction by Henry's grandfather at a cost beyond its worth—but beyond, too, what Lord Kimborough had been willing to pay for it. It had been another minor victory for the Bromleys in the continuing war between the "rival earls" of Bromleigh and Kimborough.

No one now remembered precisely how the quarrel between the two neighboring families had begun, save that both earldoms had been created at the same time during the reign of Queen Anne and that the properties involved included a strip of land along the Avon River which, through a slip of the pen on the part of the royal stationer, appeared to have been granted to both parties. The dispute over the land had continued for a generation, until that stationer's exasperated successor in the reign of George I settled the matter by the toss of a coin in the Bromleys' favor.

The Ashtons had refused to accept the settlement and continued to use the land as a right of way; the Bromleys, affronted at this "trespass," refused to negotiate a compromise, and ever since both families had perpetuated The Quarrel, as it came to be thought of, by minor skirmishing in the form of accusing a member of the rival family of cheating at cards, stealing cattle, and the like.

The most recent aggravation of The Quarrel had occurred, unwittingly this time on both sides, when Dulcie Jerome became engaged to Richard, Viscount Ashton, heir to the fifth Earl of Kimborough. Shortly after, however, Dulcie had—by sheer accident, to be sure—made the acquaintance of the Honorable Henry Bromley at a village fete, fallen instantly in love, and eloped with him.

Richard, although initially lukewarm to his prospective bride, now became incensed, accused Henry of "stealing" her, and would have challenged him to a duel had not his father forbade the meeting on the sensible grounds that Henry was much the better shot. Henry's own father had attempted to use the occasion to mend the ancient quarrel, but Lord Kimborough, considering that he had done all that anyone might expect of him in speaking so to his heir, drew the line at speaking at all to his neighbor.

Now, Henry reflected with a full sense of the irony of the situation, his ever-unpredictable father seemed to be making a last attempt at peacemaking. He turned his attention eagerly back to the reading.

". . . and to my friend and neighbor, Simon Ogilvey, I bequeath that piece of land which marches with his between Michael's Bridge and his south orchard, the separate deed to which is to be handed over to him in trust to his heirs in perpetuity."

Now everyone's attention was caught, for no one could have missed the significance of that particular piece of land—the very one in dispute more than a century ago, which had given rise to The Quarrel. To give it over in such a way to a neutral party must leave no one in doubt of the late earl's desire for reconciliation with his neighbors.

Sabina's wandering wits came back from the bright, sunny world outside into the funereal atmosphere of the library, which seemed now even more oppressive with portents of greater revelations to come. She sat up, clutching her hands together in her lap and staring intently at Mr. Quigley. Her lovely mouth and dark eyes seemed to stand out even more against her pale face, and Henry was struck for the first time with the realization that his tomboy sister had disappeared forever. Since Sabina was now four-and-twenty, this should not have been such a shock as it was, but Henry had loved the scamp Sabina had been as a girl enough to continue to think affectionately of her in that way long past her girlhood.

To be sure, she had taken on a greater responsibility when her mother died and left the management of the household to Sabina at the tender age of fifteen. And she must have grown up forcibly when Peter Ogilvey was killed not six months before they were to be married. But Henry had been off on a protracted honeymoon at the time and, even had he been able to hurry back from Jamaica to comfort her, Dulcie had pointed out, their own happiness might only have served to deepen his sister's misery. And so he had not been there, and when they met again, Sabina had seemed fully recovered from her loss and once again the merry companion he had always found her. Peter's death must have had some effect on her, but these things crept up on one so subtly, how was one to know when youth and innocence had gone forever?

". . . from the income from my estates at Redmond and Killingborough . . . ," Mr. Quigley was saying now in a higher, clearer voice, as if he expected to be interrupted at any moment, ". . . in trust for my daughter Sabina Marie and, in the event of her marriage . . ."

Henry scowled. What was this? He glanced at Sabina, who seemed to be equally in the dark but expecting the worst. Could their father really be cutting his most loved child, his "pet," as Randolph had called her in full truth, off with the most niggardly of small allowances if she did not marry? Even if she married, it seemed, she would have no more than a competence!

But Mr. Quigley was not finished yet.

"In the event of Sabina Marie's marriage to the Honorable Robert James Owen Ashton, Captain in the 1st Regiment of Dragoons, I leave her the income from the above-named estates unconditionally, and in addition a one-half part of the income from my estate at Carling and the use of the house and grounds there to her and the issue of said marriage, if any."

Mr. Quigley took a deep breath and looked cautiously around him for some reaction to this final revelation. For a full minute there was none, until Randolph remarked, with unwarranted composure, "He must have been delirious."

Sabina remained seated, her face paler still with that look of shock and her hands clenched so tightly together that the knuckles showed white. Henry stood up and snatched the will from under the solicitor's hand to read the incredible passage for himself.

"This can't be," he muttered, even as he read the words that told him it could be.

Everyone but Sabina seemed to find their voices just then and broke into a low but intent exchange of speculation, which Mr. Quigley and the new Lord Bromleigh together tried in vain to stem.

"Did you know about this, Fletcher?" Randolph accused his elder brother.

Dulcie moved to read over her husband's shoulder. Alicia remained placidly seated beside Lewis, who grinned impishly up at the rest of them.

"He always said he wanted to mend the quarrel . . ." Sabina said at last, in a voice that seemed to come from so far away as to be barely audible. Henry dropped the will and went to her as she rose from the window seat. Yet when he put his hands on her arms, she appeared not to notice, but moved with deliberate steps toward the desk, where she looked first at Fletcher, then at the solicitor.

For a moment, Henry had a clear look at his sister's eyes, and he remembered then that the only difference Sabina had ever had with her father had been over The Quarrel. She had believed passionately that the Bromleys had always been in the right of it, and it had offended her sense of family honor even to hear her father consider making overtures of peace to the Ashtons. It must be doubly a shock, Henry thought, for her to hear now that not only had her father not taken her views into consideration, but that she was his chosen instrument of reconciliation. What could the earl have been thinking?

The buzz of speculation concentrated itself now on

Sabina. They all moved closer to her, as if encircling her with their concern. Sabina's gaze darted from one to the other, then around the room, like an animal when it senses a trap. Suddenly, she gave a strangled cry and, pushing her way between Henry and Dulcie, pulled open the library door—revealing a much astonished footman on the other side—and ran out, leaving the door flung open behind her.

"Sabina, wait!" Henry called, running after her.

"Sabina!" Dulcie joined in. "Come back!"

But Sabina had fled.

Chapter 2

Captain the Honorable Robert James Owen Ashton stood up to the tops of his elegant boots in mud. Bill Theak, the captain's former batman and now the keeper of a lock on the Grand Union Canal just south of the Welford Arm, admired the captain's willingness to help with some necessary repairs to the lock—even at the expense of Lobb of London's best. What was more, the captain's assistance, while it had not initially been of much value, had rapidly succumbed to experience.

Then again, he had always been like that. If something needed to be done, he did it. If the something required knowledge he did not have, he acquired it, and if in addition the job was a particularly difficult one, he simply applied more determination. That was how the captain had got himself among the leaders in the Union Brigade's memorable charge at Waterloo, and it was how he met the challenge of lock engineering.

"I think it will hold now, Bill," Ashton said, stepping back cautiously while keeping his hands on the wooden plank supporting the newly re-bricked section of lock wall. He glanced at Bill and grinned at the dubious expression on the grizzled veteran's open countenance.

"Credit me with not repeating my mistakes, Sergeant!" he said. "I know this is the very section on which I did such an abysmal job of repair last week, but I assure you I've done it properly this time!"

Theak considered this for a moment, then gingerly let go of the plank, stepping back quickly into the mud at the bottom of the lock, as if in expectation of the wall falling in on him again.

But this time it held. Captain Ashton gazed at it with a satisfied expression for a moment before suggesting that they climb out to inspect the section of bank which had washed away in the overnight rain and had been the original cause of the breach in the wall.

"I need no further proofs of your steadfastness in the face of danger, Sergeant," Ashton said as he clambered clumsily but efficiently up the bank, "and it lies beyond the call of your duty to me to stand there awaiting disaster."

"Aye, sir." Theak relaxed a little but wasted no time in climbing out of the lock behind his captain, whose fine boots were now thoroughly ruined, to stand beside Ashton on the sunny towpath to admire their work.

It was not that the Honorable Robert Ashton habitually dressed in his newest superfine coat, silk waistcoat, fawn breeches, and top boots to perform manual labor. He had in fact been on his way to pay a social call, but had stopped by the lock to see if the repairs he and Bill had thought completed the day before had proved satisfactorily so. Like any other lockkeeper, Bill was anxious not to cause any lengthier a stoppage of traffic on the canal than necessary while he made repairs to the lock to which he had returned as keeper only months before.

In the interim—consisting of his six years of service in the Peninsula, for a good part of it as Captain Ashton's batman—the lock had been left to the care of Bill's aging father, whose intentions were superior to his physical robustness. The result was that Bill had been able to do little else since his return but repairs, from rebuilding and rehanging the lock gates to dredging the canal on either side to free it of debris—not to mention renovating the lockkeeper's house, into which Bill was eager to move his parents so that they would be more comfortable than on their cramped narrowboat.

It was when the captain paid a call a forthnight earlier to inquire after his sergeant's well-being that he had insisted on giving him a hand with the work.

"I swear to you, Bill"—Ashton had insisted when Theak was inclined to refuse his assistance—"I am finding the utmost difficulty in sinking back into the role of a gentleman of leisure—if, indeed, I ever filled such a role, for I find it impossible to recall ever having done so! A spell of hard physical labor will do me the world of good."

And so, Robert had reported for duty every morning, wearing a pair of Bill's old boots and a rough shirt, breeches, and stockings laundered daily by Bill's obliging mother, Rose. He joined with a good will in the work of restoring the neglected lock, with the result that it was ready to open again a week earlier than anticipated— even given minor setbacks such as this unexpected break at the captain's end of the brick wall that supported the sides of the lock.

When Bill attempted to thank him, Ashton made light of his usefulness. "Whatever help I can give is for your dad, Sergeant. He's a fine old gentleman and deserves to have a rest from his labor in his old age."

Bill was not about to dispute this statement and thus made no further attempt to voice his gratitude, particularly since he felt no small sense of guilt himself for staying away from his aging parent for so long. He was glad now to have a chance to make amends and less reluctant than he indicated to have the help of his captain.

What Captain Ashton did not tell his former sergeant was that, even more than his return to a leisured life, he was finding the resumption of his place in his family unusually difficult. Indeed, he felt distinctly out of place at Ashtonbury Abbey, the family home now presided over by Robert's increasingly stately brother Richard, Earl of Kimborough, and his high-minded sister-in-law, Lavinia. Hedged about as he was there by the proprieties that Lavinia insisted on and the rank that Richard still considered, five years after succeeding his father, to have raised him above even a congenial rubber of loo among themselves, Robert soon began casting about for a way to remove himself from this stifling atmosphere as diplomatically—but quickly—as possible.

He supposed he had never felt completely at home at the Abbey since Richard married, or he would not have gone into the army at the age of twenty, his younger-son status notwithstanding. But Robert's imposing height—six feet, three inches in his stockinged feet—and broad-shouldered strength made him a perfect candidate for the Royals, and his open, generous nature combined with a decisive will had made him both well-liked and instantly respected by the men who came under his command. He took to army life as a duck to a pond and plunged into the life with a zest he had not felt about anything else he had done.

At the end of the long campaign in Spain, he had been promoted major, but he preferred to continue wearing the rank he had gone through the war with, which unintentional modesty had contributed to his being much in demand as a staff officer in the Waterloo campaign, an honor that he had declined in favor of active service. He had thus emerged from the campaign with an enhanced reputation—but with a wounded left leg as well, which still gave him a stiff gait and ached in wet weather.

He supposed it was his own fault that he felt himself out of place in his boyhood home—he had, after all, been literally out of the place far longer than strictly necessary. He had therefore determined to give himself enough time to readjust before making any irrevocable move out of it again. But like many another war veteran, he was coming to the realization that his life could never be just as it was before, because he himself was not just as he was before.

"You should marry and set up your nursery," Lavinia had advised him in the forthright way she had of handing out counsel to other people. "You could have any local girl you liked for the asking, and I'm sure that even your leg would be no handicap were you to spend the season in London. Even the more sophisticated girls would be delighted to be seen sitting out a dance with you at Almack's."

Robert groaned at the thought of dancing attendance, figuratively or otherwise, on some empty-headed chit who only came up to his elbow. No, he informed Lavinia, he most definitely would not go to London. But it was considerably more difficult to explain why he would not heed his sister-in-law's alternative advice to "at least attend a few of the local assemblies, Robin dear, even if you do not care to appear to be casting about for a bride. The neighborhood families will be glad to see you again, for whatever reason—indeed, it is your duty to show them that courtesy."

It was when Lavinia began preaching duty that Robert ceased to listen. Since Richard and Lavinia were the proud parents of two vigorous sons, Robert failed to see that any more could be expected of him than the considerable service he had already given his country. He would like, he thought, to be married, but he recognized no duty to take a wife merely in anticipation of the unlikely event that the entire Ashton dynasty save his hypothetical offspring might be wiped out by fire, flood, or a return of the plague. He could afford to marry to suit himself.

But that was where the real difficulty lay. Another of Captain the Honorable Robert Ashton's virtues which had endeared him to his army comrades was his unswerving loyalty. But in civilian life, this virtue was proving more a liability than an asset, for Robert had unexpectedly, on his first leave home, fallen in love, and the seven years since that astonishing event had not been long enough to shake him in his loyalty to that first and—as it subsequently proved to be—impossible love. He was much afraid that it would take another seven years to find a woman who would be able to push to the back of his mind the memory of Sabina Bromley.

He had been aware since his boyhood of the century-old quarrel between the rival earls, at that time represented by his and Richard's father on the one side and the aging Earl Bromleigh on the other, but because Robert had more than enough boyhood playmates who met with his father's approval, he had never felt any necessity, or even curiosity, to cultivate the acquaintance of any of the Bromley children. Indeed, since The Quarrel did not affect him personally, he was barely aware of the rival family's existence.

That, however, was before he came upon Sabina Bromley one day at the edge of the canal. He had been out driv-

ing his new curricle—a birthday gift from his father—
when her unoccupied horse had drawn his attention. He
stopped, further arrested by the sight of an abandoned
bonnet lying by the road and, when he had dismounted, by
Sabina herself leaning over the edge of the canal. Her
thick chestnut hair tangled, her skirts stained with grass
and mud, and her bodice wet enough to reveal the youthful but already fully developed shape beneath the cloth,
she seemed oblivious to his presence.

Robert had stared at her, rapt with admiration, for several
minutes before he realized that she was attempting to drag
some heavy object up the bank.

She caught sight of him at the same moment and called
out in tones quite unsuited to the Fair Maid of Astolat, to
whom Robert had fancifully detected a resemblance in her,
"Don't just stand there, you great dolt! Help me!"

Robert grinned, thinking *So much for the swooning
Elaine!*, but then removed his coat and scrambled down the
bank to discover, first, that there were tears of frustration in
the young lady's beautiful brown eyes and, only secondly,
that the heavy object she was clutching by the lapels was a
man's body. Snapping abruptly out of his trance, Robert
gently removed her hands, picked the body up easily in his
own arms, and started back up the bank with it, followed
anxiously by the bedraggled beauty.

"Who is he?" he said as he laid the body in his curricle,
disregarding the effect of canal water on the fine new
leather seat.

"My brother," she said, biting back a sob as she reached
out to smooth a wet strand of hair off the pale face of a
young man perhaps ten years older than herself. Then she
straightened her spine and looked up at Robert. "I beg your
pardon—my name is Sabina Bromley. This is my brother
Lewis."

Robert was arrested in the act of unfastening his horses'
reins and stared at her again. So these were the despised
Bromleys! They did not appear particularly vicious at the
moment; indeed, he thought he had never seen a girl so un-

self-consciously miserable. He almost wished he could get rid of Lewis and comfort her instead.

"What happened to him?" he said.

"I don't precisely know. He must have fallen into the canal somehow. His horse came home without him, so I came out looking for him and found him lying by the bank. He's not—he isn't drowned, is he?"

Lewis's body had been heavy with water and loss of consciousness, but Robert had felt unmistakable signs of life as he carried him and was able to reassure her. Even now, he pointed out, Lewis's shallow breathing had steadied somewhat.

"Nevertheless, we must get him home quickly! That is— please, sir, if you would be so kind."

"I think we should take him to Doctor Abbott, rather. He would have to be called in any case, and I expect your brother needs to be treated as quickly as possible."

"Oh, yes—yes, of course you're right," the lady said, wringing her hands in her damp skirts and continuing to stare at her brother, seeming to forget her rescuer, who thought it best not to draw attention to himself.

Robert had delivered both Bromleys to the doctor's surgery and left Sabina there, much against his inclination to wait for her and somehow prolong their acquaintance. But he had learned something of discretion as well as valor in his army service thus far, and so reluctantly decided to wait and chance another opportunity coming along to further his acquaintance with the beautiful Lady Sabina.

Lewis had contracted pneumonia as a result of his accident, and as a result of the illness was confined thereafter to a chair and unable to walk. Robert discovered all this only at secondhand, however, for he had not revealed his own name to Sabina and swore Doctor Abbott to secrecy. He did not really think that Sabina would be so unfair as to blame him for Lewis's affliction, but he did not want her to associate him forever after with that particular family tragedy.

However, his hesitation made it that much more difficult afterward to reintroduce himself to her. She had not, apparently, inquired about him following the incident, and he was forced to conclude that she was aware of his identity after all and did not wish to be obliged to him. He thus returned to his regiment before his leave was up, as much to remove himself from Sabina's neighborhood as from any eagerness to resume his career.

But although he had removed himself from her physically, he could not forget her. The more he thought about her, as he lay nights on the hard Spanish ground and stared up at the stars, the more absurd the business of The Quarrel seemed, so that when Robert came home again three years later, it was with the determination to mend the rift between his family and Sabina's—single-handedly if need be—purely so that he would be able to court her freely.

But the first news he heard on his return to Northampton was of Sabina's engagement to Peter Ogilvey. Peter had been one of Robert's closest friends when they were boys, although Peter had purchased his colors even before Robert and they had lost touch with each other over the course of the campaign. He was forced to meet Peter at home, of course, and to wish him happy, but nothing would now induce him to approach Sabina. Peter did introduce him to Sabina's father, however, and Robert was surprised to find the old earl gracious and willing, even eager, to resolve the quarrel between their families.

Before any further effort could be made to do so, however, both Peter and Robert were recalled to duty. Peter was subsequently killed at Vitoria, but by the time Robert returned home at the end of the Peninsular campaign, the old earl was on his deathbed. Robert went in secret to see him and was gratified to be remembered, but the earl was too weak to speak at any length, much less to venture onto sensitive subjects.

With the news of Bonaparte's escape from Elba, Robert joined his regiment in Belgium. When he finally returned home for good in the spring of 1816, the earl was dead and The Quarrel seemed no closer to being mended than ever. And Sabina seemed still further out of his reach.

It was when Captain Ashton was racking his brain for a

reason to call on his neighbors on a visit of condolence that he came upon Bill Theak and his lock and discovered that he could effectively vent his frustrations on what he would a year ago have described as "sapper's duty." He was aware that he was only postponing a necessary decision about his future, but with the resilience of youth and health, he was able to put off the future—at least for a little while.

His respite was to be shorter than even he anticipated, however. After he and Bill had declared the brick wall now sturdy enough to hold back any flood, and Rose had attempted with minimal success to make his visiting clothes respectable again, and Robert had assured her that his social call could be put off for another day, the Theaks and Captain Ashton found themselves enjoying a well-earned pint of home-brewed on the deck of the *Rose Franklin*, the narrow canal boat on which all three Theaks made their home.

Bill sat back against the wall of the sleeping cabin and lit his pipe, while his father, George Theak, a man of seventy-eight summers and frail health but robust mind, presided over the little party from a canvas hammock slung between one side of the boat and the other.

"Aye," said George, finishing his tale of how he had come to be on the canal and giving the wooden hull a satisfied slap, "this old boat was the best part of my Rose's dowry."

"Do you not be deceived, Captain Ashton," Rose told him, her thin cheeks blushing girlishly pink with the attention. "The *Rose Franklin*—it was my maiden name, you know—was all my poor dad could offer, but George said he would take me just the same."

"Nay, it was the boat I was after all along," George insisted. "I can tell you that," he added in a loud whisper to their guest, "now it's too late for Rose to find herself a richer man."

He reached out to pinch Rose's cheek, and the captain thought he could be satisfied himself with the few worldly goods the Theaks possessed, if the right woman came along with them—a woman he could count on still being there forty years on, as Rose Theak was with her George.

"Of course, until my boy here decides to find himself a bright girl and start raising his own family, I can't properly retire, so maybe I'll get rich."

"More likely that than I'll get married," Bill said, well used to his father's frequent less-than-subtle hints about his lack of a wife at nearly forty years of age.

Rose got up to refill Captain Ashton's glass of ale, then her husband's and son's. But Bill left his untouched as he cocked his head to one side, listening.

"What's that?" he said, his sharp sergeant's ears catching some distant sound. The captain smiled, knowing that since they had come home, he too had heard echoes of rolling cannon that turned into mundane farm carts and musket fire that was only the volleys of sportsmen in the wood.

But then Robert heard the sound too—hoofbeats, and pounding harder than they had a call to on this peaceful summer afternoon. Both men's heads turned as a rider appeared a little distance away, going *ventre à terre* along the bank.

"It's a woman," Rose observed. She rose onto her toes for a better look.

"She's riding too close to the bank," Bill said, scowling. "It's a sharp drop there—muddy, too."

Robert was on his feet then, propelled by an urgent sense of having lived this scene before. He leaped for the shore just as the oncoming horse, spooked by an unexpected branch over the path, made an abrupt swerve. The rider clutched at the reins, but the mare skidded on the muddy bank, and before she could right herself, her rider had lost her seat and was tumbling head over heels down the bank toward the canal.

Oh, God, no! Robert thought. *Not again—not her, too!*

Chapter 3

Sabina opened her eyes to morning sunlight filtered through brightly colored window curtains. It was several moments, however, before full consciousness returned and she was able to interpret the unfamiliar sensations that assailed her in gentle but insistent waves.

She lay still at first, gazing at the window and forcing her eyes to focus normally. The curtains were red, she was able to discern at last, a kind of orange-red baize, and covered two tiny, high windows. She began moving her eyes slowly from one side of the room to the other. Objects—a red-glassed lantern, a single brass candlestick, a pair of dusty leather cushions—seemed to stand out in sharp relief, as if her vision had somehow become more acute than it was normally. The ceiling was very low, and the room was very narrow; a multitude of miniature cabinets lining both walls hemmed it in still more. Her bed was narrow, too, and it seemed to sway, like a child's cradle.

Sabina closed her eyes again, and the swaying motion eased somewhat. Her head ached intolerably.

Sometime later—it must have been several hours, for the light had moved—she woke again, startled by some faint sound in an otherwise silent room. Somewhere outside, a thrush sang merrily, but that was not the sound she had heard. She moved her head a little and was grateful to find that it did not ache quite so much anymore.

It was then that she saw him. He was poised as if arrested in the act of soaking a sponge in the enamel basin that stood on the bedside table. One hand was wet; sunlight glinted on a signet ring on the other. It must have been the clink of the ring against the basin that she had heard.

But all this came to her only slowly, from somewhere to the side of her consciousness. Her gaze was fixed on his face, which was quite the handsomest she had ever seen. His skin was lightly browned by the sun, but not so much as to make him seem swarthy—indeed not so much as to hide a faint reddening of his cheeks under her scrutiny. His very fair hair, a little longer than was worn in fashionable circles, curled over the collar of his decidedly unfashionable nankeen shirt. His mouth was well-shaped, and his nose long but not very straight, as if it had been broken at one time.

But it was his eyes that held her fascination. They were a clear light blue, slightly upturned at the corners, and the look they gave her was both anxious and gentle—almost loving. She smiled.

"How do you feel?" he asked. His voice was low and soothing and held the same concern as his look.

Not certain how she felt, she frowned. Nothing hurt, but something seemed hollow inside her.

"Are you hungry?"

No, it wasn't that. She looked around the room again.

"What is this place?"

"A narrowboat. You're on the canal."

"Why?"

He frowned. "You had an accident—don't you remember?"

"No, I . . ." Sabina looked at the stranger as an idea formed in her mind. She remembered urging her horse down the path along the canal—but nothing after that. She supposed her memory would come back when her head ceased to ache, but that did not concern her at the moment. Somehow it seemed much more important to find out who this gentle stranger was—and not to recover so quickly that she would not have a chance to know him. He might ease her mind as well as her body and let her forget, for just a little while, why she had fled her home.

Impulsively, she cried out,. "I don't remember!" She put

her hands to her temples and thought furiously. "Who are you?" she said, looking at him again. "Oh, no—*who am I?*"

He said nothing, staring at her for a moment with an oddly intent expression in his blue eyes. Then he pressed her gently back down on the bed; she obeyed his touch, laying her head back and suppressing a sob.

Why had she said that? She half rose again, to take back her words, but he had gone to the ladder leading, she supposed, to the deck of the boat. He called up to someone outside. Almost at once, an old woman came briskly down the ladder and shook her head sympathetically at Sabina, who still lay in the same position, staring up at the ceiling. The old woman bent down, lifted Sabina's head a little, and held a cup to her lips. Obediently, Sabina drank the warm, sweet liquid. A moment later, she was again fast asleep.

For some time thereafter—she no longer had any notion of time passing, or even of the changing light—Sabina drifted in and out of consciousness. When she woke briefly, the same handsome stranger would still be there, watching her. Sometimes he was just sitting there, his long legs fitting ill between the bed and the low chair in which he sat reading, and if he did not see that she had awakened, Sabina would watch him for a while, contemplatively.

Once she woke and it was dark in the room, with only a trace of light coming in between the high windows. It must be night, she thought, still feeling little concern about time. She stretched herself cautiously, one leg at a time. Nothing hurt, but she felt the end of the bed move. Feeling with her hands, she realized that the bed folded down from the wall, and a low table of some kind had been added to the end to extend it to accommodate her length.

But no, her guardian angel was tall, too—it must be his bed. She felt herself go warm at the thought that she was sleeping in his bed. She could not let this go on. In the morning, she would have to come to her senses.

Yet . . .

What harm could it do? she asked herself as she considered her little deception. She had done it, she realized now, because she could not remember being so fussed over since she was a child. And she hurt now, too, in a way not so easily remedied as childhood bumps and bruises. The simple concern in her rescuer's eyes—for she supposed he must have rescued her from whatever accident had befallen her—warmed her heart, and she found herself not only more comfortable in this remarkably confined cabin but happier as well, as if her whole world had suddenly brightened. She knew she would have to go home soon and face the future she had temporarily escaped from, but a few hours' respite could harm no one.

Besides, she wanted to know more about her handsome rescuer. She did not even know his name, although she supposed he was the owner of the boat she was on. That was all the more reason to keep her own identity hidden for now—if he should learn that she was an earl's daughter, all of this pleasantly warm comradeship would dissipate in the strain of the difference in their social stations.

For the first time in her life, Sabina found herself wondering how such people lived—people who worked with their hands and backs to make their living and had no servants to perform even more menial chores for them. Could their lives be so miserable as she had been taught, when there seemed to be so much satisfaction and affection in them? She must learn their secret.

When she woke next, the handsome stranger was gone, but the old woman was seated in his chair. She had a delicate face that had once been pretty, and her white hair was still plentiful and framed her face with a soft cloud. She was mending something that looked like a fine white linen shirt. How odd. Sabina frowned, then said clearly, "I should like to get up."

The old woman put down her sewing and assessed her. "I'm sorry, dearie, but you'd best not just yet. Can I fetch you anything—something to drink, mayhap?"

Sabina sat up. The movement made her dizzy. Then she caught a glimpse of herself in a small mirror hanging on a cabinet door. "Oh dear, I look a fright." She clutched her hair. "Please, may I have a comb?"

She looked at her hands, which were scraped but had

been treated with some kind of salve. She had gone out without gloves, she remembered.

"I bathed you as best I could," said the old lady, "but I did not want to disturb you to tidy your hair. I'll do it now, if you like."

"Yes, please."

The woman produced a set of tortoise-shell combs and a hairbrush. She gently combed the knots out of Sabina's hair, then brushed it with long, smooth, soothing strokes. Sabina felt her body relax, the tension leaving it like water flowing down a stream.

"Where is—I don't know his name, the fair-haired gentleman?"

The old woman smiled and put away her combs. Then she pushed Sabina gently back on the bed and pulled the cover up. "He'll be back soon. Go to sleep again now, dearie."

This seemed an excellent suggestion. Sabina sighed and closed her eyes.

When at last she awoke more fully, clear-headed and with the realization that she was well again, she turned her head in search of her guardian. He was there, asleep himself, his head on the floor on one of the leather cushions and his feet up on the first rung of the ladder that led to the deck. The chair in which he and the old woman had sat earlier now hung from the wall above him.

Sabina raised herself slightly and shifted to one side, crooking her elbow and resting her head on her hand. She could feel a large bump just behind her right ear, but it did not pain her, so she ignored it, being much more interested in the man on the floor.

Seeing him now more clearly, Sabina realized that it was not just the tiny room that made him seem so large—he *was* very tall, although very graceful too, even in sleep. His hand rested on the book he had been reading, which lay open on his broad chest; he no longer wore the signet ring Sabina had noticed earlier, but his unadorned hands were large and competent looking, as if he did manual work with them, yet kept them scrubbed and presentable when he could.

She sat up a little more to be able to see him better and was almost disappointed when her slight movement woke him. His eyes met hers and something seemed to pass between them in the moment before they spoke or moved, something that made Sabina feel that nothing that existed before this moment had any importance. Who he was or who she was—or said she was—was no longer of any consequence. Only the future mattered.

But that future was still uncertain.

"What is your name?" she said.

He hesitated for a moment before answering, "James Owen."

She savored the sound of it for a moment, then asked, "Where are we?"

"Tied up on the Welford Arm, not far from the junction. It was quieter here."

"How long have we been here?" Sabina said "we," but felt as if she were an observer of some little drama playing itself out on the Welford Arm of the Grand Union Canal, "Not far from the junction." She knew she was the cause of any interruption of their quiet life that this man and the old woman might have suffered. She ought to make amends for that.

"What happened to me?"

He moved to a sitting position on the floor, folding his long legs over a rag rug and resting his elbows on his knees, from which posture he looked up thoughtfully at her.

"You had an accident Tuesday afternoon," he said finally. "You were standing on the deck when the boat was moving and looked back for a moment, so that you didn't see a low branch coming up. It knocked you into the water."

Sabina sat up, astonished. She remembered nothing beyond riding her horse along the canal bank. How had she come to be on board the boat in order to fall off it? It seemed incredible that she had done so.

"What is today?"

"Thursday."

It must be late morning now—nearly two days later! She must have suffered a severe blow to have rendered her insensible for so long. Of course, the old woman had given her something—a sleeping potion of some kind—which must have prolonged her rest to allow her to recover fully. She felt recovered now—if not precisely her old self. She wished she could see what she looked like, but James Owen had uncoiled himself from the rug and stood up, obscuring the small mirror.

"Who—" she began.

"Not now," he interrupted her. "You must be hungry after your long rest. Come outside for some breakfast, and I'll tell you more while you eat."

Hungry. Sabina suddenly realized that she was ravenous. Two days! What must her family be thinking! She must find some way to get word to them without revealing that she knew who she was. But she could not concern herself with that yet. She must learn what had brought her to this pass before she could decide on her next course of action.

Furthermore, she could happily devour breakfast, dinner, supper, and quarts of lemonade all at one sitting!

James Owen reached out a hand to help her up, stooping a little under the low ceiling as he did so. She wobbled on unsteady limbs as she rose from the bed, leaning against him to regain her balance. His arm was strong and comforting. She had to raise her eyes to look at him, a highly unusual—but most delightful—sensation. Then she felt the rag rug on the floor against her bare feet. She looked down, noting as she did so that someone had dressed her in a loose-fitting white smock that was too short for her. She giggled.

"Your own clothes are dry and cleaned," he said. "You can put them on, if you like. But you do look charming in that smock."

He grinned at her, and she laughed as she held her skirts out to her sides to admire them. She felt like a young girl and liked the feeling. "I'll keep this for now, thank you."

"You go up first," he said, indicating the ladder. "I'll follow in case you lose your balance."

Sabina climbed slowly, but the dizziness did not return. When she stepped outside, however, the bright sunlight dazzled her for a moment. She put her hand up to shield her eyes and heard, before she saw her, the old woman call out to them.

"This is Rose," James said, when the woman approached and Sabina had become more accustomed to the light. Rose, who barely came to Sabina's shoulder, dropped her a deferential curtsy, but Sabina reached out to put her arms around her and give her a less formal but warmer embrace.

"Oh, my dearie, I'm so glad to see you up and about!" Rose said, flustered but pleased. "Are you feeling better? Would you like to bathe?"

"I think she'd like something to eat, Rose," James offered.

"I've no doubt she would, but I'll take her off to tidy up first, Rob—James. *You*, meantime, may get some eggs and bacon out of the larder and start cooking them."

Tiny little Rose then pushed very tall James off in the direction of the galley and pulled Sabina along to the stern of the boat, where she helped her out of her shift and into the cool water of the canal to bathe.

The water was deliciously refreshing, and Sabina, who had been taught to swim at an early age by her brothers, paddled about contentedly for several minutes. She had not forgotten that she was supposed to be not quite recovered and literally not herself yet. But the sensations of the moment—the cool water, the fresh, fragrant air were so keenly, immediately agreeable, that she almost did not want to have to set them aside.

She was even hungrier when she got out to dry herself off in the sunshine. She insisted on putting the shift back on, telling Rose that she was perfectly comfortable in it. Rose shook her head, but allowed her this whim.

Impulsively, Sabina bent down to kiss the leathered old cheek. Rose laughed and called her a minx, which somehow put the two of them in perfect harmony, so that when they returned to the bow of the boat to find James laying a table in the shade of a large willow tree protruding from the canal bank, they had their arms awkwardly but affectionately around each other's waists.

Rose went off to finish the cooking, while James sat Sabina down and poured her a large cup of coffee from a tin pot. She took it gratefully, added some warm milk, and devoured three slices of toast before Rose came back with a tray loaded down with eggs, more toast, half-a-dozen rashers of bacon, two freshly fried trout, a pot of jam, a basket of strawberries, and a pitcher of milk.

Sabina attacked this simple but generous repast with no coy exclamations about its being far too much for her, and James watched with appreciative amusement as she worked her way through it. He polished off most of the bacon and two of the eggs himself, but Sabina paid no attention to his depredation into her feast. When she had finished, she sat back in her wooden chair with a contented sigh.

"I've never tasted anything so delicious in my life," she said, closing her eyes and turning her face toward the sun. But when James had made no response to her remark after a few minutes, she opened them again and looked at him.

"Yes, I know—I don't remember any other meals."

She supposed she ought to show more concern about that, but almost—here in the morning sunshine, with a light breeze blowing off the water and James Owen sitting across from her—she felt so at home that nothing but the present seemed to matter. She almost wished she *could* forget her past. Here she felt newborn, without past or family or impossible decisions to concern herself with. Her skin positively tingled with happiness.

This blissful state could not last, of course, and even if she tried to prolong it, someone would discover, sooner or later, what had happened to her. She sighed and resigned herself to the inevitable. She knew, too, that it would be better if she controlled when and how this charming idyll would end.

But not just yet.

"You haven't even asked your own name," James said,

with laughter—and sympathy, too, she thought—glinting in his blue eyes. "Do you remember it?"

She thought for a moment. She ought to take some small step toward her "recovery," but if she told him her name, he would send for her family, and that would be the end of her holiday. She screwed up her face as if she were trying very hard to remember and said finally, "No."

He moved his large, sun-browned hand to encase her smaller one in it. The gesture made Sabina feel oddly fragile and in need of his protection, although she ordinarily would not consider herself anything of the sort. Indeed, she had always prided herself on her ability to take care of her own affairs.

"Never mind," he said. "It will come to you. Doubtless you will remember everything very soon if you do not try too hard to do so."

She smiled weakly at him. "But you must call me something in the meanwhile." Rose had called her "dearie," but that would never do, much as she would have liked to suggest it.

"What about Elaine?" he said. "Just for now."

"Mallory's Fair Maid of Astolat? She came to a tragic end, as I recall, although I daresay she did so very romantically. I had as well be Ophelia, who also had a passion for floating on streams."

He laughed and looked a little abashed. "Well, at least you remember your reading! But that was an unfortunate suggestion. Let me try again—what about Miranda, who was shipwrecked but found a brave new world?"

"Miranda I shall be then."

Oh dear, she had almost given herself away by her lamentably thorough education. This was going to be more difficult than she had anticipated. What ought she to "remember" and what would she not have known in any case? She thought it would be credible if she remembered distant events—such as her early reading—rather than the recent past. It would be better still to make him tell her about himself; she would be less likely to be caught out in an error that way. In any case, she liked the comforting idea of

James Owen taking care of her far too much to occupy her mind with any other thoughts for now.

"Whose boat is this?" she asked, steering the conversation to their more immediate surroundings. "Yours?"

"No, it belongs to Rose and her husband, George Theak. I'm the lockkeeper at Inverley, on the main canal. I was on the boat with them when the accident happened. George and his son Bill are at the lock now, minding it for me while I help Rose look after you."

Sabina accepted this as likely; she had supposed he must be connected with the canal, and a lockkeeper was at least a step up from a boatman. She repeated the names he had mentioned aloud, then shook her head and expressed regret that none of them had any association for her. She noticed that Rose had quietly disappeared, leaving her alone with James Owen, which was possibly indiscreet of her, but Sabina could not help feeling grateful.

She looked around at the boat and at the towpath along the bank. Just beyond that lay the road to Bromleigh Hall. Someone she knew could come along at any moment and see her on deck. She smiled to herself. She would, for once in her life, think only of the present moment.

"Tell me about yourself," she invited him boldly. "Were you born in this part of the county? Who were your family?"

He hesitated, pouring out another cup of coffee for them both, then clearing away the remains of their breakfast feast before sitting down opposite her again. Sabina waited as patiently as she could.

He did not look directly at her when he spoke, letting his gaze drift instead over the sun-dappled water, as if he were apprehensive about her reaction to his tale. She tried to look eager and accepting.

"I was born in Ashtonbury village," he said. "But I've not been home in some years. Both my parents died when I was a boy, and I've been in the army since I was twenty."

He paused then, and it occurred to her that he was oddly reluctant to reveal himself to her. Could he have guessed that she came from one of the great estates nearby?

"How long have you been a lockkeeper?" she asked, hoping that was neutral ground.

He smiled and said, rather ruefully, "Not very long. I'm afraid I'm rather clumsy at the work. If not for George's advice, I'd make a proper muddle of it."

"It must be satisfying work."

"Yes, I've always liked working with my hands and having something to show for it in the end."

She realized for the first time that she had never acquired any useful skills. She could not even set a straight seam or muddle through a tune on the pianoforte without a wrong note or two. She wondered if Rose would teach her to cook, although she could not imagine ever having a need to do so for herself. Of course, if she lived at Carling . . .

But she would not think about that yet.

"Have you known Rose and George all your life?" she asked.

"Nearly," he said, but did not elaborate. Sabina tried not to ask any more questions; perhaps he was one of those men who found nothing more exasperating than an inquisitive female. Indeed, he raised his hand to run his long fingers through his hair in an impatient gesture.

This drew her attention to something, and she remarked without thinking, "You are not wearing your signet ring."

Chapter 4

This was going to be more difficult than he had anticipated.

But how could he have known that she would remember
the ring he had been wearing that first day? What else
might he have done or said to give himself away?

"It belonged to a friend," he said at last. "He was killed
in Spain."

She lowered her eyes and said hesitantly, "I'm sorry. It
must have been terrible for you, seeing your friends . . ."

"Yes."

In fact, the ring had belonged to Peter Ogilvey, and her
loss was surely greater than his in that regard. Did she perhaps remember that at some unconscious level? But this
was not a part of her memory he ought to probe too closely.

There was a moment's awkward silence before she said,
"I'm so sorry, I do not mean to probe, but . . . well, everything is new to me and—"

"And you hope to find something that will stir your own
memory. That's only to be expected, and you must pardon
me for seeming to be so unforthcoming. I did not wish to
startle you into remembering something unpleasant."

She smiled weakly, and he had the sense of a curtain
falling between them. A conversation that had been easy
and enjoyable moments before had become awkward and
strained. He must end it for now, much as he disliked tearing himself away.

He rose to his feet and said, "Forgive me, but I must go
and relieve Bill at the lock."

"No!" She rose with him and clasped his hand. "I mean, please stay—or let me go with you."

He could not stay, of course, even if he wanted to, since Bill and George were minding "his" lock for him and it would seem odd if he did not return to his duty occasionally. Bill had assured him that they had more than enough work to keep them occupied, for now that the lock was open once more to traffic, there was still the lockkeeper's house to be swept out and put in order for the family's use. They could not live on the boat forever, Bill had reminded him.

He ought to go home now and then, as well. His sister-in-law had begun asking pointed questions as to where he was spending all his time. Richard, of course, preoccupied with his own pursuits, had scarcely noted his brother's absence from home except when his wife prodded him to inquire. The difficulty was that Robert did not want to go home. He wanted to watch over this enchanting creature he had captured, like some exotic water sprite, to be sure she did not fly away.

More practically, he wanted to be there when she regained her memory. Yet, every moment they spent together held the potential for disaster. What if she regained her memory all at once? Would she recognize him? He did not think it likely, yet he could not be sure. And how would he explain the Canterbury tale he had told her at the start about her falling off the boat when she was never on it? He had thought it best not to frighten her with a reminder that she might have drowned had he and the Theaks not been nearby, but that now seemed a feeble rationalization.

He wanted to prolong their closeness, yet the closer they came to each other, the farther away she might run when she realized the deception he had perpetrated on her. Would her heart remember, too, and forgive? Would it perhaps be better if he told her? But he could not bear to see that lovely warm look leave her eyes any sooner than it must. He would not tell her. Not just yet.

"You must not tire yourself, Miranda," he said. "I'll be back soon, I promise."

She smiled more easily at his use of the name. "When? Tonight?"

He smiled and raised her hand to kiss it lightly. "Well, perhaps not that soon. Tomorrow morning."

She sighed and replied in a lighter tone that told him he was forgiven, "I shall find in my soul some drop of patience."

He tried not to look back as he walked over the gangplank to the canal bank, then started up the towpath. But before it curved around a bend, he could not help turning to see if she were still in the same place. She was. She saw him and waved her hand. He returned the wave.

That gesture was somehow reassuring, although he was perfectly aware that matters could not be at a worse pass. Whatever had possessed him to lie to her? He knew the answer to that, of course—he had wanted to prolong the intimacy of their fortuitous encounter. He had thought, foolishly no doubt, that even when she regained her memory, she would remember their companionable talks and be more willing to forgive him his deception. She might even—although he knew it was too much to ask heaven for—be far enough along the road to loving him that even a setback would not make the end of the journey unachievable. But at the same time, common sense told him that the longer he persisted in keeping her in the dark, the less likely such an outcome would be.

When Sabina had tumbled back into his life, his first thought had been to inform her family, but his second thought—to keep her to himself for even a short time—followed so closely on the first that he had decided almost at once to keep his own identity from her. He only did it in order not to shock her into awareness, he explained to Rose, who looked at him as if she thought his wits had gone begging. She did not attempt to change his mind, however, only saying that he must find some way of reassuring her family until he decided to give up his playacting.

There was no question of whom he would inform of the full circumstance of Sabina's accident. Only Dulcie Bromley would understand.

Dulcie and Robert had become fast friends during the period when she was being courted by his brother, and simply because she had decided not to marry Richard after all was no reason, in Robert's view, to cut the acquaintance. Indeed, they had become, in a manner of speaking, spies in each other's camp, and both harbored the same urge to reconcile The Quarrel that had prompted the old earl to amend his will as he had. Robert suspected that Dulcie had always been aware of his feelings for Sabina, although he had been careful not to reveal them in great detail. There was too much to be lost.

He had—luckily, as he now realized—last encountered Dulcie the day before Sabina's accident upon receiving a summons from the family solicitor, a Mr. Quigley. That "a matter much to Captain Ashton's interest" awaited his attention was as much as the solicitor's brief letter had said, but Dulcie informed him of what precisely this was when Robert encountered her alighting from her carriage outside the milliner's in Ashtonbury village. She was, happily, alone but for her maid—whom she promptly sent on an errand—and she invited him to walk along with her for a moment.

"Good God," was all he could say, thunderstruck, when she had finished explaining the contents of the will to which she had been a witness when it was last amended.

"Just so," said Dulcie dryly. "I was instructed by the solicitors not to reveal this to the family, but no one thought to warn me about you. Yet, I take it that this is not entirely an appalling notion to you?"

"She will never consent," he said.

"The circumstances are not propitious," Dulcie agreed, and he had to smile at her understatement.

After some thought, he had said he would not be present at the reading of the will after all. "I cannot see that my presence will serve to do more than set Lady Sabina even more firmly against me than ever. We must contrive some way to present myself as the most favorable of her options."

Dulcie agreed to think about how this might be achieved,

but neither of them expected an answer to materialize as it did, and so soon. Unfortunately, Sabina's accident was now beginning to look to Robert more like an exacerbation of the original problem than a solution. And when he informed Bill and George that they could return to their boat the next morning, he was no nearer an answer. He went directly to the village and sent an urgent request to Dulcie for a meeting.

The two conspirators had maintained an active correspondence since immediately after Sabina's accident. Robert had given her the particulars of Sabina's condition, and Dulcie had told the family that Sabina had gone to stay with Dulcie's mother until she could reach a decision regarding her part in her father's last wishes.

"We must think of some way to restore her memory without making you the cause of her misfortune," Dulcie said over afternoon tea two hours later when they met again at the inn in Ashtonbury village.

"I fear I have already sunk myself too deep in the circumstances of her accident to extricate myself with any grace," Robert lamented. "I am fairly certain that she would not have recognized me had I walked into Bromleigh Hall on the day the will was read, but there is no question now that when she regains her memory, she will know that I have deceived her."

"It seems to me that you had a perfectly good reason not to reveal yourself to her," Dulcie said bracingly. "We should not want to *shock* her into returning to reality, after all."

"Nonetheless, I suspect that may be the best course at this juncture," he said, adding wryly, "indeed, it has been my justification for every half-truth and downright lie I have told her. But how?"

Dulcie was silent for a moment, pensively stirring her tea, before saying, "I have a plan . . ."

Robert heard her out and made further suggestions, and they parted shortly thereafter with the intention of putting their plan into action the following day.

It was not until the canal came into sight again that he remembered his goal of making Sabina fall in love with him, in the hope that she would forgive his deception when she became aware of it, as was inevitable. He had very little time left, yet too much had perhaps already passed.

Sabina paced the deck restlessly. It was nearly eleven o'clock. He had said he would come again in the morning. It was now almost noon!

She had lain in her narrow cot the night before scarcely able to sleep—or so it had seemed, for she dreamed of James Owen whenever she dropped off to sleep, only to wake herself with the joy of her dreams. She remembered coming up on deck at least once during the night, when the moon was still up and the light on the canal gave the scene a magical quality. The air was sweet and warm, and she slept briefly in a chair on the deck, until something awakened her.

It was darker then, and she felt a distinct sensation of panic, as if some disaster were about to befall her. Would she inadvertently give herself away? Would James despise her when he learned the truth? Should she tell him herself before it was too late? Or was it already?

By morning, however, she had nearly forgotten the trick she had played on James—and on Rose and George, too, for that matter—in pretending not to know who she was. That gave her slight pause, for they were nothing but hospitable toward her, and she much regretted the possibility that they might think badly of her.

Yet she vowed to put her contrition aside, and as the morning wore on could think only of seeing James again. Would he be the same? Would he make her feel as she had when she woke to find him hovering over her in concern the day before? She wanted nothing more at this moment than to prolong that feeling—even to persuade him to return it.

Despite her eagerness, she did not see his approach until he had boarded the boat, for at that moment she was waving to the crew of another narrowboat edging past them on the canal.

"You look as if you belong here, Miranda," James said beside her.

Startled, she turned laughing eyes at him. "I feel as if I do," she said. Impulsively, she reached around his broad shoulders to give him a hug, then, suddenly aware of the impropriety of her action, flushed and stepped back.

"I do beg your pardon—"

"Please do not. I am delighted."

"I mean—that is, I *am* glad to see you. I feared you would not be able to come."

"I'm sorry I could not come earlier. Is that Rose's pinafore?"

She laughed and spread out her skirts. "She let it down for me—not enough, I fear, although one of her larger jackets is precisely the right size. And of course her boots would not fit me, but happily mine have dried and not shrunk. Do you like my hat?"

He put his hand on his chin and pretended to study the wide-brimmed straw hat which covered a borrowed mobcap and said, "Very fetching."

She laughed. "Well, at least it will keep me from getting freckled in the sun."

"Have you had your nuncheon?" he asked.

"No, Rose wanted to wait for you, and I agreed."

He took her hand and led her to the corner of the deck where they had taken breakfast the day before. "Sit down. I'll help Rose with the food."

Sabina half rose, protesting, "I am much better, truly— let me help."

"Nonsense. I like to wait on you."

She blushed again and sat down, but he had not yet let go of her hand, and for a moment longer he held it as he backed slowly away, his eyes never leaving her face.

"I won't be a moment," he said, breaking the connection at last. Then he disappeared into the galley.

A short time later, he emerged with a straw hamper covered with a cloth and held it up for her inspection.

"Sustenance. I told Rose we would walk up into the hills to eat it. Are you up to such exertion?"

She smiled. "I think so—if you carry the basket, of course. I think I prefer to take advantage of my invalid state a little longer."

He returned her smile. "I should mention, by the way, that Rose offered to chaperone us on this venture, but I assured her that I could be trusted. Of course, if you . . ."

Sabina laughed and shook her head. He picked up a blanket before leading her across the gangplank and a few steps up the towpath. Then they turned off the path at an angle up a slight rise, James protectively on Sabina's downhill side in case her footsteps were as yet unsteady. She put her hand through his arm, as if to lean on him. She did not really need the support, but she liked the feel of his strong arm holding her and wanted to retain for a little longer that novel sensation of fragility and being looked after.

When they reached the top of the rise, a charming view of the Avon valley spread itself before them. In the distance, the water of the canal glinted in the sun, but otherwise there was no sign of human habitation. James stopped beneath an oak tree just coming into its summer fullness of leaf, and spread the blanket on the grass. Sabina pulled off her hat and flung it on the ground, but remained standing a moment longer, her gaze drinking in the peaceful view. Then she turned and caught him looking at her, a longing yet wistful expression in his blue eyes.

"It's as if—as if we were the only two people in the world," she said, sinking down onto the blanket beside him.

"I wish we were," he said softly. He leaned across the hamper and took her face in his hands.

"Perhaps we *should* have brought a duenna," he whispered. His mouth moved closer to hers and she waited breathlessly for his kiss. But then he only touched her lips lightly, teasingly, and pulled away again. Disappointed, she opened her eyes and found him unpacking the hamper.

"I'm starved," he said, not looking at her now. "What about you, Miranda?"

"I don't think I've stopped eating since I met Rose, but everything she makes is so delicious that I can't resist it." She laughed, trying to match his mood, and patted her waist. "I daresay I've put on inches. I shall never get into my own clothes again."

That was the wrong thing to say, for it obviously reminded him of the world they were trying to forget for today. His expression became somber, and she felt he had somehow moved even farther away from her. This was not what she had intended—somehow she must make him forget everything but her!

She said little as he spread the feast between them on the blanket and they devoured the bread and cheese, cold chicken and meat pies, and fruit compote that Rose had packed. When they had finished, James poured a cup of cider for her and then lay back on the blanket and closed his eyes.

She gazed at him for a long time after his steady breathing told her he had fallen asleep. She was not offended by his doing so in her presence, for she liked the idea that he was comfortable with her. She wished it could be this way after he learned who she was, but she feared it could not be. What would he think of her? Would he be angry at her deception? Would the difference in their stations be, after all, the stumbling block? Would he regret the necessity of their parting or be relieved to be rid of the need to make a decision about their future?

A radical notion came to her suddenly. What if they need not part? If she refused to marry Robert Ashton, she would be left penniless—well, nearly so, in comparison to her previous comforts—and more nearly a match for James Owen, lockkeeper. He was certainly a well-schooled and well-dressed lockkeeper. Or would her name still be an obstacle? Peter Ogilvey had not been a peer's son, after all, and no one had objected to that match. She imagined herself living on her own narrowboat or in a lockkeeper's cottage—she must ask him to show her his—and for a moment, the world did indeed go away and she could imagine living only on love.

"Why are you smiling?" he asked, and she realized that he had been awake for some time. "Have you remembered something?"

The sun was lower in the sky now and cast golden light over the landscape and the distant water of the canal. Still smiling, trying to hold on to the charming image in her mind, she shook her head.

"Not precisely. But my life since I came to you feels so . . . so familiar, somehow. It is as if we lived it before."

"Perhaps we did," he said, smiling, "in some distant time and place."

"A distant time, yes," she said, taking up his fancy, "but not a distant place. Perhaps we lived on this very spot in medieval times."

"Why not before the Conquest?"

"Oh, no, then we would have been painting our faces blue or some such silliness. I refuse to think I ever had anything to do with people who did that."

"But you feel a kinship to some medieval Miranda?"

"Yes, I think so. I lived in a castle nearby—in ruins now, of course—with my mama, who was a queen, and my brothers, all gallant knights." Sabina began to enjoy embroidering her tale. "My father was a tyrant yet loving to his children. He gave me everything I wanted but insisted on choosing a husband for me. You were my knight in armor—and when I would not marry the wicked lord from across the border, you fought him."

She stopped when she saw a slight frown crease his forehead. She was about to ask what was wrong when, seemingly with a conscious effort, he cleared the frown and smiled instead.

"Wrong regiment," he said. "I might have been a knight errant, I suppose, and carried you away from all that. I can see myself traveling about seeking adventure and rescuing fair maidens."

He plucked a nearby daisy and presented it to her. She took it and, holding it to her breast, struck a dramatic pose.

"You rescued me, but I shall be your last maiden. No more errantry for you, sir."

"Ah, Miranda, you take all the romance out of knighthood."

"Do you mean you would prefer riding out in all weathers, and never having a proper bed to call your own, to cozy domesticity with me?"

"With all those brothers hovering about, we would have to find a castle of our own in order to live happily ever after." He was gazing at her with that intent look again, but she chose to disregard it. She did not care for anything but enjoying this moment while it lasted.

"You would fight a dragon for me," she said dreamily, "one that guarded a golden castle, with diamonds in the turret windows, and we would move into it after you slew him."

"Then I would lock you up in it to be sure you never went off with some other knight."

She began to tire of the game and leaned over him and took his hand.

"You would not have to lock me up. I would stay for you—always."

He attempted to pull his hand away, but she held it fast and raised it to her face. She looked into his eyes as, boldly, she rubbed his hand gently across her face, feeling its roughness against her cheek, its warmth against her mouth. She pressed her lips to his palm.

He did pull away from her then, and sat up abruptly, almost upsetting her balance. Sabina, although surprised at her own temerity, could not back down now.

"James, please—"

He stood up, and she rose too, without his help.

"I cannot take such advantage of you!" he exclaimed, running his hands agitatedly through his hair. "You must regain your memory before we can think of— Anything else would be villainy on my part and foolishness—at best—on your own."

"Oh, no." She took his hand again and held it to her breast. "It is not events or history or dates that matter, my dear, but feelings. I know—I feel—that it is right for us to love each other."

She looked up appealingly into his blue eyes, and he could not resist her. Drawing her a little closer, he bent to kiss her mouth gently, as if he were afraid of the result. But she felt no such hesitation; her hands crept up to the back of his neck to hold his head near hers. She felt the silk of his hair against her fingers, the faint, sweet scent of cider on his breath. He sought her kiss this time, and this time he responded fully to her eager, yet hesitant touch. Lost in the delightful sensations his warm mouth evoked from every part of her, she heard a voice deep inside her saying, *Yes, this is real. He does love me.*

It was nearly dark by the time they returned to the narrowboat, walking slowly, their arms around each other's waists.

"Let's have another picnic tomorrow," she said dreamily as she stepped onto the deck.

He smiled. "I can think of no more delightful prospect. Unfortunately, I promised Rose I would go with her to Market Harborough tomorrow. She wants to visit her grandchildren, and I need to buy supplies for the lock."

She clapped her hands delightedly. "Oh, but that sounds almost as enjoyable as a picnic! May I come? How long will the trip take? It must be miles."

"It is—nearly twenty. We may have to stay overnight in the town. Should you mind that?"

Her arms crept around his waist and she smiled up at him. "We shall be together the whole day. How can I not look forward to that?"

A look of sadness washed over his face for an instant, and was gone before she could be sure she had seen it, but all he said was, "I hope you will not be disappointed."

Chapter 5

There had been a rain during the night, so that when Sabina came up on deck early in the morning, the mist had not yet lifted from the water and the sun shone only fitfully through the trees. Nonetheless, she thought the canal at this hour a beautiful sight and chided herself for never noticing it before. Of course, she did not normally leave her bed this early, but the grounds of Bromleigh Hall must also provide such vistas and the sun must shine as lovingly on them as it did here.

She found Rose and Bill nearly ready to start and George waiting patiently at the rudder. She looked around for James. A horse's whinny drew her attention to the bank, and there she saw him harnessing the two horses that would draw the boat for the first stage. She waved, and he waved back.

"James will start us off," Rose told her, "and then Bill will take over walking the horses in an hour so you and James can have breakfast together. Would you like something now? I can make a bit of toast and butter."

"Oh, no, you are much too busy, I'm sure," Sabina said. "Anyway, you showed me how to make coffee. I'll do that for you, if you dare trust me."

Rose smiled sweetly at her. "Thank you, dearie. That would be a help."

Everyone was occupied for the next few minutes and there was no time for further conversation. When Sabina had made the coffee, she brought the pot on deck and gave everyone a mugful. She drank hers while leaning on the railing watching James walking steadily alongside the horses on the towpath. Occasionally, he glanced at her and smiled, and she felt warmed just knowing he was aware of her presence.

It was pleasant, she realized, to have someone she could count on to care for her above all others. She had always been able to approach one of her brothers or their wives or even their friends if she needed anything, or only wanted to talk. But none of them was her special companion. Fletcher and Alicia had each other, as did Henry and Dulcie. Randolph was alone by choice, and his pursuits and friends took him away from home more often than not. Sabina no longer knew what his life was like outside Bromleigh Hall, but she knew that she was not part of it.

Henry and Lewis were connected by that special bond that twins always seemed to share. She had sometimes wished she were a twin too, so that someone would know her thoughts as well as she did and would listen to her sorrows as if he shared them. She thought love must be like that, for she had felt it with Peter Ogilvey. But she was beginning to suspect that what she had thought was love for Peter might have been only friendship, a friendship that might not have survived marriage. Perhaps it was just as well . . .

No, she could not think that. They had shared more than most married couples did, and there was no reason to suppose that they would not have had a good marriage. She must remember him like that and not wonder what might have been.

She sighed and finished her now-cold coffee. She must not dwell on the past today. It was too perfect a day—one that would live in her memory forever, because James was the best part of it.

An hour later, when they had reached a convenient landing where Bill could change places with James, he came back on board and pulled up a chair beside her and Rose.

After kissing both ladies on the cheek, he sat down and helped himself to a plateful of breakfast. As they ate, he told Sabina about the canal, with some assistance from Rose.

"A great deal of the canal from here to Market Harborough is new since I went into the army," he explained. "Indeed, at that time it was not possible to travel to Market Harborough by canal, was it, Rose?"

"Not entirely. The lock wasn't open yet at Foxton, nor was the Husbands Bosworth tunnel."

Sabina said she looked forward to seeing these wonders of modern engineering, but just now it was hard to believe that the entire distance might not be like the part of the canal they were sailing on. It meandered picturesquely through open fields with wooded hills to the east and occasional open views over the Avon valley to the west. James pointed out church steeples, a windmill, and other landmarks, and Rose never failed to be able to name each of them.

"I should know them," Rose said. "I've lived on this canal or the rivers hereabouts all my life. In fact, I was born on a boat—not a narrowboat, though, a river trawler it was. I had eight brothers and sisters. We learned our letters from pub signs and the broadsheets pinned up at markets. We were what some might call poor, but it was a good life."

"Where did you meet George?" Sabina asked, fascinated.

Rose laughed. "I saw him on the deck of another boat, going the other way on the Trent, near Nottingham. He saw me too, and jumped off at the next landing. He borrowed a horse and came back to ask my name.

"We were married a month later."

Sabina pressed Rose for more stories which, blushing, Rose claimed she could not remember. But Sabina's interest flattered her, and she gradually revealed the details of her long and seemingly uneventful life, during which she had never left England, or ever seen the sea or Wales or Scotland or even London. Nevertheless, Sabina envied her contentment with everything she had seen and done and wished again that she could be so easily satisfied—or rather, as contented with what she had rather than always wishing for a past that was gone forever or a future that might not be what she thought she wanted.

Presently they came to the cutting that announced the

tunnel, more than a half mile long, which had been dug through the low hills west of the village of Husbands Bosworth. The towpath continued into the tunnel, and Sabina saw that Bill was now carrying a lighted lantern so that he and the horses could keep their footing on the damp ground.

Inside the red brick tunnel, sounds seemed magnified, and even the slight lapping of water against the boat and the clip-clop of the horses' hooves sounded loudly in the dim light. James put his arm around Sabina's shoulders as they stood watching the mouth of the tunnel recede into darkness, then leaned over to kiss her lightly.

"I wish we could be together like this always," he whispered.

Some note of sadness in his voice told her that he did not believe it was possible. She knew he was very likely right, but she was not ready to let the fantasy go just yet. She turned to look ahead.

"You can see the end of the tunnel coming," she pointed out. "Let's look ahead, James, not back. I shall never forget the past days, but we must hope fortune will continue to smile on us."

He hugged her and said, "I shall always hope so."

When they emerged into the wooded cutting at the other end, James changed places again with Bill, and Sabina insisted on walking beside him for a while. They held hands as they strode alongside the horses.

"It's been a long time since I saw any of this," James remarked as they passed open fields with no sign of human habitation for miles around. A kingfisher flew up from the reeds along the bank, and they watched its green-and-blue flash across the sky until it dove again for its dinner. It was as peaceful a scene as Sabina had ever seen, at least from this perspective, and she found it confirmed both her desire to live James's life with him and her certainty that this could never come to pass. She sighed.

"Tired, Miranda?"

"No, just—sad. I don't think—I don't remember seeing any place so lovely."

He smiled. "I think I like views with a little more human life in them—a church spire, or a bridge perhaps."

"I think your wish is about to be granted," Sabina said, pointing ahead. They had just come around a wide bend in the canal, and ahead was indeed a bridge. A young man was leaning over it, watching a barge loaded with wool pass underneath. The barge passed the *Rose Franklin* with several yards to spare, and James said that they would change horses not far ahead.

This was accomplished in a canal-side version of a coaching inn. James went inside to order ale for everyone, which he presently carried out to the deck overlooking the canal, where Sabina and the Theaks had drawn up chairs.

"For me?" Sabina said when James placed a small tankard in front of her.

"Don't tell me you have never drunk ale—and this is the best home-brewed in these parts."

Sabina looked at her friends and found them all watching her solemnly, but with various degrees of mischief in their eyes.

"Oh, you think I won't drink it, do you?"

She sipped the ale, which was dark and foaming, and was surprised to find it tasty—not at all like the watery ales she had stolen a taste of from the kitchen when she was a child. Perhaps it was a grown-up taste, after all. She took a long swallow.

"Brava, Miranda!"

They lingered a little longer, and George displayed his mastery of river wildlife lore when several swans swam toward them to catch the crumbs of bread Rose and Sabina threw at them.

"Them's young-uns," George said. "You can tell by the brown bits on their feathers. They'll be white next year. This lot haven't mated yet."

"Is it true that swans mate for life?" Sabina asked, glancing at James, who pretended not to see her but was smiling just the same.

"Oh, aye, most ways. Sometimes you get a rogue among

them—a rake, you might say—that'll steal another swan's mate or destroy his nest."

"Much like some folks," Bill observed gloomily.

When they reboarded the boat, James moved their chairs toward the bow so that they could watch oncoming traffic. He remarked that parts of the canal had been widened since he saw them last.

"But Bill tells me there has been a great deal more traffic since the war, and it does not seem to have abated with the peace—a good thing for those whose livelihood depends on the canal."

"Like you and the Theaks."

"Yes, and not just lockkeepers and boatmen. The canal companies employ clerks and laborers. We'll see the carpenter's shop and blacksmith's forge at the Foxton staircase."

"How far is it to Foxton?"

"About five miles more, I believe. Then we leave the main canal and take the Market Harborough arm."

They had a nuncheon on the boat before this landmark was achieved. As they neared the locks, George blew on a horn, much like a coach horn, to signal their arrival. Ahead Sabina saw a hill sloping downward from them, studded with a "staircase" consisting of two sets of five interconnecting locks. She could not imagine how the narrowboat would be maneuvered down this incline, but George, having been displaced by his son at the rudder, came to stand by her and explain what was going on and point out the essential features.

"There's two sets, see, so boats can go up and down at the same time. Traffic's light today, so we'll have the lock to ourselves, soon as yon barge clears the pond at the bottom. It's seventy-five feet down."

When their turn came to descend the staircase, both Bill and James sprang into action, James jumping onto the grassy verge of the lock and Bill taking the rudder to keep the boat steady as they entered the first lock.

"I taught the boys to steer," George said, unruffled by the

excitement. "They know if they scrape the boat, they have to repair it."

Sabina smiled at his calm confidence in his teachings, but Bill did indeed keep the narrowboat on an even keel within the lock as James heaved on the beam that closed the gate behind them. Then James cranked the handle that opened a part of the lock gate through which the water flowed from one level to the next.

"You'll see better when the water goes down a bit more," George said. "See there? Them panels at the bottom of the gates is called paddles. They let the water out."

When they were fully inside the lock, with the wet wooden gates towering over them, Sabina felt the water level lowering under them.

"Now I know what a 'sinking sensation' really is," she said, laughing but holding firmly on to the deck railing.

Then James worked the next gate and she saw it begin to open. The boat passed through to the next lock, where the water was at the same level as in the lock behind them.

"The most important thing to remember is to close everything behind you," George told her as the water in the second lock began slowly falling under them. "Like closing gates to a field when you ride through—you don't want anything that don't belong there getting in or out of the field—or the lock. Leave a lock open, you can drain a whole section of canal."

The whole operation was repeated four more times until they finally emerged into the pool at the bottom of the staircase. Bill gave the rudder back to George and climbed onto the towpath to hitch up the horses for the next stage. James, panting from exertion, reboarded the boat, doused his head with a handy pail of water, and sat down beside Rose and Sabina with a sigh.

"Well, Miranda, are you impressed?"

"I certainly am. Good heavens, I had no idea boating was such hard work!"

He laughed. "Admittedly, locks like this are few and far between." He ran his hands back over his damp hair and heaved a sigh. "And a good thing, too."

"Six miles now to Market Harborough," George called from the stern.

Following this excitement, the Market Harborough arm seemed very tame, flowing much like a river through a variety of rural scenes. At times, woods or hills coming down abruptly to the canal hid the landscape from view, but elsewhere the fields fell away from the canal, leaving open vistas.

Sabina settled into a chair and soon found herself nodding off from the effects of sun and excitement. She was awakened suddenly from a nap she had not intended to take by the hail of a passing boatman. She sat up and saw that they were nearing Market Harborough, a bustling little market town dominated by a tall church spire.

She looked around for James and saw him at the bow of the boat, looking ahead for their landing place. There was a great deal of activity near the basin, so she did not dare distract him.

When they were safely tied up, however, he turned and looked for her.

"Well, Miranda—did you have a pleasant nap?"

"Why did you let me nod off like that? Such disgraceful behavior!"

"Nonsense, you needed it. You may think you have all your strength back, you know, but fatigue catches up with one in inconvenient ways sometimes. I remember nearly falling off my horse once in Spain after I hadn't slept for two nights. Poor Salamanca was just as tired and barely achieved a trot."

Presently, they were standing on the wharf, having secured the narrow boat. They agreed to meet Rose and Bill at the Angel Inn in two hours to compare notes and decide when to set off on the return journey. Sabina thought that James's mind was elsewhere during this discussion, for he looked distracted and only nodded in agreement when any suggestion was made.

He was no more voluble when they set off on foot to explore the town.

"What's the matter, James?" she asked.

He looked at her, and after a moment of seeming indecision, smiled. "I beg your pardon. I was only thinking what you might like to see in the town. There are any number of famous sights—St. Dionysius church, the old school . . ."

"Which is closest?"

"The church, I think."

"Then let us go there first."

He took her hand and they set off down the street. Sabina had passed through Market Harborough before, but had never really looked at it. It was a busy, crowded place, particularly around the large central square, yet it had a certain elegance. Old timbered buildings lined the cobbled streets, and numerous old inns had their doors opened invitingly to the street. Fragrant smells drifted out and mingled with the sweet smells of fruit and vegetables on the farm barrows that lumbered past, bringing supplies to inns and markets.

It was quieter in the church close and nearly silent inside the ancient building itself. They sat down on a pew toward the rear and gazed upward at the delicate tracery around the windows. Occasional muffled footsteps from somewhere beyond the nave was the only sound other than their whispers. Sabina was glad she was with James in such a lovely, serene place.

"Have you ever been here before?" James asked.

"No," she said, gazing about. Then she remembered. "At least, not that I recall."

"There is nothing quite like an English church," he said. "I thought Spanish cathedrals were grand, but they seemed—I don't know, not so friendly as our village churches, even such a venerable old one as this."

Sabina remembered that she and Peter were to be married in the Ashtonbury village church, a tiny building with barely enough pews for her family, let alone his. She had always been fond of that church, but she had not been in it since.

"What's the matter, Miranda?" he whispered.

She realized that she was on the verge of tears and quickly wiped her hand over her eyes. "Nothing. I was being silly. It's only that I feel so—alone, with no family and no past."

"You aren't alone, Miranda," he said softly, then leaned over to kiss her. "You will find your past soon. You have us in the meanwhile."

She leaned into his kiss, grateful for the brief oblivion it gave her, but the sound of a door closing somewhere in the church brought her back to reality.

"Oh dear, how improper we are being."

He smiled. "Who is to know?"

She glanced around. "Only God, I suppose."

"Somehow, I don't think He is offended."

They sat for a few minutes, saying nothing. Then she became aware that he was watching her, and she turned to look at him. She studied his face, a little browner today after so long in the sun, his slightly crooked nose more evident in the dimness of the church. His mouth curved slightly upward when she turned to him, although his blue eyes were unsmiling. Suddenly she had a premonition that this would be the last time they looked at each other in quite this way.

"James, I—"

He put his fingers on her mouth. "No, don't say it. I can say it—I love you, Miranda—because I know I always shall, whoever and whatever you may be. But you must not promise yourself when you may be promised already, or may find your circumstances to be such—"

"They aren't. I'm not."

Oh, why could she not confess now? It was not too late, surely? What if she pretended to remember on the return journey, or even here in town? Yes, she would do that! she thought, her heart leaping with excitement. If—when—an opportunity presented itself, when something—anything— happened that might seem to jog her memory, she would let it. She must be alert and not let any opportunity slip by.

But would she have the courage to make use of it?

When they finally left the church and returned to the outside world, they did not go directly to their next sightseeing objective, for Sabina, to prolong their return and search for

some means of convincing James that she had regained her
memory, began looking into shop windows and then
searching her pockets.

"I suppose I did not have any money?"

He smiled. "I daresay Rose kept it somewhere safe on
the boat. What would you like? I believe I am able to advance you whatever sum you need."

She pointed to an ivory hair ornament in the window. It
was much like one her Uncle Augustus had brought back
from India for her. Perhaps it would serve. James said
gravely that he did not think this would bankrupt the exche-
quer, and they went into the shop. Sabina tried on a number
of other ornaments, turning her head so that James could
admire them and say which one he preferred, while she
tried to think how she could put her plan into operation.

She had just decided on her choice when she chanced to
turn and saw two people entering the shop.

"Good heavens!" she exclaimed unthinkingly, for her
mind was so confused between past and present, real and
imaginary Sabinas, that she could no longer think. "Dulcie!
Henry! What are you doing here?"

There was a charged silence for a full minute before anyone responded to this surprised outburst. Then Dulcie came
forward and embraced her sister-in-law.

"Oh, darling, I'm so glad you remembered!" She hugged
the unresisting Sabina again and turned to James.

"You were right, Robin. Thank you!"

Sabina's own words had temporarily robbed her of further speech, but at this her mind suddenly snapped back
into operation and she turned toward her companion.
"Robin? What does this mean?" She gazed at him as if he
really were a stranger. "Who *are* you?"

He looked somewhat abashed, like a schoolboy caught in
a prank, and half fearful, as if he had slapped her and
couldn't believe he had done so. "Robert Ashton, Lady
Sabina, at your service."

He took her hand as if to raise it to his lips, but she
snatched it away.

"You deceived me!" she cried, unable to look into his

eyes. "If you had told me from the outset, I would never . . ."

She caught Henry's astonished glance and fell silent before she betrayed herself entirely. Could he have known from the outset who she was? And if he did, what had possessed him to lie to her, to pretend to be James Owen? It was as if Robert Ashton had murdered James Owen.

My only love sprung from my only hate . . .

"Take me home, Henry," she said in a low voice.

"Miranda, I'm so sorry—wait!"

But she ran out of the shop before she heard another word. She could not stay. She could not let the traitor see the tears in her eyes.

Chapter 6

Without looking back, Sabina strode away from the street, heedless of where she was going until she bumped into a plump lady carrying a basket over her arm.

"Look where you're going, love," said the woman, not entirely without sympathy. Doubtless, Sabina thought angrily, she and every other person within hearing distance had witnessed the scene in the shop. Mumbling an apology, she chanced to glance back. James—no, Robert, curse him—was nowhere to be seen. Obviously, he had no intention of offering an explanation, much less an apology, for his treachery. For some reason, this caused her to burst into fresh tears. She fumbled in her unfamiliar pocket for a handkerchief, which gave Dulcie a moment to catch up with her.

"Sabina, for heaven's sake, stop!" Dulcie cried, a little breathlessly. "Where are you going?"

"I don't know," Sabina sobbed and proceeded to weep into Dulcie's shoulder which, Dulcie being several inches shorter, put them both literally and figuratively in an uncomfortable position.

"Let us repair to this public house which you were sensible enough to stop before and find a private parlor," Dulcie said, leading the unprotesting Sabina inside a small, dimly lighted hostelry which, judging from the lack of any odor other than sawdust and ale, was at least clean. Dulcie went off to rout the landlady, leaving a dazed Sabina standing where she was left.

Moments later, the ladies were seated at a table in a small upstairs parlor, Dulcie pressing a glass of ratafia upon her sister-in-law with one hand and patting her shoulder in-effectually with the other. The cool interior of the inn, the silence, and Dulcie's soothing voice finally began to have an effect. Sabina's sobs subsided and she heaved a great sigh, but did not speak.

"I'm so sorry, dearest," Dulcie began. "I had no notion that our—my little plan would turn out so disastrously."

"Not in the least," Sabina said. "I daresay it is just as well I learned what a—a deceiver he is before—"

"Do not blame Robert, dearest. He only acted in what he believed was your best interest. It was I who was in error. Of course, I had no notion that you had not really lost your memory . . ."

There was nothing accusatory in her tone—indeed, she seemed to be considering this unexpected twist as simply part of a larger puzzle. But all too aware of her own fault in the affair, Sabina lashed out at the absent target.

"Do not defend him, Dulcie. He is an Ashton, and know-ing who I was all along, he no doubt had some nefarious purpose in lying to me. People who have been known to cheat at cards and steal their neighbors' sheep will stop at nothing. I daresay he hoped to take advantage in some way of my vulnerable situation. I'm sure I cannot imagine what, but then, I am not an Ashton and do not understand how they think."

"Oh, do stop talking nonsense, Sabina," Dulcie said, giv-ing in to exasperation after all. "Robert's actions had noth-ing to do with that foolish old quarrel. And do stop calling him by pronouns. He does have a name."

Sabina calmed suddenly and sighed. "Yes, but what is it? Who was it whom I—I thought to be my friend, Dulcie? Robert Ashton or James Owen?"

Dulcie left off trying to reason with her distraught friend and changed the subject.

"Well, we are certainly glad to see that you suffered no real hurt from your injury, Sabina—that is, you *look* re-markably well. I expect we could tell the family that you had simply gone away to be alone and think, or some such excuse, and no one will have any reason to suppose otherwise, if you do not wish them to do so."

She waited for Sabina to respond to this suggestion, but Sabina could only shrug. She wished she could hold on to her anger, which was more comforting than weeping like a ninny at something that was over and done with. But she could no longer think, no longer make the effort to sort out her thoughts and feelings.

"Whatever you think best."

Dulcie perused her sister-in-law's striped blouse and long green apron. "Of course, we must find you something else to wear. I'm sure that ensemble is very picturesque—quite the kick of fashion on the canals, I have no doubt—but I do not think it would be wise for you to go home in it."

Sabina dabbed at her eyes one last time with Dulcie's damp handkerchief and said, "Do you mean, no one knows where I have been? How did *you* know?"

"No one but Henry and I knew, I should say. I chanced upon Captain Ashton the very day of your accident, and he kindly informed me of your circumstances so that we need not be worried about you."

"Kindly, indeed," Sabina muttered.

To forestall another bout of recrimination, Dulcie said hastily, "Perhaps you should lie down for half an hour, dearest, while I go and find something for you to wear. Perhaps the modiste here may have something suitable made up. You have patronized her in the past, I believe. What is her name?"

"Miss Morville. On the High Street."

"Oh, yes. Well, I shall go at once. Do you care for another glass of wine?"

Sabina looked at the glass in her hand, unaware of having emptied it. "I may as well. Is it true that one forgets things when one is foxed?"

"I doubt that mere ratafia will produce oblivion all that quickly," Dulcie remarked dryly. "Henry is downstairs, by the way, if you need anything else."

With that, she adjusted her bonnet and stood up, closing

the door softly behind her as she left the room. Still unable to sort out her disordered thoughts, Sabina stared at the door, then lay down on the sofa and closed her eyes. The image of a laughing face and a tall, handsome figure against a green hillside filled her vision as quiet tears rolled down her cheeks. She paid them no heed.

Three hours later, Sabina entered Bromleigh Hall, paler but composed now, to warm greetings from the footman who opened the door and varied expressions of welcome from her brothers, who each seemed to have formed his own opinion of her flight but all of whom were, at least temporarily, taking their cue from Henry's brief negative gesture and were tactful enough not to tax her with questions.

She paused in the hall and looked around her, amazed that she had been away less than a week. It seemed she had not seen her home for months. Yet the elegant lines of the Palladian architecture were as she remembered, the long Persian rug on the floor was the same one she had played on as a girl, and the faces of the servants who found some excuse to come into the hall to welcome her were those of old friends. She began to feel the comfort of home pulling her in, soothing her lacerated heart, and refreshing her tear-reddened eyes.

Dulcie had succeeded in procuring only a light cape from Miss Morville to cover Sabina's borrowed garments, so both ladies proceeded at once to Sabina's bedchamber to divest her of these. Dulcie waited until Sabina had undressed herself down to her chemise and stockings before admitting her maid, then departed herself with her sister-in-law's discarded raiment bundled under her arm, promising to have them returned to Rose laundered and pressed.

"Oh, Lady Sabina," breathed the young maid, Emily. "We're all ever so glad to have you home again. Would you like a bath? Something to eat perhaps?"

Sabina cudgeled her brain, which seemed reluctant to make even the most inconsequential decision.

"Yes," she said finally. "That is, I should like a bath,

please. And then find me my flowered silk dressing gown. I can't think where I might have put it."

"It's nearly time for dinner, ma'am," Emily pointed out. "Should I lay out the black sarcenet, the one with the braid trim? Or would you prefer something else?"

Black. Oh, God, she had almost forgotten. Anything other than her most intimate apparel would have to be black for some time to come. She could not face it.

"I shan't go down to dinner tonight, Emily. Please convey my regrets to Lady Bromleigh—after you have seen to my bath. Oh, and perhaps you could tell Lady Henry that I do not wish to be disturbed."

"Yes, my lady." Emily, looking none too happy at the instructions she had received, nonetheless departed silently to carry them out.

Sabina wandered listlessly around her room, fingering her hairbrushes, the bed hangings, the scar on the window glass that she had carved years ago with her ring. It was all so familiar, yet at once so foreign.

After sitting in her tub until the water cooled, she ordered a tray to be sent up to her room and moved a chair to the window to nibble at her food as she gazed out at the setting sun. What had happened to her appetite? she wondered, staring at a fresh roll as if it were made of paper. The cook had sent up some of her favorite dishes, too—a little cold roast chicken, a wedge of Caerphilly cheese with green grapes, and a gooseberry tartlet. She picked up her fork and tried again.

A soft knock on the door announced Alicia, who did not wait for permission to enter, but did so with her customary air of the squire's lady ministering to the poor of the parish. She seemed not to touch any part of the room out of deference to its owner's prior claim; even her feet did not seem to disturb the floor.

"Well, my dear," she said, gliding to a tentative landing on the window seat and contemplating with a grave air Sabina's nearly full tray, "we are certainly glad to see you. Indeed, the servants have not ceased asking after your welfare ever since we heard you had had an accident." Alicia paused, apparently taken aback by this show of loyalty from persons not actually connected to the family by blood or marriage.

She soon recovered her equanimity, however, and asked, benevolently, "How are you feeling, dear?"

"Well enough," Sabina said, then looked more sharply at her elder sister-in-law. "Why? What has Dulcie been telling you?"

"Oh, nothing in great detail. Henry says you had a little fall when you were stopping at Missenhurst Grange and are still suffering from occasional dizzy spells."

Sabina did not know whether to thank Henry for the excuse he had thus afforded her to stay in her room or to curse him for meddling. It was plausible that she might have fled to the nearby home of Dulcie's parents, the Jeromes, yet how could he or any of the family think she was such a poor creature that even a knock on the head would produce so long-lasting a malaise?

But then—here she was moping like an invalid. And then—here was Alicia, the very person who would believe such a tale against all the evidence, being solicitous. She supposed she had built her own house; now she must live in it. She smiled mirthlessly at the irony of the situation.

"Shall I send for Dr. Abbott?" Alicia asked when Sabina said nothing more. "Perhaps a sedative potion . . ."

"Thank you, no, Alicia. I shall be perfectly well before long. Indeed, until my—accident—I was enjoying an active holiday, walking in the home wood and so on." Sabina found herself about to embroider another fictitious account of her past and stopped herself, coming instead to a quick conclusion. "I think I merely let myself become overtired and thus became careless. I shall come about."

Alicia accepted this and changed the subject, for which Sabina was grateful. She was not yet ready to discuss the past week with anyone, least of all with Alicia, who was everything kind but possessed of no imagination whatever. Sabina did not think she would believe the truth if she heard it.

However, her sister-in-law's social skills were highly developed, and she talked for fifteen minutes about household matters, about who had called to leave cards and expressions of sympathy on the recent sad event, and about how Randolph's valet had failed to starch enough black neckclothes on one of those rare occasions when his employer was insufficiently adept to succeed in achieving a satisfactory fall within four tries.

"Edward and Diane have been very good about observing the requirements of our period of mourning," Alicia observed, with a hint of pride in her voice at her well-mannered children. "As have Henry's twins," she then added, to be quite fair, "although they are really too young to quite understand that their grandpapa has gone away for always."

She sighed and shook her head slightly, as if in regret at the insensibility of the young. "As you know, Sabina dear, there has never been a death in the close family since Edward was born, and they were both fond of their grandpapa. Indeed, Diana shed many a tear following the event, and even Edward was melancholy for days. They still talk about him with affection, you know."

"I am certain they do."

Alicia seemed to sense that she had committed a gaffe. "Oh, I do beg your pardon, Sabina, dear. I should perhaps not remind you of your loss."

"Please do not tread on eggshells for my benefit, Alicia. Indeed, if any of the children wishes to talk about Papa, please send them to me. I will be happy to help keep his memory alive in them, if I can."

"You were always a dutiful daughter, Sabina dear."

When Alicia took her leave, promising to send up a nice cup of chamomile tea, Sabina found herself more exhausted than she would have expected from doing nothing. She glanced around, determined to occupy her mind in some way that would not leave it open to memories she was not ready to face. She pulled a novel off a shelf and sat down again by the window, determined to read herself to sleep.

But she could not concentrate, even on *Guy Mannering*. A dutiful daughter, Alicia had called her. She had always hoped she was an affectionate one, too, but perhaps "dutiful" meant the same thing to Alicia.

Henry had been less approving on the drive home from Market Harborough, calling her an "unnatural child" for taking such violent exception to her father's last wishes. He had wondered aloud why she had found it necessary to pretend to have lost her memory and pointed out in the plainspoken terms that only brothers could use that her deception had been greater than Robert Ashton's and if she did not mind her tongue, the family would think she was only having a temper tantrum and treat her accordingly.

She had put up no defense to this diatribe, having none, and Henry had apologized, even without Dulcie's prompting, as quickly as his temper had flared. Sabina recognized it now as an expression of his concern, but that did not make him any the less perceptive in his judgment of her behavior.

Striving not to dwell on her faults, she passed a restless night, dropping off to sleep only to dream of gliding over the canal in a narrowboat. There never seemed to be anyone on the boat but herself, look in vain though she might for someone—anyone—else. She then woke herself with the fright but, too tired not to sleep, dropped off again only to wake with the same dream.

The next morning, she still did not care to descend to greet the family at breakfast, but had a tray sent up to her. Randolph, the next person to visit, found her finishing her meal and regarded the tray interestedly.

"I see that your—er, adventure has not robbed you of your appetite, despite Alicia's dire prediction," he remarked. "Dare we hope that you will rejoin the living today?"

Sabina regarded her brother's impeccably tailored black coat and pantaloons and raised her eyebrows at him.

"A poor choice of phrase, perhaps," he conceded. "I daresay the obligation to wear black may depress your spirits, although I fancy it suits me. What do you think?"

He turned around, offering his slim figure for inspection, and Sabina was forced to smile. Apparently, Randolph was going out of his way to be pleasant to her today; she must therefore humor him in this rare mood. "Anything becomes you, Randolph, and well you know it, so do not expect compliments from me. I see you have conquered your neckwear."

"You heard about that little contretemps, did you? I would not have thought black muslin would be any different to my touch than white, but so it has proved. Manson has learned his lesson, however, I do believe."

"Will you take Manson with you when you remove to Stonehaven?"

"I shall be obliged to. No one else knows my tastes as well as he, and I certainly have no wish to train another man to take into account my—er, slight defects of figure in order to instruct my tailor."

"You have no defects of figure, as you well know, Randolph, and you are by far the handsomest of my brothers."

"Do you think so?" he said, pleased despite this being an acknowledged fact among them. Randolph had few faults, but a niggling self-doubt he had never been able to banish was one of them; Sabina had always suspected that it was this that drove him to taunt his siblings and make verbal game of innocent strangers.

"You should come and see Stonehaven, Sabina," he offered magnanimously. "I have begun any number of renovations only in the last week. Perhaps I may give you some ideas for improvements to Carling."

"I hardly think I want to turn Carling into a hunting box," she replied. Randolph had naturally not given the matter any thought, but she was fully aware that she might never be able to live at Carling as she had planned.

Fortunately, Randolph had numerous topics of conversation at his command and did not linger on that one. Instead, he brought his sister up to date on tidbits of news and gossip he had received from his many correspondents, an account of the horse sale in Melton Mowbray three days earlier, and an excellent Greek wine he had unexpectedly encountered in a public house there and of which he was attempting to purchase a case for his cellars at Stonehaven.

"Which reminds me that I meant to bring along a new snuff box for your approval. I acquired it the same day I discovered the wine, and it was in fact my original purpose for the outing. It is silver, with turquoise panels—exquisite!"

"Do you remember, Randolph, when I was small and found an empty snuff box Papa had left in his study? He had intended to fill it, but was interrupted by something or other."

"I remember. You took it, thinking it would make a charming house for your family of beetles."

"Well, I fancied the rubies looked just like them, and of course I had no idea what the box was really used for. Poor Papa could not imagine where it had gone and was about to overcome his scruples and interrogate the entire staff when I came along bursting to show him my beetle-box!"

Brother and sister chatted in this manner for a full half hour, which left Sabina somewhat lighter in spirit, as Randolph always did when he was witty without being cutting. Yet when he had gone away again, she found herself brooding, even becoming a little annoyed that he had scarcely even inquired after her own health. Did he not care how she felt? She knew that this attitude was entirely irrational and unjustified on her part, but none of her feelings these days were familiar to her. She wished she could return to her old self quickly. Yet, she greatly feared that she never would.

Later that afternoon, it was Lewis who came to visit, wheeling himself into her room and deftly moving his chair into position in front of her. Unlike Randolph, he wasted no time in chatter and came immediately to his point.

"How are you feeling today, Sabina? I've asked Mrs. Carstairs to send up some barley water. I'm sure you must be parched up here with practically no food or water."

"I am not precisely in solitary confinement, Lewis. You are my third visitor—or is it my thirtieth? I have lost count."

"Perhaps we ought to send for a surgeon,"—Lewis went on, as if she had not spoken, "or at least the apothecary to prescribe a restorative—or a paregoric, I can never remember which is which. Do you know, I heard about a widow in the village or county or somewhere who took her husband's death so to heart that she refused to eat and was reduced to a shadow of herself. She took nothing but goat's whey and cinnamon water and spent the short remainder of her days reclining on a sofa. They said it was a great pity, but I would call it a blessed release."

He came to a halt, but Sabina did not immediately reply. She waited for an interminable moment before asking. "Are you quite finished, Lewis? Listen carefully now—*I am not ill.*"

"Good. Then when will we see you up and about again?"

"When it pleases me to be up and about."

Lewis stared at her, his expression alternating between a scowl and a wink.

"Henry tells me you've been to see the Jeromes," he said then. "How are they all at Missenhurst?"

"In fine fettle."

"Nonsense. You were never at the Grange, although I daresay Dulcie's mother would support the tale. What were you up to, Sabina? You know what a terrible liar you are, so do not try to deceive me, of all people."

"I seem to have succeeded with everyone else," Sabina countered. "What makes you think I have been telling you all some Banbury story?"

"Never mind how I know, and stop evading the issue. The more you hedge, the more disreputable the whole adventure must have been. I know you, Sabina."

"Do you?" Sabina asked, her fragile sense of fun withering again. "I scarcely know myself these days."

Lewis's tone immediately softened, and he leaned over to take his sister's hand.

"Won't you tell me about it, my dear?"

She shook her head miserably. "I can't—not yet, anyway. I'm sorry. It's not you, Lewis, I—"

"Hush, now. You needn't go into it if it will upset you. I only came to chivy you into coming down to dinner, but since putting a pea in your shoe did not do the trick, I must beg you to come down if it will not cause you a setback—my begging, that is to say. I know how you dislike people groveling at your feet. Besides, Georgie's coming for a visit. You wouldn't like to be unwelcoming, would you?"

There was a decided twinkle in Lewis's hazel eyes when he mentioned Georgina Campion. Alicia's niece, the only child of her only brother, Georgina was a universal favorite among the family, but particularly with Lewis, since she appeared not to be at all aware of his affliction and made him join in with any mad scheme she concocted for their entertainment. Sabina had noticed some time ago, however, that Georgina was amazingly adept at challenging Lewis while never suggesting anything that was physically outside his capabilities.

"Naturally I shall be glad to see Georgina," she said. "How long will she stay? When will she be arriving?"

"Not until tomorrow," Lewis admitted. "But do come down tonight, love. It's deadly dull with only Randolph prosing on with the same topics of conversation he has been boring us with for years. You know how it is when he gets onto clothes or architecture. I vow, he would tear Stonehaven down and rebuild it from his own plans if Papa had been foolish enough to leave him enough money to do so."

Sabina laughed and promised to consider coming down to dinner, but since no one else came to ask for her company, she delayed leaving her room for yet another evening, at the end of which, however, she was so bored with her own company that sleep began to look like an attractive entertainment and *Guy Mannering* finally succeeded in sending her into slumber.

She thus slept the night through and was surprised to wake the next morning feeling more nearly herself. She told herself this was a decided improvement, but her heart felt differently.

The next day, since she was finally able to concentrate on something other than her own misery and Robert Ashton's treachery, she spent reading, and it was seven o'clock before she realized that the light was going. A moment later, Dulcie came storming into her room, a martial light in her eye.

"Really, Sabina, this is the outside of enough! You must stop sulking and come down to dinner."

"Very well."

"If you do not wish to marry in the normal way and start a family of your own, you simply must rejoin this one—did you say you would come?"

Sabina laughed. "Oh, Dulcie, do come down from your high horse. I said I would. I was just on the point of ringing for Emily to help me dress."

"Oh, thank goodness." Dulcie sank down on the window seat beside her sister-in-law and heaved a sigh. "I really did not want to rail at you, dearest, but I felt something must be done."

"You are quite right," Sabina agreed. "And I have decided that it cannot be done from this room."

Dulcie looked at her with concern growing in her eyes again. "What are you going to do?"

"I don't know. But I shall think of something."

Chapter 7

Robert Ashton gazed down the length of the dining table in front of him, mentally comparing his ancestral residence with the coziness of the Theaks' home on the water—and not to the Abbey's advantage.

Dinner at Ashtonbury Abbey was invariably in the formal style, even when only family members were present. The Abbey was a large building, built upon over the centuries since the Dissolution in a variety of fashions that tended to reflect ever more ancient times so that in its current incarnation it resembled a Crusader's castle more than a modern estate. The dining room was similarly built along massive lines, with a table that could seat fifty; even with all the leaves removed, it could hold many more than the five persons who assembled there for meals in the ordinary course of the day.

The earl's heir, Viscount Ashton, aged seven, and his younger brother, the Honorable David, aged five, did not of course dine with the adults except on those rare informal occasions when their mother was able to tolerate them. This left, in the current season, the earl and countess, the countess's mother, Lady Brendel, the Reverend Mr. Jennings, a distant relation of Lady Kimborough who chanced to be staying at the Abbey, and the earl's younger brother, lately returned from the wars, to forgather at the family board.

On the day of Robert's parting from Sabina, he was unable to participate in the proceedings as fully as Lavinia might have liked and so he was grateful for the voluble Mr. Jennings. The meal itself was somewhat overpowering in any case, consisting of numerous courses and side dishes, from poulard à la duchesse to an exquisitely grilled breast of lamb in mint leaves. Lavinia employed a French chef, not so much because she cared particularly about what she put in her mouth, but because she could boast about him—in a subtle way, of course—to all her acquaintances. Alfonse stayed because he was allowed to experiment as much as he liked so long as he provided one good English dish at each meal, and because the earl at least appreciated his efforts and told him so.

In the general way, Captain Robert too was a notable trencherman, having learned when food was short as well as unpalatable to make full use of it when it was plentiful. However, he was notably remiss in contributing to the polite conversation which his sister-in-law decreed was as essential a part of civilized dining as good food. She had for some time been discoursing upon the paucity of high-minded activities to be found in the neighborhood without offering any suggestions of her own or volunteering her own home for activities in the advancement of literature or science, but only Mr. Jennings appeared to be interested in the subject.

"I was privileged to hear a lecture by Mr. Southey while in London," this gentleman remarked. Having made short work of his grilled trout, he daubed his lips genteelly with his napkin and cleared his throat importantly in an irritating way that could not help draw the attention of the other diners—the earl's younger brother excepted—to his remarks.

"That is, I should say"—Mr. Jennings tittered delicately—"when *I* was in London. I daresay I might call on the Southeys at any time while they are domiciled in Greta Hall, which, as you may know, lies a mere twenty miles from my own home. However. What was I saying . . ."

There was a momentary silence until Lady Brendel offered politely, "When you and Mr. Southey chanced to be in London at the same time . . ."

"Oh, indeed, yes, how absurd of me to lose my train of thought . . ."

Since Mr Jennings's train of thought, once set firmly in motion, ran very well on its own, Robert felt no obligation even to appear to be raptly attentive to his words. Instead, he allowed his mind to wander back to his last sight of Sabina Bromley. Did she really despise him as much as that look seemed to say? Was she able to forget, for he certainly could not, the very different look she had given him the day before on the canal bank? She had told him that she loved him; she had initiated the declaration.

Why, if she did not mean it?

He told himself that he had every right to be as angry as she was at his "betrayal"—she had, after all, deceived him about her loss of memory. To be sure, she had not recognized him as a member of the Ashton family, and he had deliberately led her to believe he was someone else. Yet, why had she concealed her own identity in the way she did?

"My dear Robin," Lavinia was saying, "I wish you would let me plan a ball, or at least a small dinner party, for you."

He was fairly certain that he had not heard any introduction to this topic, so he asked, quite naturally, "Whatever for?"

"It must seem unusual that we have not yet done so," Lavinia explained, as to a slightly dim child. "It should not be thought that your arrival was not an important family occasion—which of course it was, and it must be seen to be so by the rest of the world as well."

"I am perfectly capable of announcing myself. I will even, if it will allay your social concern, say that I did not wish any fuss to be made about my return."

"Yes, but it isn't just that," Lavinia went on. "You have not met our neighbors for years, some not at all. There are a number of pretty, eligible young girls—"

"Oh, no, Lavinia! I will not have you parading matrimonial candidates through my own home for my inspection. That is the outside of enough."

"But surely you will wish to marry and settle down now that your military career is at last at an end. You said as much when you first arrived."

And so he had. That had been rash of him, Robert now

knew, but at that time he had had only one candidate in mind, and she had now declined the post.

A thought occurred to him. Could she have known who he was, after all? He did not guess that she had not really lost her memory—even when they were playacting and she had drawn a picture that seemed very much like her life as he was aware of it. Could he have been equally obtuse in thinking she had not recognized him?

But the puzzle remained—why?

Lady Brendel had by this time entered the conversational lists. A formidable aristocrat with an aquiline cast of countenance and a penchant for varying shades of purple in her garb and personal adornment, even to the feathers in her turbans, she began describing in excruciating detail the various entertainments she had had the pleasure of attending or hosting in London last season and in which she had every intention of indulging herself again.

"Perhaps, Robert, you would like to spend a little time in town with us?" she offered. Robert made an effort not to wince, but she must have sensed his withdrawal, for she went on, "Or with my other daughter and her husband, Lord Northrup, who would be equally glad to have you. You may even come to us during the summer, when London is thin of company, of course, but it is always possible to arrange a small entertainment at home. Would that suit you better?"

"Thank you, Lady Brendel, but I fear I would damage your reputation as a hostess beyond repair."

Lady Brendel smiled at this witticism. "Dear me, no—as if anyone could! That is, *you* surely would not do so."

Robert knew better than to fob Lady Brendel off with vague assurances that he would consider her kind invitation, and so he only smiled noncommittally. The ladies appeared to be in unison in deciding that there was nothing to be gained by pursuing the subject further at this time, but Robert knew he had not heard the last of it.

The conversation turned to other topics, and Mr. Jennings obligingly resumed his observations, which were innumerable, so that Robert was allowed to finish his meal in silence. The dinner ceremony concluded with a crème plombières praliné, which Mr. Jennings disposed of with his usual dispatch. Lady Brendel, declaring that she never ate sweets, ate hers anyway. Lavinia picked up her fork, but did not touch it, and Mr. Jennings eyed her plate covetously. Robert quietly signaled a footman, who brought Mr. Jennings a second helping.

He must, Robert thought, write to Dulcie Bromley this very evening to learn how Sabina's return had been received by her family and whether her attitude toward him had softened in the least. If it had, he would approach her, apologize again, and attempt to start afresh. If not—well, he would find another way. He would not give up.

"We had given him up for dead after all that time," Lady Brendel was saying. This succeeded in penetrating Robert's reverie, and he wondered if they could possibly be talking about him again. It seemed not, however.

"He turned up after battle of Victoria—is that right, Robert?"

"Vitoria."

Lady Brendel appeared not to hear the distinction and went on, "Yes, and in perfect health, although it appeared he had lost his memory and was laid up in a field hospital for weeks before someone was able to identify him."

Robert shook his head slightly to clear it. It must be only coincidence that they were speaking of a loss of memory. Or perhaps he had heard incorrectly. He must stop brooding on what had happened or he *would* begin hearing things. He was more used to taking action.

But it seemed that the ladies were taking action of their own, however indirect. Having engaged his attention again, Lady Brendel inquired of her daughter if the gentleman in question was not the same Captain Tennison who had married Salford's eldest daughter, the one whose hair was never properly dressed but who had a very fine, clear complexion.

"Indeed, yes, and a most eligible connection it was. I believe she is already increasing with her second."

Robert was aware of Lavinia's views of marriage, an institution which she considered necessary for the propagation of a solid bloodline and nothing more. She was aware that her contribution to her own marriage was superior in the matter of pedigree to her husband's—at least in her opinion—but she did not hold that against him, feeling that the combination of their inheritable traits was a happy one and was alone responsible for the good health, pleasing looks, and observable intelligence of her male progeny. It naturally followed that her brother-in-law should also make such an alliance, and had she been brought to understand that he intended to marry only for love, she would have pitied him.

Robert wondered idly about Sabina's views on love matches. Did she envy George and Rose Theak, as he did? Did she believe in lifelong fidelity? He knew for a fact that, having produced two male children, Lavinia had no further interest in the marriage bed and that Richard was less distressed than relieved by this attitude. He also believed, although he did not know for a fact, that Richard still harbored a tendre for Dulcie Bromley, for he had chosen a mistress—a discreet lady whom he had set up in an impressive mansion near Rugby—who was the image of his former fiancée.

Robert had thus far avoided discussing the terms of Earl Bromleigh's will with his brother, but he knew that he must do so quickly, for it would be bound to become common knowledge before very much longer. Therefore, when the ladies had left the gentlemen alone with their port, he addressed his brother.

"Richard, there is a matter of some importance that I must discuss with you."

The earl finished lighting his cigarillo—one of a supply, very fragrant but much despised by his countess, which Robert had sent him from Spain—and turned to the third gentleman in the party, who had leaned forward expectantly at Robert's words. "I trust you will not take it amiss, sir, if I ask you to leave us alone."

Mr. Jennings appeared not to have heard, but when the

silence began to lengthen, he reddened slightly and stood up. "Yes, yes, certainly. I beg your pardon, I am sure."

"Winston will see that you have your port and anything else you may require in the library."

When Mr. Jennings had gone out, murmuring flustered apologies and looking distinctly disappointed, Richard stared into space for a moment, his arresting light eyes blank, then turned to his brother.

"Doubtless you did not wish the good parson included in the conversation. Everything he hears goes directly to Lavinia. Not that she might not have to hear in any case, if what you wish to discuss concerns her in any way."

"Not directly, but I daresay she will have to be informed at some point."

Robert had been admiring his brother's ready assumption of authority and the unobtrusive way he wielded it. He must have acquired this assurance with his title, for Robert remembered him as being a somewhat solitary boy, who appeared not to care whether he was included in the other children's games or not, with the result that none of the other boys paid the least mind to him. Perhaps the title had given him the self-confidence he had once lacked. Robert had seen similar transformations in army officers who, when they bought their commissions, had no experience or talent for leadership, but then found the knack for it buried somewhere in their personalities. He had always been un-critically fond of his brother, despite his apparent lack of warmth, but now he began to admire him as well.

"Does this have to do with Earl Bromeigh's will?" Richard asked, when Robert did not immediately broach the subject that had prompted him to ask for this interview. He raised his brows in surprise.

"You know?"

"I *am* a magistrate, remember. Very little of this sort of thing escapes my notice."

"Then I beg your pardon. I should have informed you earlier, but I thought—I hoped everything would have worked itself out by this time."

"And it has not?"

"The lady does not wish to marry me."

"That is scarcely to be wondered at, surely. She *is* a Bromley." He looked at Robert, his light eyes unreadable. "Do you wish to marry *her*?"

"Yes."

Richard digested this for a moment, and Robert had the impression that his answer was unexpected. Unlike Lavinia, who had married into the family and taken on its prejudices as her own, Richard's sense of family loyalty was strong but practical. He continued the quarrel with the Bromleys because it was a tradition. Yet he was ready enough to spurn tradition when it became burdensome; he had, indeed, not hesitated to banish some traditional, but hideous and moth-eaten, wall hangings from this very room when he assumed the title.

Robert had hoped to enlist his brother's aid in his crusade against at least this one vexatious tradition if he could, but Richard had, possibly also as a result of his solitary childhood, always considered himself above any kind of common brawl, which he doubtless saw this issue developing into all too easily.

"I should counsel patience, my dear Robert," he said now, not unexpectedly. "As I understand the terms, she will be much the worse off than you if she does not agree to marry you."

"There is a little more to it than that," Robert said, and explained as briefly and unemotionally as he could the incident on the canal. At the end of his tale, Richard looked as if he had swallowed something distasteful. But if he were disappointed to find any member of his family involved in such a disgraceful imbroglio, he was tactful enough not to say so.

"In that case," he said, stubbing out his cigarillo as if to declare that he washed his hands of the whole affair, "I must leave you to decide what would be the best course of action for you. I fear this kind of thing is wholly outside my experience. Of course, if there *is* anything I can do to help . . ."

Robert smiled and shook his head. "Thank you, Richard.

I wish there were, but I fear you are right. I must work this out for myself."

"Do keep me informed, however," Richard said, rising from his seat.

"There is one thing," Robert said, before Richard reached the door to the parlor where the ladies awaited them.

"Yes?"

"Please explain the situation as best you can to Lavinia. I am afraid that is wholly outside *my* capabilities."

Richard smiled wryly. "This is one situation in which I will take your military advice, dear boy, and get over the rough ground as quickly as possible."

Robert grinned and put his arm around his brother's shoulder. "You're a good fellow, Dickon, in a pinch."

Robert thought it a politic move on his part to get himself out of the house early the next morning, before Lavinia awoke, in case Richard had been brave enough to broach the subject of his unsuccessful courtship of Sabina Bromley in private the night before. He did not think he could face Lavinia's reaction over the breakfast table.

He saddled his horse, Salamanca, and took him out for a long ride over the still misty hills. The stallion knew the ground better than he did by now and, being given his head, in turn allowed Robert to empty his mind of all thought, the better to look at the new day in a clear light.

He rode first to his favorite vantage spot, a slight rise behind the Abbey which overlooked the Avon valley and on a clear day, gave a view well into Leicestershire. It showed him clearly that "green and pleasant land" of Blake's that he had missed so much in Spain's dramatic but barren mountains.

He continued through open fields, giving Salamanca his head, and rode into Ashtonbury village. It was seven o'clock by now, and he decided to break his fast at the Feathers rather than return home. Even if he did go home, he reflected, he would no doubt be there well before anyone but his nephews was awake and thinking about breakfast. Besides, he had become fond of the village since his return to England. It seemed to him to represent everything that was best in English life and English people, and he had lived without both long enough to appreciate those qualities of cohesiveness and neighborliness without intrusiveness that characterized English villages.

And he knew there was always a welcome at the village inn, where the master at least pretended to remember him from his previous visits and the hostess took a motherly interest in his welfare. Apart from that, the food was plentiful, excellent, and not French.

The Feathers was situated at the end of the High Street under a sign featuring two large plumes and a small coronet between, a design that Robert suspected had some connection to the rival earls, but he had not yet worked it out. The inn was a low, timber-framed building with benches provided on either side of the door for the regulars and a dim interior which on rainy days required candles to be lit all day long. The ale, however, was exceptionally good.

When Robert pulled up and dismounted, his mind on a pint of the best, an unexpectedly familiar voice greeted his ears.

"Hullo! There's a horse I know. Where's the rider? D'you suppose he's been thrown?"

"Nicky, by all that holy! What are you doing here—and up at this hour?"

Robert came around to Salamanca's other side, where he found Nicholas Glyn, Viscount Markham, standing at a typical posture—hands on his hips and a grin on his tanned face—and flung his arms around him. The former lieutenant was no longer in uniform, having exchanged it for biscuit-colored pantaloons, a pearl-gray coat over a darker gray waistcoat, a spotted neckcloth, and a bell-topped beaver hat. In his hand, he carried—when he was not swinging it to illustrate a point—a cherrywood walking stick with a carved ivory grip.

"I haven't been to bed yet, of course," his lordship announced cheerfully. "Here, steady on, old fellow, I ain't in the Royals anymore and don't have to put up with abuse from superior officers."

Robert stepped back and admired the ex-cavalryman's modish apparel while the tall, black-haired, and exceptionally elegant viscount struck a pose before him. "I see that you are a civilian again—although I hesitate to call you a gentleman in that getup. When did you sell out?"

"Oh, months ago, but had to spend some time with my family or I'd be disinherited. These fellows have just come home, however." He motioned to the gentlemen standing next to him. "You remember Charles Trent and Lambie Williams? We're all going to Wales by way of Derby to see them both safely home. Can't trust them to find their way on real roads, you know. Like as not to gallop across every field of rye they see."

Robert acknowledged the two officers still in uniform, one a thin redhead, the other a muscular Welshman only slightly shorter than his tall English fellow officers, both of whom were well known to Robert from certain disreputable escapades in the field having nothing to do with battle.

"Don't listen to him," Mr. Trent advised. "This is a forced march if ever I endured one. Couldn't even bring my man along to give me a decent shave in the morning."

"No one's going to notice if you don't shave for three days, boyo," said Mr. Williams, "but those of us with real beards are likely to be mistaken for footpads along these Sassenach back roads. I won't feel safe until I'm on Welsh ground again."

"Where you can plot against us in that heathen language of yours," Mr. Trent rejoined.

Robert recommended that they all pay a visit to the local barber, who had a wicked way with a razor. The viscount gave him a dubious look, but Robert only smiled angelically and led the threesome into the inn. They sent the landlord scurrying for a mammoth breakfast, during which the old friends shared the news of absent friends and old escapades since they had last seen one another.

Two hours later, they were again standing outside the inn

attempting to say good-bye. The viscount flung his arm around Robert's shoulder and promised to write.

"Don't gammon me, Nicky. You know you never do, or you would have let me know you were coming through Leicestershire."

"An oversight only, dear boy. Couldn't find any paper, and my pen needed mending."

"Look here, Nicky, I wish you wouldn't go just yet," Robert said. "There's plenty of room at the Abbey for you all, and I can use the company."

Viscount Markham gave his friend a shrewd look and asked, not without sympathy, "Lady didn't wait for you, eh? Pining away, are we?"

Robert shrugged. "It's a long story."

At that moment, Mr. Trent came up waving a handbill. "Look at this, Markham. There's a fete here day after tomorrow, with racing. What do you say we stay on a few days and show the locals how it's done?"

The viscount clapped his friend on the back, and informed him that he had just been arranging accommodation for them. "Stroke of luck here, Lambie. We get to make our billet in an abbey tonight. What do you say to that?"

"Better than a convent," said Mr. Williams, speaking from experience. "The wine will at least be drinkable."

Chapter 8

Once Sabina made up her mind to come down to dinner, it was only a matter of days before Dulcie Bromley was able to persuade her sister-in-law to accompany her and their visiting cousin into the village to perform a few minor errands. It was only after they had returned to Bromleigh Hall that Dulcie realized that Sabina had been willing to go only because she had determined to put the whole incident of her accident behind her and carry on as if nothing had changed since the day her father's will was read. Unfortunately, Dulcie understood this only after Sabina's carefully constructed self-deception had begun to fall apart around her.

Sabina had always said Georgina Campion had been born, like Beatrice, in a merry hour. She never failed to bring sunshine into the house with her when she came to visit, for which all the Bromleys felt grateful. In deference to the family's obligatory state of mourning on this occasion, she had arrived clad in sober black, but her cousins, led by Lewis, had rapidly teased her out of it, saying they would not have her at meals unless she showed off her latest gowns for them, the more colorful the better.

Georgina obligingly went immediately up to her room and changed into a green-and-white sprigged muslin day dress with a wide sash and ruffles along the hem, which was universally approved. Georgina had an excellent fashion sense, and this costume went so well with her strawberry-blond curls and green eyes that she made Sabina feel positively dowdy despite her superior height and better figure.

Nonetheless, and although she had announced that she would not continue to wear black within the confines of Bromleigh Hall, either, Sabina made no demur when her maid proffered the despised black bombazine on the morning of their expedition to the village. She said only that she preferred one of the lighter-weight silk gowns, then donned it complacently and added only a small cameo brooch by way of ornamentation. She even ascended the carriage with her bonnet veil down and when, half a mile down the road, she unpinned this and stuffed it into the pocket in the door of the vehicle, Dulcie made no comment, seeing this as a minor setback. In any case, Sabina's complexion was so pale as to leave no observer in doubt of her continued grief at the loss in her family.

It was a bright, almost relentlessly cheerful day, and all three ladies soon succumbed to the mild weather and had the coachman put down the top on the landaulet so that they might enjoy the soothing effect of the sun on their faces.

"Summer is my favorite season of the year," Georgina declared, putting her face up to the sun in total disregard of the danger of freckles. "Lewis says he likes autumn, because the air is so brisk and bracing, but I must be a very indolent sort of person, because I prefer the warmth of summer."

"I agree," said Dulcie, "although I might have a small partiality for spring, when everything is new and green. Of course, the twins were born in spring, so that may influence my preference."

"We should have brought them along with us!" Georgina said, referring to Dulcie and Henry's six-year-old boys, Ian and Ivor.

"Oh, I think not," said their fond mother. "They would be bored with shopping. Anyway, Henry promised to help them to build a treehouse today, and I'm sure that is a much more agreeable prospect than a tame carriage ride with their mother."

"Which is your favorite season?" Georgina asked Sabina, who had thus far listened in silence to the conversation.

"Let me guess—you go out riding in all weathers, so you must prefer the greater challenge of winter!"

Sabina had to laugh at that. "I know I must seem a very wintery sort of person just now, but actually I agree with Lewis. There is nothing like a ride through the woods with dry leaves underfoot and the sun shining through the bare branches."

"Well, today is a fine day for a drive to the village," Dulcie observed. "I wonder if Randolph has already collected the post. I was hoping for a letter from my mother."

"Telling you how they have set the house aright again after my disruptive descent last week?" Sabina said. Dulcie looked bemusedly at her for a moment before she remembered the story that had been given the family about Sabina's accident and took the hint.

"Oh, I'm sure it was no trouble at all, Sabina dear."

Sabina smiled wryly, but said no more, as Georgina began waving to people she knew as they neared Ashton-bury.

As the party approached the village green, a murmur of voices could be heard, and when applied to, their coachman remarked that the annual village fete was being held today, and a fine day it was for it.

"Oh dear," Dulcie said. "I suppose we must avoid the High Street then. I cannot think how I could have forgotten the day. Put us down at the Feathers, John, and we will walk to the shops by way of Bosworth Lane. Does that seem agreeable to you, Sabina? Georgie?"

Georgina expressed herself happy to follow Dulcie's lead in anything, and Sabina murmured her consent, but noted that her sister-in-law did not meet her eyes. She did not for a moment believe that Dulcie had forgotten the fete, since the Bromleys made a point of taking an active part in each year's event. To be sure, since this year's planning had unhappily coincided with the late earl's final illness, none of the village officials had approached the family about their participation, but Sabina knew that Dulcie would, at the very least, have sent some of the servants to assist with setting up booths and baking cakes to be sold and painting banners. She would certainly not have forgotten when the event was to take place.

Sabina had no notion of what Dulcie intended by this minor deception, but she was in a mood not to question anything. Indeed, she preferred not to exercise her mind in any fashion, for lately she had found that whatever she turned it to invariably led down a path she did not wish to follow.

She did not, as it happened, discover that Dulcie had any ulterior motive. Their few errands accomplished, the ladies returned to the Feathers to recoup their energies with a cup of tea before starting for home. They seated themselves by one of the few small windows, with a view of the High Street. Sabina was a little surprised to find that the slight exercise of walking from shop to shop—not to mention doing so in Georgina's bracing company—had already revived her flagging spirits, and she gazed about with unexpected interest.

"Oh, look," Georgina said. "There are booths set up along the green. Would it be all right if we had just a quick look to see what is being offered?"

"You may do so, of course, dear," Dulcie said. "We'll follow along behind."

"And hold your purse," Sabina added, "lest you be tempted to extravagance."

Since Georgina was an only child and the apple of her father's eye, she was more than able to fund any extravagance she cared to name, so this admonition was greeted with no respect whatever. "Pooh," said that young lady. "How could I possibly be extravagant at a village fair? This is scarcely Bond Street."

"I wouldn't know," Sabina murmured as she and Dulcie repaired to one of the benches outside the inn while Georgina went ahead to pore over the bangles and beads at one of the stalls on the green. "I've never seen Bond Street."

Dulcie looked stricken. "Oh dear, I'd forgotten that. You did not have a proper come-out, did you, Sabina?"

"Oh, I did, but only at the Leicester assemblies. Very

tame it was, too, but at the time I did not wish to be away from home for even a few months."

"Are you sorry now?"

"Not for that, no."

Dulcie decided against inquiring further into this remark and tactfully changed the subject.

"Shall we invite some young people to the Hall to amuse Georgina?" she asked. "It need not be anything formal."

"I think Georgina came to visit *us*," Sabina said, smiling. "Lewis, in particular."

"Oh, I see." Dulcie was pensive for a moment, watching their cousin bartering cheerfully with an old man selling hand-woven reed baskets. "Henry said the same thing, but I was not sure what—"

"What she would see in him? You have only to watch them together, Dulcie. Georgina has loved Lewis since she was five years old, and his disability has had no effect on her feelings. Indeed, it matters only to him. You'll see, she will wear him down."

"I'm sure I hope so."

When Georgina came back to show off her purchases, Dulcie asked her, "Would you care to watch any of the activities? We could find a spot at a discreet distance. I expect no one would disturb us."

"Oh, let's do!" Georgina exclaimed.

Sabina had been on the point of disclaiming any desire to watch small children dirtying themselves in sack races, but was reluctant to spoil her young cousin's amusement. Additionally, just at that moment, a group of soldiers in uniform came around the corner and walked in their direction, talking animatedly among themselves. They were, Sabina saw as they came closer, cavalry officers, and one of them was Captain the Honorable Robert Ashton. As he passed near their bench, his eyes met hers briefly before he turned away as if he had not seen her, and he and his friends continued on their way.

Georgina glanced admiringly after the officers, then turned as if to ask about them. Just at that moment, Dulcie, who had been occupied with choosing cakes from a tray brought out to them by the waiter and had missed this little scene, turned to her companions again, and Sabina said to her, "I believe there must be racing of some sort to be seen. Perhaps we can watch for a short time."

"The very thing!" Georgina agreed, then added slyly, "How did you know about the racing, Sabina?"

Sabina looked her cousin in the eye and said in Alicia's most quelling manner, "There is racing *every* year."

Dulcie signaled the waiter again, who confirmed that some officers who chanced to be passing through the village had agreed to display their equestrian skills and join some of the local young men in a race.

So it was that an hour later, the Bromley ladies sat in their open carriage under a conveniently shady tree not very distant from a paddock in which three or four officers were taking turns putting their mounts through their paces. They were obviously well acquainted with one another, and Sabina found herself envying them their cheerful camaraderie and wishing she had friends with whom she could be so at ease.

She had Dulcie, of course, who was all anyone could wish for in a sister, but her first loyalty, naturally, was to her husband so that Sabina could not call on her whenever she wished, nor had they entirely the same interests in common.

Dulcie was teasing Georgina about the handsome black-haired officer who attracted as much feminine admiration as his fine black horse did from the gentleman, but Georgina declared him to be "nothing out of the common way." Sabina saw nothing unusual in Georgina's sole dissent from the general opinion about the officer in question, given her undimmed loyalty to Lewis. One of the lieutenant's fellows, however, was another matter.

"Oh dear," Dulcie said. "I do believe that is Robert Ashton on the big white stallion. I don't think he has seen us, Sabina—do you wish to leave?"

"Our departure at this point would doubtless attract more attention than our staying," Sabina said. "Do not concern, yourself, Dulcie. I shall not burst into tears again. Ever."

Her sister-in-law squeezed her hand sympathetically, and Sabina felt a pang of guilt for supposing even for an instant that Dulcie had planned any of this. After all, there was no way she could have known that Captain Ashton would be here; they were scarcely acquainted. Georgina studied her slightly flushed face again, and Sabina had the distinct impression that her seemingly flighty cousin had the ability to see into her soul.

The display of clever steps having concluded, the officers offered to take on any challengers in a race, the small fee paid by each racer to be put into the fund for the restoration of the church belfry. The lieutenant with the roguish grin proved to be the most attractive target of challenge, and every other race was his, for no one seemed able to beat him. Captain Ashton evoked sufficient interest, however, for the onlookers to see him win twice and lose by half a length once—to an elderly gentleman who looked by his bearing in the saddle to be a veteran of another, earlier campaign.

"They are remarkable horsemen," Dulcie observed. "I suppose it is no wonder that they accredited themselves so well in the charge at Waterloo."

"The Union Brigade's charge?" Sabina asked interestedly. "I did not know James—Captain Ashton took part in that."

"Oh, yes. Henry read me the account in the newspapers. I would not have remembered except that my maid is acquainted with a kitchen maid at Ashtonbury Abbey, and she repeated the story when the captain came home. You know how servants like to spread such tidbits about local people—especially about a member of such a prominent family."

"You need not sing the Ashtons' praises, Dulcie. I am aware of your partiality in that direction."

"Not at all. I married Henry, you may recall, and I daresay Richard no longer gives me even a passing thought."

Georgina eyed her elder cousin with interest. "Did you ever love him? How came you to be betrothed to him?"

"It was an arranged match, of course, but I was not opposed to it. I had never felt the slightest *tendre* for anyone else, and I supposed myself immune. I had also heard that within such marriages both parties are free to follow their own lives, once an heir has been produced. I was very young, and I fancied this an advanced idea which would suit me down to the ground."

She laughed. "Of course, after I met Henry, the idea that any husband of mine would fail to dance attendance on me from daybreak to dusk was an appalling notion. I am perfectly capable of reminding him, should he be remiss in this regard, that had I married Richard, I should have been a countess by now. Oh, look, the blacksmith has raised a challenge to all four officers!"

This indeed proved to be the case, for, like many another villager, the waiter from the Feathers had laid aside his toil to watch, and he came to inform the ladies of the details of the challenge, also advising them that the blacksmith's name was Jack Belfield. Dulcie thanked the obliging waiter for the information and requested their coachman to give him a seat beside him to watch the race, a vantage point the waiter was happy to take up. He struck up a lively conversation with the coachman, and the two were shortly making wagers on the race, an activity to which the ladies turned discreetly deaf ears.

"Now, we know Captain Ashton," Dulcie said, "and I believe the bruising rider with the black hair is Lieutenant the Viscount Markham. Therefore, the stout gentleman and the thin, redheaded one must be—since apparently they have all sold out and we need no longer use their ranks—Mr. Trent and Mr. Williams."

"You are as good as a playbill, Dulcie," Sabina said, falling into the spirit of the occasion despite herself. "Which do you fancy to win against the blacksmith?"

"Do you care to lay a small wager among ourselves?" Dulcie asked. "I confess, I am partial to the black-haired viscount."

"Then you must give me odds. He has won every race he has run thus far."

"Yes, but his horse must be tired, and both the blacksmith and his mount are fresh," Georgina observed. "How do you fancy Captain Ashton's chances?" she added with a mischievous glint in her eye.

Sabina was mightily tempted to back one of the other gentlemen, but instinct—and her father's advice remembered from when she attended her first race meeting—told her not to bet for any other reason than that she was sure she had a winner.

"Enough to place a wager on him," she said.

They pooled the remaining shillings in their purses and settled their wagers among themselves just as Mr. Trent's showy bay leaped from the starting gate, getting a fast lead on Jack Belfield's sturdy roan—which he quickly lost, the blacksmith finishing several lengths ahead. The crowd cheered wildly for their own champion, and Sabina saw Captain Ashton exchange an enigmatic look with his friend Markham. Suddenly she knew how the race would end.

As the waiter had explained, the blacksmith would be declared the victor if he beat three of the four officers. Mr. Williams was in the saddle next and gave a good account of himself, finishing only half a length behind Jack Belfield's roan, which left it up to the remaining two officers to maintain the reputation of the corps.

After a rest and a round of ale, the blacksmith and Viscount Markham raced, and again Markham won handily.

"The roan must be winded," Dulcie said.

"So must be the cavalry horses," Sabina countered. "They have all run several races. Only Markham's black seems inexhaustible."

She held her breath when Robert Ashton mounted his big charger. He looked as if he was enjoying himself immensely and responded with good humor to the jibes of his fellow officers and the encouragement of the crowd. He, too, was a local champion, Sabina realized, wondering how that had come to be.

Captain Ashton signaled his horse into a few turns that looked remarkably like a bow to the crowd, and the blacksmith called out, "Aye, m'lord, he can dance—but can he run?"

Markham laughed at that and shouted, "He's seen through that trick, Robin! Show him what else you have up your sleeve!"

Ashton grinned and brought his horse up to the starting mark with no further displays of virtuosity. The race was over in a minute, but to Sabina, holding her breath, it seemed to take an eternity.

The two riders left the start at the same instant and stayed together for the first quarter of the course. Then Captain Ashton, on the inside, pulled ahead briefly before being overtaken in the third quarter. Just before the finish line, the captain put on a burst of speed, but so did the blacksmith, and in the end it was Jack Belfield's muscular roan that won by a nose.

The crowd cheered both riders around the track again in a triumphal march, which the horses seemed to enjoy as much as their riders. Dulcie held out her hand, and Sabina put two shillings into it. She looked up again and thought she saw Robert Ashton wink at her. Doubtless she was mistaken, she told herself. Just as she was mistaken in thinking that he had deliberately held back a fraction of a second at the finish to let the blacksmith finish first.

"So you see my difficulty," Robert said to Viscount Markham as they made their way homeward that evening, laden with honors and goodwill and numerous toasts from the villagers.

Mr. Trent and Mr. Williams had elected to spend the night in the village, having been invited to any number of local entertainments by the other participants in the races, but Markham had professed a preference for the comfortable bed he had been given the previous night at Ashtonbury Abbey. Declaring that he must be getting soft now that he was a civilian again, his companions agreed to meet him at the Feathers early the next morning to resume their journey to Wales.

"What I could see was that she is every bit as stubborn as you are," Markham said on hearing his friend's tale of his unlucky courtship. "Much better-looking, of course. A real stunner, in fact."

Robert smiled. "I'll concede that readily enough. And I'm afraid her stubbornness is a family trait, particularly well developed in her."

He outlined the history of The Quarrel to the viscount, who declared it to be a great deal of botheration over dead people and dead issues, but Robert assured him that it was far from moribund.

"Her father had wanted to make peace, and I had hoped myself to win Sabina by somehow resolving the differences between our families. But her loyalty is stronger than her reason, and I am not willing for her to blame me for what she would consider a betrayal of her family—which is how marriage to me must appear to her."

"There must be some way to win fair—if stubborn—maid. It does seem that she has some feeling for you."

"She does that, but just now it is so far from love that I fear it will be near impossible to turn it in that direction. A resolution of The Quarrel would certainly make our future life together more comfortable. Neither of us would need to be estranged from our families, and it must be a good thing if other members of both families got along—or at least spoke with one another. However, I am prepared to abandon my family if I must—excepting my nephews, but that is another problem altogether."

"There ought to be a way to do both," Markham said. "Mend the quarrel *and* woo fair maid."

"So I thought, but how? Do I leave her be and hope she sees the error of her ways, or go after her?"

"I've never known you to turn your back on a challenge, Robin. I'd say, think of it as a military campaign. Plan your attack carefully—and spring it quickly."

"Aye, General. If only I could think of a plan of battle."

"Make her jealous."

"With whom? There's no one else in the neighborhood who'd let me use her that way."

"Oh, I don't know. That little barmaid . . ."

"I'm sorry I asked."

They emerged from a wood just then and Markham, spotting a clear field before them, called out "Cavalry, charge!" before setting his horse to a gallop and leaving his friend in his dust. Robert wasted no time in taking up the challenge, but was not surprised to reach the end of the field well behind the other man.

"Unfair!" Robert called, laughing. "You cheated."

"Of course I did. I can win over almost anyone except you, so I must take what advantage I can. Anyhow, what can you do? Report me to my commanding officer?"

"I shall put a notice in all the papers."

"That won't tell anyone anything they don't know already." He stroked his horse's neck and whispered loving words in the black's ear. It twitched expressively, and Robert would have sworn the horse understood him.

"I say, look there, Robin—what river is that?"

Robert looked down from the rise they were standing on and smiled. "That's no river, that's the Grand Union Canal."

"You don't say. Didn't you tell me you had been putting in manual labor at some lock? I knew there was a sparsity of serious amusements in these parts, but I thought that was going a bit far for a little fun."

"Come down with me," Robin said. "I'll show you the results of my labors and make you jealous."

Markham took up that challenge as well, and before long was being introduced to the Theaks and given a tour of the boat and lock. He teased Rose about her apple cheeks, making her blush, and went out of his way to be deferential to George. Bill, of course, he was already acquainted with, and the two reminisced over a cup of cider about their adventures in Spain, some of which put Robert to the blush.

The sun was well down toward the horizon before they tore themselves away, Robert saying they would offend his sister-in-law if they were late to dinner again. Rose got a little of her own back by declaring that the viscount could doubtless charm any hostess out of taking offense at anything he did, but Markham conceded that Lady Kimborough might be an exception to this rule, and bade his present hostess a fond good-bye.

On the remainder of their journey, Markham expressed his delight at meeting the Theaks, but Robert found that his friend had not forgotten their earlier conversation in the course of the afternoon's bonhomie.

"There are other ways to make her jealous than of another woman," he observed after they had ridden along for some way in companionable silence.

Robert turned his head. "What do I have that she does not? That she could possibly envy?"

"You'd know that better than I. Think about it. If she came to believe she would be missing something rare—other than your charming person, of course—she might be more willing to consider overlooking your innumerable faults."

Robert was silent for a few moment and then said, "You may be right."

"I'm always right," said the viscount confidently. "You can expect me back through here a month from now—and I'll expect *you* to at least be betrothed by then!"

Chapter 9

In the days following the village fete, Sabina found it impossible to return to the uncaring, unthinking state she had forced herself into following her return from Market Harborough. Instead she indulged in melancholy thought and futile self-recrimination, relieved only by wistful daydreams of what might have been.

Early in the morning, before her mind was fully awake, she drifted happily in that state between sleeping and waking, where she seemed able to transport herself easily to the canal and the narrowboat. There she saw Rose and Bill Theak and heard the birds' call from the bank and smelled the coffee brewing in the painted tin pot Rose used.

And there was James Owen, lovingly watching over her. She smiled in her sleep and then, only reluctantly when Emily knocked tentatively on the door, put aside her dream and rose to another endless day.

But even the prosaic events of a day at home could not prevent her from seeing reminders in every cloud and tree of her time on the boat. And of her time with James Owen.

He had been so considerate when she was ill, and then so gentle when he looked into her eyes and said he loved her. But no—he had not actually said so. Had he? She racked her memory, but on this matter it was indeed faulty.

She did remember that he had drawn back from making any commitment to their future together until she had regained her memory. Surely that indicated some consideration on his part for her vulnerable state. And she did remember that he had kissed her—or had she kissed him? She felt her face grow warm with the memory. How brave she had been when she did not know what courage was!

I wish we could be together like this always, he had said as they stood together on the narrowboat that day. James Owen had said that—only hours before Robert Ashton betrayed her.

She could not yet bring herself to think of James Owen as being one and the same with Robert Ashton, although when that name entered her consciousness, it no longer automatically aroused anger or resentment in her. Perhaps, if she could keep that lack of emotion about him, she might be able to do something to break this stalemate that was rendering her incapable of action. She could not be herself again if she continued to mope about like this. She certainly could not wait for him to suggest a next step—*his* future, after all, was not at stake. *He* could resume his old life with perfect ease.

He had not tried to communicate with her, either, which must prove that he had no intention of apologizing for his deceit. *I'm sorry, Miranda.* Very well, she would give him that. He had called out to her as she hurried to get away from him at that shop in Market Harborough, and she had not stopped to hear any more. She supposed she ought to take the next step, but how? How could she apologize without abasing herself, without laying herself open to further hurt?

The answer came to her one evening, just as she had blown out the candle by her bed.

Of course! He could not refuse. It was the only solution. Her mind whirled with the possibilities, and she felt she would never be able to sleep this night for thinking about how she would present them to him. But within half an hour, she was deep in blissful unconsciousness.

She spent more time in carrying out her decision than in making it. First she must think of a neutral place for them to meet—she would not go to Ashtonbury Abbey, so she could not ask him to come to Bromleigh Hall, and she most certainly would not meet him on the canal. Not there, not where the memories would rise up like ghosts to haunt her.

Her mind's eye roamed over the nearby country and then lighted on the perfect place. This problem solved, she spent an hour writing and tearing up letters before finally settling on the simplest of polite requests:

Dear Captain Ashton:
I would be grateful for a word with you. I shall ride out to Carling tomorrow and hope to meet you on the path near Michael's Bridge at noon.

> Yours,
> Sabina Bromley

This missive dispatched, she then put the matter from her mind as settled. She must face yet another endless day before she saw him, but this, she was surprised to find, was suddenly less of a chore.

She called Emily to help her with her hair, and the little maid, apparently taking this interest in her appearance as a sign that her mistress was herself again, chattered away as she plied brush and comb. Her mind elsewhere, Sabina scarcely heard, but smiled and agreed at appropriate places so that Emily was then able to report to the housekeeper, Mrs. Woodruff, that all was well with Lady Sabina, and "before you know it, there'll be no holding her back and we can fret about her just as we used to."

Sabina, having arrayed herself to her satisfaction in a black-and-white striped day dress with a black collar, went looking for something to do. She found Georgina and Dulcie in the family parlor, a bow-windowed room that looked out over the home wood and was pleasantly sunny today. The two ladies were engaged in mixing potpourri, and their table was covered with bowls of dried rose petals, narcissus, spices, and herbs.

"Oh, hullo, Sabina," Georgina said, glancing up. "Here, smell this."

Sabina obligingly put her nose into the bowl Georgina held up to her, which contained an array of petals.

"Too delicate," she pronounced. "It won't keep its fragrance very long."

"Oh dear," Georgina lamented, "I was afraid that was so. I shall have to add some cloves, much as I dislike to do so. But it is a pleasant fragrance, is it not?"

Sabina agreed that a cologne of that particular recipe would be very agreeable.

"I shall make a note of the mixture, Georgie, before you discard it," Dulcie said. "I have been meaning to purchase some fresh oils and elixirs," she added, "to mix special perfumes for all of us—us ladies, that is to say, although I daresay Randolph would help us if we gave him some. What do you think, Sabina?"

Sabina pulled a chair up to the table and said that was a splendid idea for Christmas gifts. She joined in the mixing and, grateful that neither lady had made any remark about either her absence or her apparent recovery, was able to laugh and exchange silliness with them comfortably for another hour.

When Georgina stood up, stretched, and said she simply must get some exercise or she would grow too fat to fit into her new clothes, Sabina offered to go for a walk with her.

"Oh, good," Georgina said, "You know all the paths, and you don't dawdle. I need a brisk trot today."

"I shan't join you, then," Dulcie said. "I like to dawdle."

"Then you may go to the greenhouse and look to see if there is any more rosemary," Georgina told her. "I have an idea."

"I dare not ask what it is."

"Oh, it is no secret. I only thought it would be fun to mix up a scent that reminds one of the baking and cooking that goes on for Christmas. I daresay the gentlemen like *those* fragrances well enough!"

Dulcie shook her head, and Sabina laughed as she and her cousin departed by the garden door. They were soon walking as briskly as Georgina could wish, for her legs were not nearly as long as Sabina's, through the wood and up the rise behind it.

At the top of the rise, Georgina called a halt and said she simply must rest for five minutes. They sat down on the grass and talked about nothing for twenty minutes, during which Sabina began finally to feel as if her life was as happy as it had always been and that nothing had changed. She knew that it had, and when they returned to the Hall, there would be reminders everywhere that her days as a carefree girl were over, but she was glad she could remember them easily after all.

Glancing down the hillside, she saw Michael's Bridge in the distance and thought about what she would say to Robert Ashton tomorrow. Even that did not depress her spirits, and at the end of the day, she was able to pass another comfortable night, from which she woke the next morning refreshed and confident of success.

She rode out with a groom in attendance an hour before she needed to, in order to exercise both her horse and herself, but when she approached the appointed meeting place over a rise and saw Captain Ashton leaning on the gate to the bridge, his big white horse nibbling the grass nearby, she dismissed her groom. This worthy, accustomed to Lady Sabina's predilection for roaming about the estate unescorted, departed without protest. Indeed, he had been surprised to be asked to accompany her in the first place, and exercised his mind on the return journey on the question of whether the lady intended him to report her meeting with a gentleman when he returned to the Hall, and if so, what reason she could possibly have for it. On the whole, he thought it safer to hold his tongue.

Sabina had taken the groom only because he chanced to be hanging about the stable with nothing to occupy his time, and having dismissed him, she thought no more about him. Indeed, she found herself growing oddly short of breath as she approached Captain Ashton who, lost in contemplation of the stream beneath the bridge, appeared not to hear her until she was reining her mare to a halt. Then he turned around, and for a moment, she seemed to stop breathing altogether.

He really was as handsome as she remembered. Dressed informally in well-worn riding breeches, a corduroy coat, and a red kerchief knotted carelessly around his neck, he nevertheless presented a graceful picture. Sabina remembered her knight errant and tried not to smile; she did not think they wore riding breeches under their shining armor.

Their eyes met briefly before she dismounted, an exercise with which he did not assist her. She was disappointed not to feel his hand on hers again, even for so mundane a reason, but she dared to hope that he was as anxious about this encounter as she was.

Once on her feet, she looked at him again, searching for something familiar in his look. But there was nothing. His gaze was cool, as if he were deliberately keeping the warmth out of it, and when he spoke, his voice was carefully neutral, betraying no indication of his feelings at this moment.

"Lady Sabina." He took her hand and shook it formally, letting it go almost at once. She stood up straighter and tried not to let the sigh of disappointment escape her lips.

"Captain Ashton. Thank you for—making yourself available."

"How may I serve you, ma'am?"

"May we not walk as we speak, sir? I find I am still restless despite my ride."

They set off along a path leading into a spinney. Sabina had deliberately chosen this bridge, because it crossed not the canal, but a tributary stream of the Avon, and there was no towpath along the water. It was, however, a pleasant, verdant spot, and she hoped this would help her cause rather than distract from what she had to say.

"I saw you at the fete the other day," she said.

"I know."

"You—and your friends—appeared to be enjoying yourselves hugely."

He smiled slightly at that. "It is difficult not to enjoy

oneself with men one has been through so much with—particularly when they are as fond of merriment as Nicky—Viscount Markham, that is—has always been."

"I envy you that kind of friendship."

He glanced sharply at her, and she wondered what had startled him about that remark. Could he possibly be less indifferent than he appeared? Could he care at least a little about her happiness?

"You and the other ladies seemed to be good friends also."

"Dulcie is my sister-in-law and Georgina—the young woman in the blue stripes and ridiculous hat—a cousin, but yes, my family are my friends as well."

She walked a little farther without speaking, swinging idly at branches along the path with her riding crop. He kept up easily with her long stride for a little way, then stopped, forcing her to halt also.

"What makes you restless, Sabina?" he asked in a different, but no more encouraging tone. She told herself that his use of her Christian name was at least not discouraging.

"I have a proposition to put to you, Captain—Robert. I hope you will consider it—dispassionately."

"A proposition?"

"A proposal, let us say."

"Pray present it."

Gathering her courage, she resumed walking. He still did not touch her, but as they negotiated the narrow path, her skirt occasionally brushed his leg, and once or twice he stepped ahead of her to move a branch out of her way or point out a protruding root. She found this almost more distracting than physical contact, so that when they reached a small clearing in the middle of the spinney, she stopped and faced him.

"I daresay you have been apprised of the terms of my father's will—that is, as they concern you."

"I have."

His responses were maddeningly brief and unadorned. She supposed he was waiting for her to state her proposition before he committed himself to any expression of greater interest.

"Naturally," she said, attempting to get to the point but finding it nearly unapproachable, "I have been somewhat—anxious about the matter myself. You understand, it affects me more directly than it does you."

"I would say it affects us both equally."

"If they are carried out, certainly. If not, only I shall suffer."

"Suffer? Surely not. I was not led to believe that you would be cast out penniless into the world should you refuse to marry me."

"No, no—certainly not. But—well, I would lose a great deal of what I hold dear. I could manage on a fraction of the allowance I have been receiving—indeed, I am not at all profligate—but I should not enjoy the freedom I have had at Bromleigh Hall all my life. Until now."

"The earl would not deny you access to your childhood home, would he?"

"The earl . . . ? Oh, Fletcher. No, I suppose not, but it would not be the same. I could not continue living there as if I were a poor relation, and I would not be able to live at Carling, which would have been my second choice in any case. Indeed, I had fully expected to remove to Carling when my father recovered from his illness. Or did not, as it transpired."

"And Carling is . . ."

"A house which was once occupied by my great-aunt and would have been mine in the normal course of events. It is located near Swinford and thus not a great distance from home—that is, from Bromleigh Hall—so that I should be able to visit the family whenever I wished and still be my own mistress."

She glanced up at him, but he continued to wait with polite interest for her to reveal her proposal.

"It is a lovely house, quite my favorite of all of Father's properties. You will agree, I'm sure, when—if—you care to visit it." She felt herself babbling and stopped to take a deep, composing breath.

"I expect you are wondering where all this is leading."

He smiled then, and for a moment she hoped that he did have some sympathy for the difficulty she was having in making any sort of appeal to him. She looked away from him, however, determined not to think of him as James Owen. If she did that, she would find herself begging, and her pride would never forgive her that.

"In short," she said all in a rush, "I wish to propose an arrangement between us that will, I hope, benefit us both as well as fulfill my father's wishes."

She paused for another breath. "I am proposing a marriage of convenience between us. We could be married quietly at Bromleigh Hall—or at Ashtonbury Abbey, if you prefer—but after the ceremony we would each be free to live our own lives. Separately."

She dared a glance at him, but his expression had scarcely changed. He was, however, not smiling.

"Suppose one of us wished to marry someone else?"

This possibility had never occurred to her. She had never had any intention of marrying, at least she had not since Peter—but that possibility was no longer available—and she had supposed that Robert had no such interest either. She had certainly never heard that he had expressed an interest in any local girl.

Her imagination began to run wild. Good heavens, could he have become involved with some woman in Spain? She felt oddly disappointed at the possibility that he might prefer someone else, even if he could not have her.

"The expression on your face is a wonder to behold," he said, a slight smile returning to his lips. "Let me disabuse you of the notion that I have any interest in marrying anyone else. But why should I marry you?"

She was taken aback. "Why? But—I thought you would be eager to mend the quarrel, as my father was."

"I'm sorry, Sabina, that your father felt it necessary to use you as the means by which to resolve the differences between our families. I know he would not have done so had he known what the results would be."

"How do you know that?"

"I suspect there is a great deal about your father that you did not know, but one thing is that he and I became friends—or nearly so—before he became ill. Unfortunately, I was obliged to return to Spain before we could further our acquaintance. But in Spain, my dear Sabina, I learned how supremely unimportant such things as that quarrel are. You, apparently, have not yet learned that lesson."

"But don't you understand what I have been saying? I am trying to resolve it."

"You are eager to carry out your father's wishes because you loved him. You would also very much like to live at Carling on an income that would keep you there in comfort without the indignity of having to accept an allowance from your brother. But I believe that you would prefer to do all that without giving any ground to the enemy."

She could scarcely believe her ears. How did he know all *that*? He could not have learned it from her father. Had he been listening to gossip or pressing her friends for the intimate details of her life? But she had just told him that her only friends were her family. She did not understand.

"But what would the advantage be to me to marrying you, given that I do not give a fig about The Quarrel? As you rightly pointed out, only you would suffer by our not marrying. I am perfectly content in my single state and certainly have no reason to change it for a very *in*convenient marriage."

"But I thought—I mean, I do not intend to deny you any profit from the venture. I would make over to you the income from Carling, and I daresay my brother—"

"I have always enjoyed an ample income, and my prize money from Spain is invested in the funds and doing very well. I don't need money, and even if I did, as a business proposition, your offer is of little value."

"Well, then—will nothing induce you to consider my offer?"

"I might be tempted."

"By what? Oh, is it the appearance of such an unusual arrangement? I suppose—well, Carling is a large house. I would be able, perhaps . . . That is, if you wish to live under the same roof . . ."

"Have you no pride, Sabina?"

"I beg your pardon?"

"No, perhaps you do not." His eyes had finally lost that blank, carefully schooled expression. There was unmistakable anger in them now. "But I do have mine. I love you, Sabina. I have always loved you, and about that one thing I have no pride. But I will not marry you unless it is a true marriage—in mind, body, and soul. We could marry, and we could be happy, but only if we marry for love, Sabina, and for no other reason."

He moved closer to her. She tried to back away, but his arms went around her and held her fast. "You remember love, don't you, Sabina? It tastes like this . . ."

His mouth closed over hers then, and for a moment, she let herself remember, let herself feel the warmth stealing through her at his harsh, yet gentle kiss. But then he deepened the kiss, and she pulled roughly away.

"You deceived me!" she hissed. "What assurance do I have that you will not do so again?"

He stepped back and looked at her, angry again. "*I* deceived *you*? Have you told your family about your loss of memory, Miranda? Or are you too ashamed at your own deception?"

"I did not do it deliberately to deceive you!"

"And I did not act to hurt you. But it appears we have hurt each other. My apology was no doubt grossly inadequate, but I repeat it now. I'm sorry, Sabina. I wish I could take it all back. Nearly all."

"You made me love you by deceiving me!"

"Yes. I'm sorry for that, too. But you did love me. Me, Sabina, not James Owen."

She could feel herself on the verge of tears and the pride he said she did not have would not let her show them to him. "No, not you," she whispered, pain clutching her heart. "James Owen was another man, and we met in another time. That time is gone now, I see that."

She began to run then, out of the spinney and down to

the bridge where she had left her horse. She did not look back until she had mounted the mare and headed on the road home.

Then she glanced back. There was no sign that he had ever been there.

Chapter 10

Following his encounter with Sabina, Captain Ashton found himself missing his comrades in arms. He could have used Nicky's carelessly given but always sage advice—particularly when the matter concerned the ladies. Richard was equally discreet, but his brother had counseled patience, and Robert did not think he could remain patient very much longer. And it was certainly no use to apply to Lavinia, on the grounds of her being female, for she would only cast aspersions on Sabina's character and say there was nothing else to be expected from a Bromley.

He could only search his own soul for an answer. Taking Salamanca out for his early morning ride the day after Viscount Markham and his other friends had left for Derby, Robert pulled up on a rise overlooking the Laughton Hills, the direction in which he knew Carling lay, and stared at the dawn landscape contemplatively.

Should he have accepted Sabina's proposal, hoping that love would win out in the end? No, he had his pride, too. And he had done enough damage already in the name of love; he could not be sure that Sabina would not come to hate him even more if she were forced to endure his presence, if in name only, every day of her life.

Gazing down into the nearer distance, he caught the glint of sunlight on the canal. He smiled. He had not seen Rose and Bill for nearly a week. He would go there and refresh his mind and spirit; perhaps then he might come up with an answer before it was too late to sway Sabina in any direction at all.

On his way down the hill, however, he had a sudden

thought and turned back toward the Abbey. His nephews had been begging him to take them on a picnic; now was as good a time as any. Besides, he had been intending to introduce the boys to the Theaks.

As he rode up the drive, two small bundles of energy burst out of the woods to run beside Salamanca to the house. Geoffrey, the elder and already tall for his age, won the race as usual, with his younger brother, his blond curls in disarray, gamely catching up at the end.

"Halloo, Uncle Robert. Can we have a ride?"

"Gosh, sir, he's a big fellow, isn't he?"

Only Robert's battle-trained horse kept him from being thrown or the boys from being trampled. When he had dismounted and handed the reins to a grinning groom, however, he scolded them just the same.

"No, you cannot ride Salamanca until you learn how to behave around horses. Do you remember nothing I have told you?"

Lord Ashton, aged seven, protested, "We were just glad to see you, sir. We forgot that we should not make sudden noises near horses. But Salamanca must have heard all sorts of loud noises in battle, didn't he?"

"He did, but he is an exception. And flattery will avail you nothing, young sir."

"Please, please, sir," pleaded Davey Ashton, aged five, apparently believing that begging was more acceptable than flattery, particularly when accompanied by little jumps as he tried to reach Robert's hand. "Can't we just sit on the saddle with you for a little while?"

"Perhaps."

"When, sir? Today, sir?"

"Very well, sir. Today, sir. Geoffrey, go down to the stables and tell Foster to saddle Salamanca again after he has had a little rest. He should also make the donkey cart ready, since I cannot take both of you up at the same time—that *would* be asking a great deal even of a battle-hardened cavalry horse. We will go out as soon as I have had some breakfast."

With a whoop, Geoffrey ran off to the stables, while

young Davey hurried to keep up with his uncle's long strides. "May I have some breakfast with you, Uncle Robert?"

"I suppose you may, toad-eater. But haven't you eaten already? I believe your mama likes your company at breakfast, doesn't she?"

"Not really," Davey said wisely. "She just wants to be sure we're up and properly dressed. Anyway, that was *hours* ago. I'm hungry again!"

Robert grinned. "You may make a soldier yet, young 'un."

He picked up Davey and set him on his shoulders for the walk to the house. Davey squealed with delight and pulled on his hair, but Robert no longer minded. When he had first returned home, both boys had been in awe of him, having heard exaggerated tales of his heroism in the field from the servants. It was some weeks before they dared even speak to their legendary uncle, but Robert was patient and wooed them by speaking to them as if they were intelligent enough to answer for themselves, even if Lavinia often responded first or the boys were too timid to speak up.

Gradually, however, Geoffrey's admiration had turned to adoration, and the younger Davey followed his lead in this as in most things. It was all Robert could do then to stay off the pedestal they erected for his use without giving his nephews a distaste for him. This he contrived by offering them advice and lessons in all the things their mother thought too dangerous or too vulgar for young boys—particularly the sons of an earl—to know or hear.

But Robert had not entirely forgotten his own boyhood, and he knew what an adventure it was to brave the woods at night, or learn to shoot a gun, or ride on a horse bigger than one's own docile little pony. He was invariably careful also to teach the boys to be cautious in strange places, to handle weapons with respect, and to be both kind and firm toward animals. Lavinia would have to be content with that.

Now that he had won their loyalty, Robert had another goal in mind. Their parents might be content, if not determined, to carry on the rivalry between the Ashtons and the Bromleighs, but Robert was equally determined not to let it continue into the next generation.

Thus far, he had merely mentioned the other family casually in conversation, when pointing out where their land began and—just as important—where the Ashtons' estates left off. Careful probing elicited the information that the boys had not yet been made aware of The Quarrel, and Robert was grateful for the first time for their father's indifference and their mother's disinclination to raise distasteful subjects within the hearing of innocents.

Indeed, Lavinia confirmed this by confronting him in the breakfast parlor, while the boys were in the stables, with her impressions of Earl Bromleigh's will.

"I assure you, you are well out of it, Robin dear," she said as confidently as if he shared her opinion. "Why you should have been involved in the first place, I fail to understand."

"I would have thought that to be obvious," Robert replied, offering to pour Lavinia a cup of cocoa. She shook her head, and he put the pot down. "There is no other eligible Montagu for Miss Capulet to marry."

She frowned. "I do wish you would not use literary allusions, Robin. I am never certain what you mean by them."

"I use them hoping to make my meaning clearer," he said, "but forgive me if I have failed. I meant in plainer English, that Earl Bromleigh hoped to resolve the differences between our families by joining our houses through my marriage to Lady Sabina."

"Nonsense. It cannot be done so simply. Anyway, what if you refused?"

"I have not refused. She has."

Lavinia stared at him in amazement. Robert noticed for the first time that her eyes bulged slightly, making her look remarkably like a distant relation of the Prince Regent. He wondered why she had not claimed such a kinship; perhaps she considered the disreputable prince a connection she would not care to make.

"I cannot credit it," she said finally. "Richard told me

only that that particular clause in the will would likely be legally overturned."

Robert inwardly applauded his brother's ingenuity, but he preferred that Lavinia not labor under any illusions about him.

"I do not wish it overturned, Lavinia. At least, not until I have exhausted all other means of persuading Lady Sabina to marry me."

"I do not know how you can lower yourself so. The Bromleys will hold this over our heads forever."

"What if they do?" Robert asked, becoming irritated.

"I daresay we can rise above it," Lavinia conceded, "but one would not wish to offer even the smallest reason for the Bromleys to feel superior to the Ashtons."

"Why should they?" Robert retorted. "They are not dukes or even marquesses. Nor are we, for that matter. It seems to me that we are far more alike than not."

"Nonsense. There is no question. Why, Earl Bromleigh—indeed, there is another odd thing about them. Why do they not call themselves earls *of* Bromleigh? I'm sure their style is outmoded and ridiculous."

Robert had to laugh at that, which did nothing to appease his sister-in-law. "It *is* ridiculous, Lavinia, can't you see? These petty differences cannot justify this continued estrangement, and any others are far in the past. Even Richard, who has more right than any of us to hold a grudge, does not."

"I do not wish to discuss this further," Lavinia said, rising from her chair. "In any case, I see the boys coming back from the stables, and I refuse to sully their innocent ears with such sordid gossip."

"Gossip, indeed. What a whisker."

"Good day, Robert."

With that, the countess departed, her head held high, as if to impress an audience of Bromleys with her personal superiority, if not that of certain black sheep regrettably still cluttering the family escutcheon. Robert smiled to himself, but then, when his nephews came racing into the room and jumped onto his knees, he put out of his mind Lavinia and her dogged determination never to see any side of an argument but her own. He would not "sully their ears" with anything sordid, but he would teach them about The Quarrel in his own way.

Indeed, he had already added some information about the Ashtons' differences with the Bromleys to his other lessons to the boys about the world beyond the Abbey, dismissing it as a tradition not much different, or more real, than the ghost of a nun said to haunt the east wing, the only part of the house that still contained the stones of the original abbey.

Robert was now attempting to work out a way for Geoffrey and David to meet Edward and Diana, Earl Bromleigh's children, and Dulcie's twins without making an occasion of the meeting. But since neither set of siblings ventured into the village nor anywhere else except under heavy escort, this seemed unlikely to come about soon. In the meanwhile, Robert's excursions with his nephews were conducted in an ever-widening circle around Ashtonbury Abbey. Sooner or later, he hoped, it would encompass Bromleigh Hall.

An hour later, the little expedition of one horse, two boys, and a donkey cart driven by Foster, Robert's groom, set off for the canal, a coin toss having settled which of the boys should have the pleasure of riding before their uncle first. Davey, not very sorry to have to wait, for he liked to "help" steer the donkey cart, sat beside Foster on this conveyance as the quartet made their leisurely way along the canal.

"Where are we going, Uncle Robert?" it finally occurred to Geoffrey to ask.

"I want you to meet some very pleasant people who own a boat."

"Oh, sir, what kind of boat?" Davey asked eagerly, nearly letting the reins drop.

"Ah, a future navy man, I see. It is a narrowboat."

"What sort of boat is that?"

"Dear me, Admiral, you do have a great deal to learn before you take up your sailing career."

"I know!" Geoffrey crowed. "It is the kind of boat they sail on the canal."

"Right you are, my boy. But one does not *sail* a narrowboat. It is pulled by horses."

"A boat pulled by horses?" Davey's imagination balked. "How can that be?"

"You shall see," was all his uncle would tell them.

What they saw when the lock came into sight was George Theak whittling in a chair on deck, Bill lying on his stomach with his head in the hatch and a hammer in his hand, and Rose seated beside George, painting a tin washbasin with a bright floral design. Rose and George stood up and waved when they saw Robert and the boys coming toward them. When Robert dismounted from Salamanca, tied him to a tree, and called out, "Permission to come aboard, sir!" Bill scrambled to an upright position and ceremoniously bowed them over the gangplank, raising his hat politely to Geoffrey and David in turn.

Introductions were made all around, and for a moment the boys stood politely, trying not to look too eager to run off and explore the boat.

"What is that you are whittling, please, sir?" Davey asked George, who still held his knife and a block of wood which as yet had no defined shape.

George leaned down toward Davey. "This will be a boat like the *Rose Franklin*," he said, then held up the elongated piece of light wood. "This be the bow, see, and that the stern, and here in the middle is the cabin."

Davey stared at the wood, trying to see a boat in it. "May I watch you, sir?"

Bill interrupted. "That sounds to me like a pretty tame entertainment for two lively young fellows like you. Why don't we show you around the boat first. Then when you're tired, you can sit with us for a while and watch George work."

Those were magic words, upon which the boys eagerly turned to their uncle for permission, which was readily given. After consultation among the Theaks, Rose was delighted to show the boys the most interesting features of the boat. Bill would then give them a tour of the lock, and George would later direct a voyage of the narrowboat as far as the Welford arm and back. Foster declined an invitation to join in these activities, saying he would take the donkey cart back to the Abbey and return for the young gentlemen in time to get them home for dinner.

Robert sat down with Bill and George for a smoke, during which they could hear delighted shouts from below when the boys discovered the beds that folded down from the wall and the myriad of tiny cabinets lining the cabin, all of which they had to open and explore and close again with a bang.

"I trust they won't do any damage, Bill," Robert said. "I think they are small enough not to be able to actually sink the boat by putting a foot through the floor."

George laughed. "You should have seen Bill when he were a boy. He ran around boats as if they was dry land and was even more lively than your nephews."

"Yes, but there was only one of him."

Davey came shooting up the ladder just then, with Geoffrey bringing up the rear for once, and began shaking his uncle's chair in his excitement, while Geoffrey lifted the lid of the box of feed for the horses, inspected the contents, closed the lid again, and sat on it.

"Whoa, there, young man!" Robert reproved his younger nephew. "If I go overboard, will you jump in and save me?"

Deflated, Davey let go of the chair, saying shamefacedly, "No, sir. I'm sorry, sir.—anyway, I can't swim." He glanced longingly at the canal.

Bill and Robert looked at each other for a moment before Bill said, "The pond at the bottom of the lock is calm and shallow enough, and the water is warm."

Davey had been holding his breath, but now burst out with, "Oh, Uncle Robert! Oh, Mr. Theak! Will you teach us to swim?" He shivered with anxious anticipation, and even Geoffrey looked eagerly at his uncle for confirmation.

"Only if you keep your clothes dry and do not—I say again, *not* tell your mother about it."

"Oh, no, Uncle Robert, we won't say *anything*," Geoffrey promised, and Robert knew he was as good as his word. The boys always behaved angelically within their mother's hearing, and if Lavinia wanted to believe they were that way all the time, Robert would not disabuse her.

Rose produced some towels, and the boys set off for the lock on foot, Bill explaining to his eager listeners that the boat could not be tied up very close to the lock or it would be in the way of any traffic coming through. The pool was where the boats finished up after passing through the lock, Bill told them, and from there they set off on the next section of canal. It the boys were very lucky, he said, a boat would come through while they were visiting, and they could see the whole operation and learn how the gates were operated.

Rose and Robert, meanwhile, went into the galley to prepare a nuncheon. Robert offered the hamper full of supplies he had brought, and Rose exclaimed delightedly over the bounty it revealed.

"I could not very well impose two hungry boys on you unannounced *and* expect you to feed them too," Robert said, unpacking a variety of foodstuffs.

"You mean, three hungry boys."

Robert laughed. "You have me there. Nonetheless, I've paid for my food with hard labor. I take it there have been no further difficulties with the lock?"

"No, Bill is very pleased with the repairs you both made. Everything looks to be good for another ten years, he says."

They spoke a little longer of impersonal topics, Rose bringing Robert up to date on the state of the lock, George's health, and her pleasure at being able to work on such simple chores as decorating the boat without wondering whether the hold would spring a leak or some other disaster occur. At last, however, they had to speak of the subject they both had on the top of their minds.

"Is Miss Bromley well?" Rose asked, taking the easiest

approach in case Robert did not wish to discuss his feelings directly just yet.

"She was well enough yesterday," he said. He hesitated for a moment and then sat down on the cot beside the pantry where George customarily slept. "Well enough to berate me with considerable energy."

Robert had written Rose a note explaining the scene on the dock at Market Harborough, so that she was aware of the reasons for Sabina's quarrel with Robert, but she had not seen him since then. Robert described briefly his meeting with Sabina in the spinney, and when he came to an end, there was silence between them for several minutes while Rose counted mugs and napkins and Robert waited patiently for her attention to return to him.

"I don't know what to do now, Rose."

"It does not seem that Lady Sabina wishes to put an end to the quarrel between your families," Rose ventured.

Robert laughed wryly. "I do not think it is her greatest concern. She is more taken up with her quarrel with me."

Rose frowned and considered this. "That must be because she has some strong feeling for you. It may be anger now, but anger, like love, does not simply go away. It must be replaced by some other emotion."

"I have told her my feelings. I have asked for her love. What more can I do?"

"If she is not willing to change anger for love, you must find something else that she will accept, and hope that it is a step closer to love. You have been loyal for many years, Robert. I think you can be patient a little longer. Try to discover what she fears more than loving you, then try to make her see how you can save her from that fear."

"That sounds a harsh recipe."

"It is. But I think she is even more stubborn than you are. She needs to be shaken from whatever path she has set herself on, even if she recognizes that it leads nowhere. But I also think she still loves the man she fell in love with here on the canal, and she knows that love lives inside her somewhere. It only needs to be brought to light again."

Robert rose from the cot, careful not to bump his head as

he moved to give Rose a hug. "I shall think about what you have said, Rose. Thank you."

Rose turned around to look directly up at his face. "I want to see you happy, my dear. And Lady Sabina, too, for she came to be like a daughter to me while I knew her. But remember—be patient."

He smiled. "Which is more than my nephews will be if they come back to find their nuncheon not awaiting them. Did I tell you that my brother's heir is showing disconcerting signs of being as imperious as his mother? The other day, he ordered me—ordered, mind you—to play spillikins with him. I was quite taken aback to be ordered about by a lad who scarcely comes up to my waist."

"Did you refuse?"

"On pain of court-martial, yes."

"I am beginning to see why you brought them here. You want them to see that while they may be princes in their own world, its boundaries are very small."

"Wise Rose. Will you help me tame my nephews?"

She nodded. "First we must feed them. Then they will be malleable."

Chapter 11

Sabina made up her mind to tell no one of her encounter with Robert Ashton and his refusal of her offer. It would be too humiliating.

But no, why should she feel so when it was he who was at fault? *He* had refused her sensible and, indeed, generous offer. She had spent the remainder of her ride to Carling mentally berating him as unreasonable, unfeeling, and deceitful, and repeated this litany of faults to herself in order not to forget them. But her mind, on her heart's urging, insisted on amending them.

He had not been unreasonable. He had agreed to meet her, after all, and he had heard her out. He was not unfeeling. He had said he loved her. . . .

But how could she be sure he meant it? His kisses certainly felt as if he meant it. Even Peter Ogilvey had not made her feel quite like that, although she had thought she loved him. But why would Robert not agree to marry her if he did love her? He had deceived her before—but no, she could scarcely accuse him of faults she herself held in abundance.

He had said he loved her. If she had been in his position, would she have accepted such a marriage? She was uncertain. Yet, she could understand why he refused. If it were she, she would have feared that a marriage which began in such a manner could not improve—or at least not without a great deal of heartache. Love was fragile and might not survive such a trial. It was not yet even sufficient for trust.

When she finally returned to Bromleigh Hall, having deliberately exhausted herself by riding for miles and stopping to call on every tenant family she could find at home, Sabina retreated again to her room and did not go down to dinner that evening. The next day, however, Dulcie came up to her late in the morning and would not leave until Sabina was dressed and ready to take the noon meal with the family. She gave in and, pale but composed, entered the dining room with some trepidation.

Fortunately, it proved to be an informal family affair. Lewis and Georgina had gone off together to scour the lending library in the village for something neither of them had not yet read twice, and Randolph was spending the night at Stonehaven. Therefore the luncheon party consisted of only Sabina, Dulcie, Henry, Fletcher, and Alicia, whose children came hurrying into the room just after Sabina. Their tardiness distracted attention from Sabina as they were mildly chastised by their mother and given a stern look by their father, by which time their aunt had quietly seated herself and allowed Henry to pass her a plate of cold meats.

As a footman poured a glass of lemonade for her, Alicia asked, in the same solicitous tone she had used for as long as Sabina had known her, "Are you feeling more the thing today, Sabina dear?"

"Yes, thank you, Alicia."

"I am glad to hear it. You do not mind the children joining us, do you?"

As Diana, age twelve, and Edward, age nine, were well-behaved children on the whole and were now eagerly—but with impeccable manners—attacking their meal, Sabina could only assure her that she did not mind in the least. Indeed, apart from their value as foils to deflect the adults' attention from herself, Sabina liked Edward, and particularly Diana, for she knew what it was like to grow up with brothers. She and the increasingly pretty—and already tall and slender—girl were good friends. Edward, poor dear, was short even for his age, and Sabina hoped her assurances to him that he had plenty of time to catch up with his father would not prove hollow promises. At least, since Henry's twins were born, he was no longer the youngest as well.

"I see you have had your hair cut," she said now to Diana.

"Do you like it?" Diana appealed to her aunt over her soup spoon. "Mama thinks it far too short in the back, but it's ever so much more comfortable in warm weather."

"And very fashionable, too," Sabina said, although she had no notion of what the latest mode in coiffures might be. She made a mental note to herself to subscribe to some of the fashion journals, for Diana's sake.

She helped herself from a platter of cold meats and whispered to Alicia, "It could be worse. She might have heard about Caroline Lamb's scandalous crop!"

Alicia managed a smile at that. "You are quite right. I should be grateful for small favors."

"Speaking of Lady Caro—" Henry began.

"Please let us not," Fletcher interrupted, "in range of impressionable ears."

As the impressionable ears were tuned rather to whispers and giggles between themselves, Henry continued unimpeded. "I have obtained a copy of *Glenarvon*, if anyone cares to borrow it. After I have finished, naturally."

"What is *Glenarvon*?" Fletcher asked, looking up from his game pie to see all the adult heads turn toward him in amazement at his ignorance. Even Sabina had heard of the epistolary novel whose recent publication had set the *ton* abuzz with speculation as to the identity of its characters.

Dulcie explained Lady Caroline's thinly fictionalized account of her affair with the poet Lord Byron as delicately as she could, barely touching on the facts of the scandal, which were, of course, well known even in the wilds of Leicestershire, Fletcher's ignorance notwithstanding.

"Can she write?" he asked irrelevantly.

"What difference does that make?" Henry countered. Fletcher gave him the same glare he had favored his son with earlier, and Sabina giggled. She was discovering, somewhat to her surprise, that she had missed the companionship of family mealtimes. She gazed about her with new eyes, seeing her familiar napkin ring, the dented silver vase in the center of the table, the spot on the wainscoting where a twelve-year-old Sabina had thrown a strawberry at Randolph and missed; perhaps she valued such times and such familiar possessions more now that she was in danger of losing them.

Before she could reflect further on this melancholy prospect and sink herself into the dismals again, Fletcher said to her offhandedly, "Since you are obviously feeling more yourself today, Sabina, I wonder if I might have a word with you in the library after luncheon?"

This brought Sabina back to earth with a thump. She did not know why Fletcher wished to speak with her, but it could only have to do with her current untenable position in the family. She hoped that Fletcher would not feel called upon to harangue her to do her duty.

In the end, her eldest brother did appeal to her sense of duty but in only a mild way in the course of an amiable conversation that Sabina could find nothing in to object to.

When she entered the room, Fletcher asked again after her health and, upon receiving a reassuring murmur, said, "Please feel free to confide in me, Sabina. Believe me, I quite understand the awkward position you find yourself in."

"You do?"

Fletcher looked rather awkward himself for a moment. "Well, I suppose I cannot presume to know your feelings, but it is apparent even to me that Father's will has caused you distress. I'm sorry."

"Thank you, Fletcher."

"The thing is, Sabina—what do you intend to do?"

"Do?"

He ran his hand through his hair in an exasperated gesture, and she realized that she was scarcely helping him maintain the sympathetic attitude he had determined to display. A part of her mind distanced itself from the proceedings as a way of easing the distress she knew the subject could cause her, and she observed her eldest brother as from a distance. He had, she knew, been preparing himself for his role as the next earl for some time. She had always known that he would succeed in doing honor to his father's precedent, but she also saw now that he was not entirely sure of himself. It warmed her heart toward him that there was still something of the boy in Fletcher, and she determined to be of more help to him.

"Blast it, Sabina, you must know what I mean. As head of the family, I will certainly attempt to assist you in whatever course you choose to follow—if only you will give me some indication of what it is! Do you wish to continue living here? Would you prefer removing to Carling? Do you have some other intention?"

Sabina ran to her brother and hugged him briefly. "I do beg your pardon, Fletcher dear. I did not mean to be deliberately obtuse or unhelpful. To be frank, I have been racking my brain to come up with an answer, but what I should most like I fear will be out of my reach financially if I do not agree to the terms of the will."

"And what is that?"

"I should like to live at Carling. I have decided that I do not wish to marry—anyone—and will be perfectly happy to spend the rest of my days there. You know, as Papa did, that it is my favorite house—apart from this one, of course."

"Not an extravagant desire, I suppose," Fletcher said dryly. "At least you do not wish to spend the rest of your days touring the East or living in a villa on Capri or heaven knows what else."

Sabina smiled at that. "You know I have never taken extravagant notions like that."

"No, but I am given to understand that a female in your position might behave in an extraordinarily—well, never mind. I should know you well enough to know you are not that kind of female. You would at least engage a companion, I trust."

Sabina held her breath. "Fletcher, do you mean—are you saying that I *could* live at Carling?"

He tried to look important and magnanimous at the same time, but the smile would not stay suppressed. "I have discussed the matter with Mr. Quigley," he told her gently, "and although it appears we cannot raise your allowance, if it is not beneath your pride, we could contrive to pay the expenses of keeping up the house so that your income would be for your personal use only."

Her hopes rose still more, until he added, "Of course, there is one thing you must do . . ."

Sabina's heart sank again. "What is that?"

"You must at least nominally fulfill the conditions of the will by asking Captain Ashton to marry you. I will, of course, approach him first and make him understand that you do not wish him actually to accept; I should not think it would make any difference to him. I'm sorry, but I'm afraid his asking you and your refusing will not suffice. I know it is a difficult thing to ask, but I daresay you need not approach him personally at all. An exchange of letters . . ."

Sabina shuddered. She had thought the scene in the spinney was the greatest humiliation she had ever suffered, but she saw now that it could have been much worse.

"I have already asked and been refused," she said.

Fletcher raised his brows in astonishment. "But—how did this come about?"

Sabina briefly described her encounter with Robert in terms that her brother might find some sympathy with, bringing her account to an end before the tears she felt welling up inside her overflowed.

"So you see," she said, taking a deep breath, "that condition has been met."

Fletcher was thoughtful for a moment. Then he put his arms around his sister and held her while her tears finally spilled over.

"I'm so sorry, dear. It must have been difficult in the extreme to have to lower yourself so."

Sabina said nothing, muffling her sobs in Fletcher's waistcoat. He was generally highly intolerant of hysterics in anyone, and despite her agitation, she could not help being grateful to him for his sympathy today.

"Thank you, Fletcher," she said, gaining control of herself and pushing away from him. "I do beg your pardon. I seem to burst into tears at the least kindness lately. It is too mawkish of me."

"Not at all—only natural. You have always been more tenderhearted than you cared to let on, and I would not like to see you changed, even by an emotional crisis such as this has doubtless been. I am only glad I can relieve it in some measure."

He looked down at her consideringly, then kissed her cheek and said, "I shall leave you now. When you are feeling more composed, come and see me again and we will begin arrangements for your move to Carling."

"Thank you, Fletcher." Sabina kissed his cheek. He left the room, saying he would see that she was not disturbed, and she sank into the sofa, put her head back on the comforting old cushions, and breathed a sigh of relief.

She was free! She need not have put herself through that awful scene with Robert Ashton. She did not have to marry him after all.

She wondered why she did not feel more joyful.

Henry had watched Sabina leave the dining room, going to her meeting with Fletcher much as Joan might have faced the stake, then turned to his wife for guidance.

"We must do something," Dulcie said determinedly, having also noted Sabina's departure, which had set her forehead in a frown. "We cannot let poor Sabina fret herself into illness and unhappiness."

Henry gently smoothed the lines from his wife's brow with his finger. "Unfortunately, it seems that everything we have done thus far has only made matters worse."

"That is because we have tried too hard to spare Sabina's feelings. We must be bold. Let us call a family meeting. Lewis and Georgie should be back shortly."

Thus it was that an hour later, the family—excepting Sabina, of course, and Fletcher—met in Lewis's room to decide their sister's future. Lewis rolled his chair next to the sofa, where Georgina took up a position beside him. Dulcie sat in a straight-backed chair, and Henry stood behind her. Randolph, who had unexpectedly returned to the

Hall with the family letters he had found waiting at the village posting inn along with his own, was reluctantly inveigled into joining the gathering.

"We can scarcely decide her life for her," he said now, when Henry put it in those terms, intending to be jocular but apparently not succeeding. "She would never forgive us—even if she fell in with whatever harebrained scheme we might come up with to trick her into going along."

"I hope we have learned our lesson about attempting to trick her," Dulcie said, and Henry nodded.

"What do you mean, Dulcie dear?" Alicia asked.

Henry realized suddenly that Dulcie had not meant to say that. Or had she, even unconsciously, wanted to talk about Sabina more openly and so let fall something that would allow her to do so? The others were as yet unaware of Sabina's adventure on the canal and of her true relationship with Robert Ashton. Dulcie looked up at her husband questioningly.

"I think you had better tell them," he advised, aware that he was bound to make a mull of it if he tried.

And so Dulcie told Sabina's family that her accident had occurred at the canal and that she had been rescued by Captain Ashton, who was fortuitously nearby at the time, and stayed with a lockkeeper's family who treated her kindly.

"I *knew* she hadn't really gone to Missenhurst," Lewis exclaimed, thumping the arm of his chair with his fist, "but she wouldn't tell me where she really was."

"Please do not let on that you know now," Dulcie begged, leaning forward to clutch Lewis's arm. "I'm sure Sabina knows that it would have to come out sooner or later, if only through a slip of the tongue such as I made tonight. But give her time to adjust to having her secret made known."

"But, Dulcie," Alicia asked, still bemused, "why did Captain Ashton not bring her home immediately?"

Dulcie explained about Sabina's apparent loss of memory, but did not, Henry noticed, come right out and say she had been pretending. Rather, she hurried on to explain, "She did not recognize Captain Ashton, which I suppose was no real test since she had not seen him since—well, I don't know that they ever did meet before that."

"They did," Lewis put in. "Sabina doesn't remember, but it was Robert Ashton who rescued me when I had *my* fall into the canal. Or at any rate, it was he who drove me to Dr. Abbott's surgery. I got it out of Abbott later, but Ashton had asked him not to reveal his name to Sabina, so I never mentioned it either. Now I wish I had."

There was a brief silence as everyone digested this. Then, apparently coming to the same conclusion at the same time, they all spoke at once.

"Dulcie, why has this all been kept such a mystery?"

"If Ashton saved her life, why is she angry with him?"

"Is he willing to marry her?"

"Why won't she marry him?"

"She's more than likely just being stubborn again."

"It seems to me that he has behaved as well as anyone could, given Sabina's attitude."

"Quite right. I think we've all misjudged the man."

Dulcie answered these questions as well as she could without breaking Sabina's trust entirely and speculating aloud on her true feelings and her grievance against Robert Ashton.

"Henry and I do believe that she does not despise Robert as much as she lets on, whatever her feelings about his family. That is why we are asking for your suggestions for bringing her to see reason—and to see that her happiness may lie with this marriage. Even if she does not give in to your father's wish that she marry Captain Ashton, you must all agree that we cannot let things go on as they are. Surely, it would be better for all concerned to make peace with the Ashtons."

Since no one volunteered any further suggestions, Dulcie went on: "I would go so far as to say she is in a fair way to being in love with Robert, although I beg you—you in particular, Lewis—not to question her on that head. Unless—has anyone heard her say anything at all that might give us a hint?"

When this question was similarly met with only a shaking of heads, Dulcie grew impatient.

"Well, say something, won't you? For example, do you think a change of scene would help Sabina see things in a new light? It's a pity she can't spend the coming season in London, but she won't be out of black gloves yet by September. Still, she did remind me that she had never been there. Perhaps she regrets not having a conventional come-out."

Lewis snorted contemptuously. "Not our Sabina. She has always been most content the closer she is to home. Until now, at any rate, and the current situation has little to do with place."

"Can we suggest some new activity to occupy her mind?" Henry ventured. "Charitable work, or a new pastime? She told me only recently in fact that she was sorry she never learned to draw, and I can't even interest her in a hand of cards these days."

"That is the most idiotic suggestion I have heard thus far," Randolph said in disgust, moving back into the light. "She still has Carling—at least in the same way Great-Aunt Mary did. I expect she will be spending more time there in the future. If we can persuade Fletcher to allow her to make some improvements to bring it more in accord with her own tastes, perhaps that will keep her occupied."

There was another awkward pause then. At last, Georgina, who had been listening in silence, spoke up.

"I know you said, Dulcie, that you did not wish to—I believe the word was *trick*—Sabina again, but it seems to me that you are treading far too carefully around her feelings. For myself, I think she would *like* us to do something definite—something *bold*, you said, something she perhaps cannot bring herself to do for herself to further her relationship with Captain Ashton."

"We can scarcely propose to him on her behalf," Randolph remarked unhelpfully.

"But we do not know his feelings," Georgina said. "At least, I do not. Does anyone know him better?"

She looked directly at Dulcie who, after the question had

hung in the air for a moment, confessed, "Well, I suppose I do. We have—spoken from time to time."

"About Sabina?" Lewis asked, his interest piqued.

"Yes."

"And?" Randolph demanded. "*Does* he want to marry her?"

"Yes."

Henry jumped in to save his wife from further questioning. "I think we can safely say that Robert will go along with any reasonable scheme we may concoct."

"Well, why did you not say this in the first place?" Lewis asked querulously.

"Perhaps there is some way to bring her to see Robert Ashton in a more favorable light," Alicia ventured.

Dulcie and Henry exchanged glances, and it was Henry who remarked that he was quite certain Sabina was not set against Captain Ashton personally.

"Then what, pray, is the difficulty?"

"She feels it would be—disloyal to the family to marry a Kimborough."

No one responded to this at once, since the rivalry between the two earls had been part of their lives for so long that they no longer questioned it. Forced to do so, neither a compelling reason to abandon the quarrel nor a willingness to appear weak in the eyes of the other family appealed to any of them, even though each of them was now prepared to admit that Robert Ashton was not such a bad sort after all.

Georgina, however, harbored no such prejudices. "I *do* know about The Quarrel, and if you want my opinion of *that*, it is a great deal of stuff and nonsense! What's more, I believe it is partly your fault—all of you Bromleys—that Sabina is in this—this hobble. If you love her, you *ought* to do something to get her out of it!"

"Your father *did* make his will as he did with the express purpose of resolving The Quarrel," Dulcie, another outsider in the group, reminded them.

"So he did," said Lewis. "Georgie, you are perfectly in the right—if unflattering to family tradition. Dulcie, I'm sorry, but I fear the rest of us have forgotten our part in putting Sabina into this fix in the first place. Should we then make some overture to the Ashtons—a peace offering of some sort?"

"They wouldn't accept it," Randolph said. "Why should they? There is nothing in it for them."

"We might at least extend some gesture of goodwill," Alicia said. "A dinner party, perhaps?"

The others glanced around, looking for approval of the others, but Alicia, the acknowledged mistress of the social life of Bromleigh Hall, was already caught up in her own plan.

"It would of necessity be a small party," she said, "since we cannot be entertaining on a grand scale as yet. I may be able to convince them on that head, emphasizing that it will be only the two families and there will be no cards or musical entertainment offered—unless, of course, we can contrive to make them feel sufficiently welcome to linger for a time after dinner."

"We must leave that up to them, I think," Dulcie offered.

"Naturally," Alicia agreed complaisantly. "I will say only that we are simply attempting to carry out Father's wish that we become a little . . . friendlier with our neighbors."

"So long as they understand that we are not conceding any blame or fault," Randolph stipulated.

Alicia put on her diplomatic smile. "You may depend on me, Randolph dear."

Chapter 12

Captain Ashton reached Northampton just before dark, having left London that afternoon. He drove himself in the same light curricle he had left Ashtonbury Abbey in, a minimum of baggage piled beside him, after deciding on the spur of the moment to accept Lady Northrup's written invitation—no doubt instigated by Lavinia and her mother, but generously worded just the same—to stop with them in town for as long as he liked. He still had no desire to go to London, but he was desperate enough to hope a change of scene might at least clear his mind.

It had turned out to be less of an ordeal than he supposed, and he had stayed for nearly a month. But the tug of home—and the more acute desire to see Sabina, for any reason—was more powerful than any attractions of the capital.

It would have been more sensible, he supposed, to delay his departure until first light the next morning, but he had had his fill of visiting and sightseeing and even the friendships he had made or renewed, and once having made up his mind, he did not stay five minutes longer than he needed to throw his belongings into his curricle and harness the horses.

He had driven several teams hard and now, at last, had exhausted himself. He handed the reins to an ostler and went into the inn. He did not care if they no longer had any rooms available; he could sleep under the stars perfectly well. But he was hungry enough to fix his own supper if the cook could not be aroused.

Had it been less than a month since he left Leicestershire? It seemed forever, although now that he had put some distance between himself and the metropolis, that time seemed at last to be fading into insignificance. It had seemed an eternity while it lasted.

It had been Lavinia's persistent hints, suggestions, and unvoiced disappointment in him which had driven him to depart for London after a particularly trying breakfast, although it was also true that he had simply been unable to come up with any other plan. Even Dulcie Bromley had admitted that it would not hurt to try absenting himself for a short time in the hope that it would make Sabina's heart grow fonder.

On his journey down, Robert had mulled over the advice he had received from various quarters and found it all wise but somehow impossible to follow.

I should counsel patience, Richard had said. This was eminently sensible, given that there was little fear of Sabina's falling in love with someone else—so long as patience did not stretch to years. Time was notoriously debilitating to all passions. In any case, Robert's patience was not boundless.

Plan your campaign, Nicky had advised, *make her jealous*. But Robert did not know how to make Sabina believe he was interested in another woman without taking unfair advantage of another woman just for the sake of the charade. As for making Sabina envious of him in some other way—what did he have that she might covet? His freedom, perhaps. But despite the restrictions of her father's will, she doubtless commanded as large a fortune as he did, more than enough to make her independent. He had never believed that money was all it took; one needed a certain indifference to convention. Sabina admittedly lacked that; she would not be so committed to The Quarrel if she could easily set tradition aside.

Make her see what she fears more than loving you, Rose had said. He did not believe that Sabina feared anything else. Yet, he was leaving her now in the hope that losing him, if not the worst fate that might befall her, might at least make Sabina think again about what she really felt for him.

Not that she would ever lose him. He could never leave her. He would always need to be near her.

Robert's Aunt and Uncle Northrup welcomed him warmly to their mansion in Brook Street and, forewarned by her sister, the Countess of Kimborough, Lady Northrup had secured invitations to more events than Robert could possibly attend in two weeks—the time he had told Dulcie he would stay away and assured Lavinia was more than enough to make his presence felt among those people she felt deserved to be gratified by the attentions of an Ashton. However, he did not promise to dance with any debutantes; apart from the awkwardness resulting from his wounded leg, he knew better than to raise any hopes where none could possibly be fulfilled.

"It is a pity," said Lady Northrup, "that the Season will not begin properly until September. London is distressingly thin of company just now—except for those of us who are too indolent to travel to the country or abroad for the summer, that is. But I daresay you would much prefer not to be overwhelmed by dinners and balls, Robert dear. A few soirees and a card party or two will be much less taxing."

Despite his hostess's assurances, it seemed to Robert that there were a great many people still residing in the metropolis even during the sultriest weather, and he found himself invited to any number of events to which he could not put a name but which involved walking, riding, eating, or playing cards, in some combination. He also found himself smiled at by hopeful mamas, glared at by resentful young men, and surrounded by variously pretty females who were by turns demure, daring, and doting. He could not remember any of their faces even the next day, although he dutifully followed Lady Northrup's lead in leaving his card at their residences.

Occasionally, he would catch sight of a taller, darker girl on the other side of a room or a dining table, and for a moment his heart leaped. But it was never her.

"My dear boy," Lady Northrup said to him one night when they had just come home from an evening at the opera, "you are breaking hearts all over town. You could have any one of those charming young things to hold in your palm and make her heart whole again, if you will only choose. What about Miss Hutchings?"

"Too short."

"They are all too short for you, my dear, gigantic Robert. Surely it cannot be your only requirement in a wife, that she be tall?"

Never having considered what his requirements for a wife were, he could think only of those qualities, good and bad, which were Sabina Bromley's. Never having considered what he wanted, he had known exactly what it was when he first laid eyes on the right woman. And any substitute must be a poor one.

"I'm sorry, Aunt. I fear I am doomed to remain a bachelor. But I thank you for the opera. I enjoyed that immensely."

"Yes," remarked Lady Northrup dryly, "I noticed that you actually watched the stage and listened to the music. Poor Lady Haversham was madly signaling to you from her box the entire time, and you never noticed."

"I *am* sorry. Ah . . . who is Lady Haversham?"

Lady Northrup had to laugh at that, and Robert was glad to know that she was, after all, very little like her sister. She could at least accept his feelings, if not understand them, and she was never offended by his lack of social graces or interest in what everyone else in London seemed obsessed by.

"Very well, Robert. I wash my hands of you. I should say, I hereby cease taking any responsibility for your entertainment, although of course you are welcome to stay with us as long as you wish if you find amusement that is more to your liking in town. I shall not, needless to say, confess my failure to Lavinia or your brother."

Robert smiled, then rose when she excused herself to seek her bed, and kissed her on the cheek. "Thank you, Aunt. I *am* sorry to be such a poor prospect."

"Do stop apologizing in that exasperating way, Robert. But do not forget to say good-bye when you decide you have had enough."

"I won't."

Nonetheless, Robert unexpectedly found a reason to linger when he decided to look up some of his army fellows. It occurred to him that dining with them at their clubs or inspecting the horseflesh at Tattersall's with some former cavalrymen might prove much more to his liking than sitting about in cramped drawing rooms. And so it transpired. For a few blessed days, he felt as if he were on leave and would be called back to duty at any time, but in the meanwhile he intended to enjoy himself with no thought of the coming campaign.

One morning, however, the future intruded on him again. He had presented himself at White's Club, early for a luncheon appointment, and found Mr. Augustus Gerard, late of the 12th Light Dragoons, lounging at his ease in the library. He looked up when Robert came in and greeted him cheerfully.

"Robin, old man, I know just the girl for you!"

"No, you don't, Ger. Take my word for it."

Robert was about to sink into a chair, but stayed his descent momentarily, hoping to escape another foray into this tiresome topic. Augustus waved at him to sit down.

"Hear me out, old fellow. Besides, you Union Brigade fellows still owe the 12th for services rendered."

"And never let us forget it."

Augustus grinned, having raised the reminder to his satisfaction. "Here's the thing, Robin. Jane's a great gun, not looking for a beau, but she's in desperate need of a man like you. You would be doing her a great favor by living in her pocket for a week or two."

Intrigued in spite of himself, Robert seated himself and said, "Very well, tell me the whole, for I cannot imagine what you are thinking."

Captain Gerard explained that his cousin, Lady Jane Portman, had been in Paris after the surrender, where she fell in love with a French émigré who had just returned from exile and was attempting to reclaim his estates.

"Her father heard about it and made her come home, intending to put a stop to the affair."

"Why? He sounds eligible enough to me."

"But he's French, you see. It don't matter to my uncle if he's as rich as Croesus or as highborn as the Prince Regent or that he fought against Boney. He won't have his girl married to a frog."

"I take it Lady Jane thinks differently?"

"Of course—you'll understand when you meet her. In fact—and I tell you this in strictest confidence, Robin— they are already married. Did the thing secretly in Calais before she came home. She thinks that as soon as Marius settles his affairs and she can present him to her papa, all will be well. And if my uncle still don't approve—well, she's prepared to do without his approval. Personally, I think she should tell the prosy old bore that she don't need his blessing, because she don't, but she says she sees no reason to make an enemy of her own father—"

Robert interrupted this speech, which seemed to be developing into familial complaints of the kind he was all too familiar with.

"And how do I fit into this romantic tale?" he asked.

"Jane's mother is after her to go out in society and be squired about by some eligible fellows and as soon as can be to get herself betrothed to some Englishman—preferably one who can trace his line back to the Conquest. The Season's not even started, and Jane's already having a time of it to fend off the fortune hunters."

"An heiress, is she?"

"Came into the world hosed and shod, as they say."

"Pretty?"

Captain Gerard hesitated at this, but cousinly honesty prevailed. "Well, she ain't bad looking, and I'll go bail she won't go to fat or get horse-faced when she's older. A long meg, she is, but nice eyes, if I do say so, and not stupid."

"And when does *Monsieur le mari* arrive to claim his English bride?"

"That's it, you see. He should be here by now. Jane's hoping it won't be more than another week—certainly before the Season starts, or she'll really be in the soup then, what with the relations expecting her to be entertaining any number of more suitable offers by that time."

Sensing he had caught his friend's interest, Augustus leaned forward to make a last appeal to his chivalry. "What do you say, Robin? The two of you are in the same boat in a way, aren't you? Neither of you is looking to enter the marriage mart, but you're stuck here in town for the time being with relatives breathing down your necks. Like I say, you could save each other a deal of botheration."

Robert considered for a moment. If Lady Jane was willing to go along with this little deception—and it was no means certain that Gerard's assurances of her agreeability meant that she had even heard of his plan—a mild deception, short of term and innocent in intent, might indeed be to his benefit as well. Besides, he had no other reason to hang about London for another week that was in the least appealing.

"All right, Ger, introduce me to your cousin."

This was accomplished the same evening at a musicale sponsored by Lady Jane's hostess, a Mrs. Callendar, who had apparently once been her governess. Robert was interested to see that her cousin's description did Lady Jane Portman little justice. True, she was not a diamond of the first water, but she was a willowy creature with fair hair, a fine complexion, and a pair of large, candid hazel eyes that smiled when her lips did. More important, she was intelligent and not hesitant to show it. And she was almost as tall as Sabina Bromley.

"Good evening, Captain Ashton," she said when he presented himself at Mrs. Callendar's Mount Street home, an address which indicated that the family had been fond enough of their former employee to set her up in style on her retirement. "Gus has told me *all* about you."

She smiled impishly at that, and Robert had to smile back. "Surely not *all*, Lady Jane. He doesn't *know* all, despite his air of doing so."

"Yes, he is looking a little smug this evening, isn't he?" the lady said, taking Robert's arm to lead him into a large parlor where a dozen guests of varying ages and relationships to one another were gathered. Robert knew none of them other than Lady Jane and her cousin, but he was glad to see there was not even one other eligible young lady present. Furthermore, the tone of the evening appeared to be relaxed in the extreme; introductions were of the most perfunctory nature, several conversations were going on at once, and his hostess gave Robert only the most cursory, if cordial, of greetings before inviting him to help himself from the various refreshments displayed on a sideboard.

"I hope you do not mind our taking advantage of you in this way, Robert?" Jane asked forthrightly, as they filled their plates from a selection of oddities ranging from cheeses and cold meats to chocolate-dipped crystalized fruits.

"Not at all," he said candidly. "Believe me, I sympathize with your—er, plight. And you are doing me a great favor in return."

Jane seated herself on a sofa and indicated that he should join her. "Would you care to tell me about it? I will not be offended if you wish to keep your affairs to yourself, of course."

Robert did briefly outline his difficulties with Sabina Bromley, and when Jane listened sympathetically and did not swoon and exclaim that she had never heard such a romantic tale, he began to feel even more at ease with her. He apologized for being unable to dance well, and she assured him that she would much rather sit and talk, and perhaps tomorrow he would be good enough to take her for a drive, for she had been feeling closed in ever since coming to town.

This completed Robert's capitulation, and since Jane was an accomplished hostess in her own right, having run her diplomat uncle's house in Paris, and was well-read in two languages, he found the evening passing more quickly than any five minutes since he had arrived.

What was more, he knew that Lady Northrup would hear

about his apparent fascination with Lady Jane and report it back to Lavinia, and he would be spared that most dreaded of all male predicaments, a nagging female.

By the time he rose the next morning to pick Jane up for an unfashionably early ride in Hyde Park, he was feeling positively chipper, a fact that Lady Northrup did not fail to notice on his return for a late breakfast.

"Well, Robert, I suppose I ought to be offended that you enjoyed yourself most at an affair that I did not arrange for your amusement—and a mere musicale at that—but then Sophie Callendar has always prided herself on her unconventionality. You *did* enjoy yourself, did you not?"

"Yes, Aunt, thank you. I'm sorry you were not there, but I daresay you have already heard all about it."

Lady Northrup laughed and confessed that she had made it her business to do so. "And I assure you," she said, "that I will be happy to write to Lavinia at once to reassure her that I have been doing my duty—even if I have not."

"Thank you, Aunt. I would be grateful—and will naturally give you all the credit when I return home."

"I don't know what you are up to with this sudden craving for society, dear boy, but I daresay *you* do. Do you have plans for this evening?"

He had indeed already contracted to meet Lady Jane at a small private dinner party at Captain Gerard's house, but aware that it would aid both his cause and Jane's to be seen together more publicly, they had agreed to go on to the theater later and perhaps even a late supper at the Piazza.

And thus it was that Captain Ashton was soon known to be "sitting in Jane's pocket" and that Lady Jane was encouraging the attentions of one of the most eligible bachelors in town. For the next week, the affair was talked about in terms of the greatest satisfaction even for those who had no hand in bringing it about. An engagement notice began to be expected even before the Season got fully under way.

Since he had few qualms about deceiving the *ton* in this fashion—for it loved nothing so much as speculation and forgot nothing more quickly than alliances that did not materialize—Robert found himself for the first time enjoying

London. He began to look at its attractions with new eyes and even to think about bringing Sabina here one day—if she could be persuaded to leave Leicestershire—to show her around and shower her with expensive trinkets from the shops to which he escorted Lady Jane. Sabina could set the *ton* on its ear, if she chose.

Engaged in this pleasant speculation, he almost lost track of the days, and it was only when he called for Lady Jane one morning to take her riding that time again took up its course. He found her in a euphoric mood, waving a letter at him as she came to greet him in the hall.

"Oh, Robert, I must tell you—oh, do come into the library." She glanced at the interested footman still hovering near the door and contained herself until a door was closed between them and the servants.

"Marius will be here tomorrow!"

Robert felt an unexpected twinge of jealousy. It was absurd, of course—this was what they had both been waiting for, and Monsieur le comte de Abbreville had timed his appearance to a nicety. But Robert suddenly realized that he had enjoyed Jane's company more than he had expected and would be sorry to lose it. He smiled just the same.

"Dearest Jane—I'm delighted to hear it."

She threw her arms around his shoulders and hugged him impulsively. "Thank you, Robert. I do hope you will like him."

"I? What has my opinion to do with anything?"

She gave him a searching look. "But we are friends, are we not? I want my friends to like my husband, and I want to keep my friends despite my marriage. You will remain my friend, won't you, Robert?"

He smiled. Of course, he must. How could he think that Jane would forever disappear from his life when her Marius returned to claim his bride?

She gestured for him to sit down. "I'm so sorry, Robert. I quite forgot that although my future is settled—or at least, looking much rosier—yours is not. Will you go home now? Have you done sufficient penance in exile to satisfy your family—and make Sabina miss you? I know I should be desperate by now, if I were her."

"Would you be, Jane?"

She put her hand over his. "Any woman whom you love must be desperate to be with you all the time, Robert, believe me."

"I've been told that absence makes the heart grow fonder."

"Nonsense. I know from experience that absence only makes the heart lonely. My poor heart would not have survived this summer without your company, Robert, but you must now think of your own loneliness. It will come back, you know, although I think I have helped you to forget it for a little while, just as you have done the same for me."

He raised her hand to his lips and kissed it lightly. "You have been a lifesaver, Jane."

"I'm glad. But I think you must go home now, Robert— at least, after you have met Marius—and claim your lady. No weapon is more powerful than a loving and faithful heart to win a woman, Robert, and while absence may make Sabina miss you, your presence will win her heart. Go to her, dearest."

He realized all at once that this simple advice was what he had felt would eventually prove the key to Sabina's heart, no matter what elaborate stratagems and deceptions he or anyone else invented to bring it about.

He kissed Jane on the cheek and squeezed her hand affectionately. "I'll go at once, Jane. Thank you."

And despite his impulse to leave London that very day, Robert did stay to meet Jane's Marius, and was relieved to find that he liked him as well as he did Jane. They all spent a good part of two days together, until it became obvious to Robert that even Jane was eager to leave, to take her husband to Devon and present him to her father. He wished them luck, promised to visit when they had settled into a home of their own, and finally set his mind toward home.

Thus it was that Robert and his uncle were sitting at the breakfast table the next morning, reading the various daily newspapers in companionable silence. When Lord

Northrup put down *The Times* to refill his coffee cup, Robert folded *The Morning Chronicle* and looked up at his uncle.

"I believe I shall return to Ashtonbury Abbey today, Uncle, if that is not too impolitely abrupt a departure for you."

"Not for me, dear boy. Expected it two days after you got here. But do talk to Althea as soon as she gets up. She won't take kindly to finding you gone when she comes down to breakfast."

"I would not dream of upsetting her."

"Good boy. You'll mention to Richard that I'd like first dibs on Firefly's new foal, won't you?"

"I will do that."

"Good, good. Didn't think that was the sort of thing you'd forget—not like chits' names, eh, boy?"

Robert smiled. "I am a sore disappointment to Lady Northrup, I fear."

"Not at all, boy. You gave her a week in the limelight. She enjoyed being your sponsor, even if you did not give her a chance to choose a wife for you."

Lord Northrup raised his newspaper again, remarking by way of ending the conversation, "Expect you've had one picked out all along, eh?"

"Yes, sir."

"Good, good."

Robert woke before dawn, as the sounds of morning activity at the Old Oak Inn in Northampton began to penetrate the darkness, and sat up expectantly. He got up and rang for a waiter, then dressed hurriedly, threw his things into his traveling pack, and wolfed down the hearty breakfast the waiter produced. Half an hour later, he was driving north again.

It was still early morning when he began to recognize landmarks and calculated that he could not be more than an hour's drive from home. He slowed the horses to an easy pace and put his mind to how he would approach Sabina. Would she have missed him as much as Jane had assured him she would? Would she have heard about Jane and felt a little jealous? He could not imagine how she would have heard anything, but conventional wisdom said that her jealousy could only work in his favor.

Nonetheless, Sabina could not be relied on to react conventionally to anything. She might refuse to see him. He would have to find a way to see her where she could not get away from him and therefore must give him a chance to speak.

He was considering how he might lure her to the canal again when he arrived at home to a boisterous welcome from his nephews, a nearly warm welcome from his sister-in-law, a quizzical glance from his brother—and an invitation to dine at Bromleigh Hall on the silver tray in the hall.

Chapter 13

"Will it *never* stop raining?" Sabina inquired despairingly of her sister-in-law.

She had not seen or heard from Robert Ashton for three weeks and refused to admit even to herself that she missed him or cared where he was or what he was doing. Further, her plans for her new life at Carling Manor were progressing apace, and her present enforced idleness ought, in view of her own professed desires, to be something in the way of a well-earned rest.

"It has not been raining for very long," Alicia observed sensibly. "Although it did wake me when it started—it could not have been later than four o'clock this morning, for I remember that it was very difficult to fall asleep again. I may as well have risen then, for I have no energy today."

"That is the trouble with rainy days," Dulcie added. "Not only does one feel too languid to do anything, but gray days are sad days, I believe, making one think of the winter and cold weather to come."

The ladies were ensconced cozily in the library with a fire to add to their comfort and put the lie to their gloomy expectations of a turn in the weather. Indeed, upon being applied to by the countess, the head gardener had predicted cheerily that the weather would clear later in the day and that autumn was still a "goodish way off, my lady."

"What does Edina have to say?" Alicia inquired.

Sabina had reluctantly accepted Fletcher's insistence on a companion, unable to think of any relative outside her immediate family with whom she would care to live. At Alicia's suggestion, however, she was considering her cousin

Edina Bromley, a childless widow who took an even greater interest in family history than Sabina did, and had invited her to spend a week at Bromleigh Hall. The matter of engaging Edina as her companion was touched on only delicately, but Sabina suspected that her cousin would understand the invitation clearly enough.

In the meanwhile she had already received several letters from her cousin following her own brief letter of invitation. Edina's letters were gossipy and friendly and contained no hint that the writer considered herself a poor relation dependent on her noble kinswoman for support. Indeed, she seemed to have a degree of personal pride, neither excessive nor overbearing, of which Sabina approved. She could not bear a poor-spirited woman, who could not find occupation for herself and might never let Sabina be alone. She was beginning to think that Edina might do well enough as a companion.

Nonetheless, she had been gazing at the crossed and recrossed lines of her cousin's latest missive for some time, no longer seeing them—although she would never have confessed this to the countess.

The letter contained the information about Edina's scheduled arrival time at Bromleigh Hall. Another page was taken up with her profuse thanks to Fletcher for making his town carriage available for her journey to Leicestershire. As usual, all the correspondence and organization of this favor had been undertaken by Alicia, and Edina must have guessed this, for she added a gracious note to Lady Bromleigh.

"She thanks you for your hospitality, Alicia. She will arrive a week from Tuesday and is excessively grateful to be able to ride in comfort in Fletcher's carriage."

Dulcie smiled. "I suspect that 'excessive' is putting it mildly. I hope you will not find Edina's effusiveness overwhelming when she is finally with us, Sabina."

Sabina shrugged. "I cannot know until I meet her."

"Well, if she does prove trying, a word in her ear should be sufficient to curb her enthusiasms, I think. Edina is perhaps foolish, but I do not believe she is stupid."

"She is a very amiable woman," Alicia put in. "I have never heard her utter a word of complaint or criticism of anyone."

"Just the same," Dulcie observed, "she is a poor relation and well aware of it. I believe condescension would hurt her more than a little kind advice."

Dulcie and Alicia continued their conversation, apparently unaware that Sabina had ceased to take part. Instead, she stared out the window, as if to dispel the mist by the very intensity of her gaze.

She tried to empty her mind of all thought, in order to look at things afresh and try to see more hope in them. In this she was only partially successful, as the words spoken between the other ladies began to intrude on her concentration. She knew they were discussing Edina, but she could not help hearing their words in terms of her own behavior.

". . . despite her foolishness because she truly has the happiness of others . . ."

Why was it so difficult for her to think of the happiness of others? Sabina wondered. She had always considered herself a loving, generous person. Surely she had been when her father was alive? Yet, she saw now that she was no better than the Ashtons, or at least . . . well, not Robert. She could not fault him for not attempting to mend the family quarrel.

". . . none of us can expect to be beloved of everyone . . ."

She had chastised herself ever since that dreadful scene in the spinney for wishing to be loved but not making any effort to be loving. She need not have treated Robert so shabbily. She had not set out to do so. Where had she gone wrong?

She was on the verge of getting up and announcing that she needed some fresh air, rain or no, when Dulcie's twins came into the room, shepherded by their nurse, a cheery old lady, nearly as wide as she was tall, known to Ivor and Ian as well as to their father and uncles as "Muffin."

"Mummy, see what I've made!" Ivor exclaimed, waving a sheet of drawing paper at her.

"Me, too!" Ian exclaimed, attempting to climb up into his mother's lap as well. Ivor having firmly established a beachhead there, however, Ian had to settle for his Aunt Sabina's more ample skirts. She put her arms around her towheaded little nephew and kissed the top of his head, drinking in the clean, sweet, soapy smell of his velvety skin and fine hair. For the first time in her life, she wondered what it would be like to hold her own child like this. It was a pleasant picture.

Ian had no such sentimental thoughts, however, and squirmed as he tried to show her a pencil drawing of some sort of animal with very large, dark eyes and pointed ears.

"What a beautiful horse!" she exclaimed, freeing one hand to hold the drawing up admiringly.

"It's Bunny—my pony," Ian informed her, pointing to the animal's forehead. "See, that's his diamond."

Sabina glanced over at Dulcie, who mouthed "thank you" at her. She had been praising Ivor's drawing without, Sabina guessed, having the least idea of what it was intended to represent.

Taking Sabina's lead, the subject of horses in art was thoroughly investigated, and Alicia told the boys that more drawing paper would be obtained for them so that they could execute studies of all the horses in the stables, if they liked. Ivor expressed a desire to broaden his subject matter, but Ian scoffed at wasting his talent on any subject less noble than a pony.

"Come along now, young gentlemen," Muffin said at precisely the moment when the countess's tolerance of talkative six-year-olds was reaching its limit. "It will soon be time for your nuncheon, and you must put away your toys first."

"Not toys," Ivor said firmly, as his nurse shooed him out the door. "Pencils. And . . . drawing paper."

"We're artists," Ian added proudly.

When the door had closed behind them, Dulcie asked Sabina, "However did you guess that it was a horse?"

Sabina laughed. "You must ask Henry about my own blighted artistic career—I had no one to appreciate that I had drawn a horse and not a cow or a goat. I was particularly proud of my houses, but everyone thought they were hayricks. I gave up my artistic career before attempting portraiture—goodness knows what would have been made of those."

Even Alicia smiled at that, remarking that she would not have dared to attempt something she had no talent for.

"Oh, but I did not know I had no talent," Sabina exclaimed. "Father always led me to believe that I could do anything, so of course it never occurred to me that I could not."

Her smile faltered slightly at the memory—and the belated realization that there was sometimes a price to pay for the arrogance of believing one was always right. Why had Papa never explained that to her?

"Are you feeling unwell, Sabina?" Dulcie asked, frowning at her expression.

Sabina recalled her smile from exile and assured her sister-in-law that she was perfectly fine.

"In fact," she said, rising, "I believe I will go and answer Edina's letter while it is still in my mind. Then I may ride down to the village to post it if the weather clears in the next hour or so."

Alicia looked up from her petit point and said, "Do be careful, Sabina dear. The rain will have left the roads muddy."

Sabina smiled. "Don't worry about me, Alicia. I don't fail at the same fence twice."

"At least take a groom with you," Dulcie called after her as she left the library, "so we will know when you come a cropper!"

The gardener was right about the weather, as it turned out. By midafternoon, a watery sun was shining through the thinning clouds, and the flowers Sabina could see from her window sparkled with drops of the vanished rain.

She obeyed Alicia's instructions to take care on the roads, but disregarded Dulcie's to take a groom with her. She kept her horse to a sedate canter, and slowed still fur-

ther as she turned onto the towpath. The air smelled as
fresh as spring, and the birds singing from the rushes along
the canal sounded as if they were delighted that the sun was
out again. Sabina felt herself in perfect sympathy with
them, and her spirits rose as she approached the Theaks'
narrowboat.

She was momentarily disconcerted when it appeared de-
serted; no one was on deck, and there was no sound from
within. Sabina reined in, disappointed, but then she heard
her name called from farther up the path.

"Lady Sabina!"

Rose Theak was hanging some shirts from a line strung
between the side of the lockkeeper's cottage and a row of
lime trees. She put down her laundry basket and waved.

Sabina waved back and rode up to the cottage. "I forgot
that you are not living on the boat any longer. Is the house
all finished then?"

"Come and see," Rose invited her, pinning up the last of
the shirts to flutter like a sail in the breeze.

When Sabina had dismounted, Rose indicated the
clothesline and said, "George likes the smell of the outdoors in his shirts, so when the weather is fine, I hang them
beneath those lime trees and they retain some of the fragrance."

She opened the cottage door for Sabina, who ducked her
head and entered the low-ceilinged parlor. It was a moment
before her eyes adjusted to the change of light, but then she
saw that the Theaks' new home was really quite cheerful.
The walls had been painted white, several braided rugs
were scattered about the stone floor, and Rose had hung
thin blue curtains and painted a border of red roses around
the doors and windows. She had not quite finished, Sabina
saw, for the design around the two small windows facing
away from the canal were only drawn on, and several pots
of paint stood on the still-raw table.

"You are so clever," Sabina said admiringly, seating herself in the chair Rose pulled away from the wall and held
out for her. "I wish I could paint."

"Did you not study watercolors with your governess?"

Rose asked, putting a kettle on the fire. "I thought all young ladies of quality had lessons in the arts."

"Oh, I had lessons certainly, but not the talent." She laughed and told Rose about Ivor and Ian and their artistic endeavors. "Fortunately, Muffin is never a harsh critic, so perhaps the boys may be encouraged to continue their efforts. I remember that it was very lowering to be pitied by my tutor. *He*, of course, was a master of every art."

"He?" Rose asked.

"Yes, I had all my lessons with my brothers—or at least with Lewis and Henry. The others were much older. I rebelled at nursery lessons as soon as I discovered that the subjects the boys were studying were much more interesting. As a result, I can do sums in my head and recite Julius Caesar's histories in Latin. Much good has it done me."

"Nonsense. No knowledge is wasted. If nothing else, it exercised your brain, just as your riding here today exercised your body."

Sabina laughed. "I think my horse had all the benefit."

Then she reached out to squeeze Rose's hand and said, "Thank you, Rose. It makes me feel better just to talk to you."

"Are you feeling sad, dearie?" Rose asked sympathetically, taking the kettle off the hob and two mugs down from the shelf.

Sabina was surprised to find herself blinking back tears. Why did the least kindness of late make her want to weep?

"Oh, Rose, I don't seem to be able to do anything right!"

Over several cups of tea, Sabina poured out the story of her meeting with Robert. She supposed that he might already have informed Rose of the result, and she did not think he would have said anything ungentlemanly about her behavior, but she had to make Rose see her side just the same.

When she had stumbled to an end of her tale, she raised her cup to her lips, found it empty, sighed, and put it on the table beside her. Rose did not refill it, somehow sensing that she did not need refreshment, but renewal.

"I think . . ." Rose began, then hesitated. When Sabina

looked at her appealingly, she went on, "I think you believe you have behaved badly and want forgiveness. You are frightened that things will not work out as well as you hope, and you are waiting for something to happen or someone to tell you that you deserve to be happy."

Sabina nodded. "I suppose so. I do feel as if I am hovering between a stormy sea and the solid shore. Perhaps I am waiting for someone to bring me safely to dry land."

"But who do you think will do this? Robert?"

"No! I mean, I cannot ask him to do more, or try harder, or say any more than he has already said."

"His family, then? Is their opinion important to you?"

Sabina thought for a moment. "I should like to be friends with them, but not if it is not important to . . . him."

"Then I think that leaves only one person who must act. One person who can end the quarrel between your families. One person who can let you love the man you love without qualms."

Sabina looked at Rose, but the other woman only waited.

"You mean—myself."

"Yes, dearie. There is no one else anymore."

Sabina sighed again. "You are right, of course. I wish you were not so wise, Rose. I do not think I can do it."

"It is only pride that prevents you, Sabina. And pride is a poor substitute for love. It will not keep you warm on winter nights or strengthen you to face life's smaller tests."

Sabina was silent for several minutes. "I don't know what to do next, Rose."

But there Rose would not help. She only smiled, patted Sabina's hand, and said, "That is something you must decide for yourself. You have nearly done so, I think, and the rest will come more easily than you expect."

She placed her hands flat on the table and rose. "Meanwhile, my lady, you may take off your pelisse and roll up your sleeves. You are going to help me paint this table."

Time passed quickly on the canal, as Sabina happily helped Rose with her daily chores. The simplicity of the work put her mind at ease, and although she had begun the day berating herself for her selfishness and had finally made up her mind to accept her fate as a poor spinster relation rather than to make Robert's life miserable with her pride, by the time she left Rose, she had come to view her fate as not so terrible after all. At least it would bring her some peace.

She was nearly late for dinner and hoped no one had begun to worry that she had met with yet another accident. To the contrary, however, when she entered Bromleigh Hall through the garden doors in order to go up to her room unseen, she heard laughter and voices from the hall.

There was a palpable excitement in the air, although when Dulcie saw her on the stairs, she said only, "Oh, there you are, Sabina. Do hurry and change. We have something to celebrate tonight!"

"What is it?"

"Come and see!" Dulcie called back, disappearing into the drawing room where, judging from the rise in the volume of voices, the rest of the family was gathered. Could they have had some unexpected visitor? Yet only Georgina ever merited this kind of jollity.

Her maid soon revealed the source of the excitement.

"Whatever is the matter with everyone, Emily?" Sabina said as the girl pulled off her boots and quickly unbuttoned her riding habit.

"Oh, my lady, it's so romantic!" Emily exclaimed, pulling off Sabina's jacket. "It's Mr. Lewis and Miss Georgina. They're to be married!"

Sabina paused in the act of washing her hands and face in the bowl Emily held out to her. She looked up, face dripping, and stared at the maid. Emily handed her a towel.

"I don't understand—when did this happen?"

"Just now, my lady. Mr. Henshaw—the butler, that is— overheard when he was asked to bring champagne into the drawing room. They made the announcement when everyone was gathered there before dinner."

Everyone but me, Sabina thought.

She supposed it was just as well, since she might well have put a thorough damper on the excitement had she been as surprised as everyone else. She was happy to welcome Georgina into the family, of course—not that she had not always seemed a part of it—but she could not help the pang of jealousy that the news aroused in her. It would not subside quickly, but when she went downstairs, she must be happy for her brother and cousin.

"I shall wear that dark green silk, Emily," she said. "And the silver eardrops—no, the emerald ones. I cannot go downstairs looking gloomy tonight."

"Yes, ma'am," Emily said happily.

Ten minutes later, Sabina had composed herself sufficiently so that when she entered the dining room as everyone else was taking their places, she was able to smile and tell Georgina when she bent over to hug her that she was glad to welcome her as a sister.

To Lewis, she said, "Well, you are a surprise, Lewis. I thought you would never come to your senses about Georgina."

Lewis grinned. "I was overwhelmed by superior forces," he confessed. "*She* proposed to me."

Georgina's musical laugh confirmed this. "Well, I could not wait any longer. I shall soon be on the shelf."

Sabina's smile at this sally was wrenched out of her at the sudden memory of her wretched "proposition" to Robert. Still, that was finally and truly behind her. Had she not just today made up her mind to accept her spinster fate and learn to enjoy it? She would be independent and comfortable, after all, and live as she chose in a place she loved. What more could she want? Tonight was the perfect occasion to forget the past and begin looking ahead.

But the loving expression on Georgina's pretty face as she looked at Lewis tore at her heart. It was all she could do not to weep.

"You are looking very lovely this evening," Randolph, seated next to her, observed sotto voce.

Sabina blinked her eyes and glanced at him. "Thank you. I could *not* bring myself to wear black tonight."

"I should think not. Even Alicia, you notice, has covered her weeds with a flowered shawl."

"It is called paisley, Randolph, as well you know."

He grinned. "I was only testing you, darling, to be sure you are truly with us again."

"Have I seemed so very far away?"

"Preoccupied, I would have called it. Not to be wondered at, I'm sure."

"But it might have become tiresome before much longer."

Under the table, Randolph squeezed her hand. "I hope you would have confided in us before coming to that state, Sabina. You know you can trust any of us, however much we tease over less important matters."

Sabina felt her eyes watering up again. "I know, Randolph dear. I'm sorry if I have behaved as if I thought otherwise. I shan't forget again, I promise."

"We only want to see you happy, darling."

It seemed, Sabina thought, that everyone wanted her to be happy but herself. Rose was right. It was up to her to decide what she really wanted and to act on it. She must seize the happiness that had eluded her because she had let it.

At that moment, Henshaw came into the room bearing another tray of champagne glasses, followed by a footman with a bucket of ice shavings and two bottles. Henry rose to propose a toast.

"Will everyone please join me in toasting the happy couple—although I personally believe that Lewis ought to be the happier of the two for finally accepting his good fortune."

"Hear, hear!" said Fletcher and Randolph in unison.

Lewis grinned from ear to ear, and Georgina blushed as more toasts followed. Much against Lewis's objections, his brothers then proceeded to reveal all his childhood peccadilloes and to warn Georgina what to expect of a husband who was invariably grumpy in the morning and insisted on lemon instead of milk in his tea.

Alicia observed that it had been a long time since there was a wedding in the family, and Sabina had to be grateful for her tact. There had not been a wedding because Peter Ogilvey had not lived to come back to her. But there had been a betrothal much like this one, different in only one circumstance—she had not loved Peter as Georgina did Lewis. She had always known that, but she and Peter had been friends and she had loved him as a friend and thought they could build a marriage on that. It was only now that she knew she had been relieved not to have to put that friendship to such a test and to face her fear that she could not be the wife Peter expected.

Her mind eased of at least that lingering burden, Sabina was able to take part in the general goodwill and felicitations being given all around her. She knew all this ought to be directed at her, and although she had never up to this moment pictured herself as the center of attention in the way Georgina was now, it was borne in on her that she was sorry she was not.

It was at that moment that she made up her mind to swallow her pride, even if she choked on it, and go to Robert to try to make it up with him.

Chapter 14

"Oh, by the bye, Sabina, we are having a few neighbors to join us for dinner tonight—just a small party. You will know everyone, but I thought I would just drop a word in your ear so that you may plan your wardrobe accordingly."

Alicia murmured this piece of news to her sister-in-law as she passed her in the hall in front of the breakfast room and was out the door to the garden, flower basket over her arm, before Sabina could reply.

She found it mildly irritating that Alicia would invite guests without asking if she felt up to receiving them, but then dismissed the matter from her mind. This was Alicia's home, after all, and she could invite whom she chose. And since Sabina had been coming down to dinner in the normal way for weeks now, she could scarcely refuse to do so tonight.

"What did she mean by that?" she asked Dulcie, who came out of the library just at that moment.

"Why, what could she mean, except to forewarn you to expect outsiders tonight. I daresay she wished to be certain you do not wear red or something equally unsuitable."

Dulcie looked at her now, surveying her dark blue riding habit. "Are you going to Carling today? Would you care for my company?"

"Thank you, but I daresay you have enough to occupy you here," Sabina returned, adding wryly, "preparing for this mysterious dinner party, that is. Perhaps I will ask Randolph to come."

"Try Henry," Dulcie advised. "He does get underfoot when there is housekeeping to be done."

"I will," Sabina replied, putting on her hat in front of the hall mirror and studying her reflection. She thought she had regained some of the usual color in her cheeks, and her eyes were no longer red-rimmed. She must be recovering. Indeed, she had been feeling much more herself since her discussion with Fletcher and had even begun to view the future with some optimism. She now had a goal and defined steps to follow to achieve it—even if it meant compromise in the matter of a companion.

She carried in her pocket the latest of several letters she had received from her cousin Edina, all of which she had politely, if hastily, answered. Today's letter, however, which she had already taken out several times to brood over in the course of the morning, had done little to maintain her cheerful outlook.

She sighed and turned toward the back of the house to make her way to the stables. As it happened, however, Henry was nowhere to be found and Randolph, one of the grooms informed her, had just driven off to the village.

Accepting the same groom's offer to accompany her only because she had decided to take some swatches of drapery fabric and wallpaper samples with her to see how they would look in her bedroom at Carling, Sabina set off, her mind vaguely troubled by the notion that something was going on that she was not a party to and that her family were avoiding her. She told herself that they were merely leaving her to sort out her feelings about moving in her own mind; they were, after all, still within reach if she wished to discuss anything with anyone.

She had begun organizing her move to Carling the very day of her talk with Fletcher and had already spent several afternoons at the house to see to any changes that might be made before she moved in and to set the servants to cleaning and otherwise readying the house, which had not been occupied since her Great-Aunt Mary had lived in it until her death three years earlier and was disagreeably dusty and faded-looking in some quarters.

Carling Manor was located only a few miles from Bromleigh Hall, on the other side of the Avon. It had been purchased by the late earl only twenty years before, mainly for its excellent coverts, and it was not therefore a traditional family property. Despite this lack of pedigree, however, Sabina found the manor house small enough to be cozy and well built enough to be dry and snug in all weathers.

The three farms situated on the estate were prosperous, and the income from them would have kept Sabina in comfortable circumstances. Unmarried, of course, the income was not hers to command, but Fletcher had kept his word to consult immediately with Mr. Quigley and an arrangement was being worked out by which she could at least pretend to enjoy independent means and live as she wished.

She refused to let her mind dwell on the inevitable farewell to her family that the move to Carling entailed, or on her happy past at Bromleigh Hall, telling herself that the move was much the same as moving to a room in a far wing of the Hall; it was not so far away that she could not still visit whenever she liked.

She immersed herself in every detail of the management of her new home, determined to arrange everything to her liking. Today, however, she found herself unable even to decide between two shades of blue curtains for her dressing room and temporarily gave up the effort. Instead, she sat on a Holland-covered chair and took out Edina's letter. It was already folded to the page that had captured her attention when the letter arrived that morning:

. . . quite the sensation when he arrived [Edina wrote in a hurried but legible scrawl], particularly since so few such handsome young men had been spotted on the streets so early in the year, but none of the liveliest young ladies seemed to interest him, until—and here is the astonishing part, dear Sabina—he was seen yesterday driving Lady Jane Portman in the park, not for the first time, and last night they were seen—*unchaperoned*—at the Theatre Royal. Now I have no objection to Jane, who is a charming girl, but she is hardly in the first blush of youth, and not at all fashionable in her looks and dress, despite her recent sojourn in Paris. Well, I daresay it is not serious . . .

Sabina was less sanguine. She might have dismissed, although with some difficulty, the news that Robert Ashton was squiring one of the Season's accredited beauties, but a girl not in her first youth—and she was conscious of her own situation in that regard—and not "fashionable" struck her as ominous. It would be precisely such a female who would be most likely to attract Robert Ashton. If he were in a humor to be attracted.

She could not be sure that he was not. She had certainly given him no reason to return to Leicestershire if he were.

She glanced at the date on the letter and saw that it had been written three days before, although not posted until yesterday. She wondered what had happened in the intervening days and looked forward to the next morning's post with a mixture of dread and curiosity.

It was in this abstracted mood that she came down to dinner that evening. She had dressed in gray silk with a discreet silver brooch at the collar and had allowed Emily to experiment with her hair, which effort had produced a flattering, high-swept style that was nonetheless simple enough to pass Alicia's stern inspection. Despite the simplicity of her costume, however, she knew the gown flattered her figure, and she had studied herself with some satisfaction in her looking glass before descending to the front hall.

She had reached the hall before becoming fully aware of voices and the bustle of someone's arrival. But then she glanced toward the door and stopped abruptly at the foot of the stairs, not certain whether to believe her eyes.

"You!"

Robert Ashton bowed. "I am pleased to see you again, Lady Sabina."

Despite his neutral tone of voice, she could see by the warmth in his blue eyes that he really was glad to see her, as if nothing had happened between them since they set foot on the wharf at Market Harborough, as if he had not been amusing himself in London with—but she would not think of that. Obviously Edina had been mistaken.

She found his warmth more disconcerting than if he had been cold or angry. He was dressed formally but soberly in pale knee-breeches that made his legs look even longer, a gray coat, and a white silk waistcoat. It was even more distressing that Sabina found his tall figure and handsome face no less attractive than ever. She felt the color rise to her cheeks and put up her chin belligerently.

"Good evening, Captain Ashton. This *is* a surprise."

He raised his brows questioningly at that, but before he could say any more, Alicia took Sabina by the arm and led her firmly, if not quite forcibly, to meet their other guests.

"Lady Kimborough, I believe you are not acquainted with my sister, Sabina. Lord Kimborough, my sister. My dear, these are our neighbors."

"The rival earl," Richard said sardonically, but genially enough, and held out his hand to shake hers. "I am happy to meet you at last, Lady Sabina."

He studied her with ill-concealed interest but not unapprovingly. Sabina shook his hand lightly, wondering how much he knew about her relationship with his brother.

When she turned to his wife, however, Lady Kimborough merely nodded her head slightly in her direction, not accepting her hand or even meeting her eyes.

"Welcome to Bromleigh Hall," Sabina said deliberately in her direction, stressing the first word.

"Thank you," Lavinia replied stiffly.

Alicia, perhaps sensing that Sabina was likely, at the least encouragement, to jump on her high horse, ushered their guests into the green drawing room under cover of uncharacteristic garrulousness. There was, however, enough skill in her conversation to draw Lady Kimborough into responding politely, if not warmly, and when Fletcher joined in, the small talk nearly approached a normal, sociable level.

Fletcher did take her aside briefly when they entered the drawing room and said, in a low voice, "Sabina, I must apologize for all this. I assure you, it was done without my knowledge. I have explained to Alicia that we had come to an arrangement, but you know how she is—nothing must interfere with her social plans once she has set them in motion."

"I'm not certain I understand you, Fletcher."

"I only mean, I would have prevented your being obliged to meet Captain Ashton again, if I could—particularly in your own home."

"Thank you, Fletcher, but you need not have interfered, I assure you."

He glanced at her as if uncertain whether to believe her, but Alicia signaled to him just at that moment and he said nothing more, only squeezing Sabina's hand briefly before resuming his host's duties.

Georgina was already seated in the drawing room, looking like a fashion plate in a simple white frock with a high neck edged in lace and demure blue flowers around the hem. Even Lady Kimborough, herself arrayed in dark blue silk and a profusion of diamonds which she must have been confident no one else could approach, appeared to approve of Miss Campion and condescended to be gracious on being introduced to her.

Each of the Bromleys joined this initial grouping in turn, until all had been suitably presented. Sabina had no doubt that Alicia had carefully choreographed the parade in order not to overwhelm the Ashtons with superior waves of Bromleys. Dulcie and Henry, the most likely to cause an eruption of competitive spirit, arrived last, bare seconds before dinner was announced and they all trooped into the dining room.

Robert had said very little during all this, but still managed to stay close to Sabina so that she was continually aware of his presence. She considered Fletcher's hurried apology. Could he have meant that this dinner party had been organized solely for her benefit? But she was unable to sort this out in her mind, for someone, usually Dulcie or Georgina, insisted on drawing her into the general conversation, and even her monosyllabic answers failed to persuade them to let her fade into the background.

When Robert Ashton offered his arm to lead her into the dining room, she hesitated, but because Dulcie and Henry were standing behind them at the door, almost as if prepared to push them through, she laid her hand lightly on his sleeve and marched forward, head held high.

As he pulled out her chair for her to be seated at the dining table, Robert leaned over and whispered, "You look lovely tonight, Sabina."

She could scarcely jump up and run away at just that juncture without upsetting furniture and physically pushing him out of the way, so she therefore simply sat down and pretended not to hear him. He smiled and took his place beside her. At least, she thought, she would not have to look at him.

The cook, told that Lord Kimborough employed a French chef, outdid himself in preparing a "proper English dinner"—according to *The Experienced English Housekeeper*—consisting of the requisite number of courses, including covers and removes in the correct order and placing of service. Lady Bromleigh had insisted, for reasons she did not deign to explain, that the interval between courses was to be kept to the absolute minimum, with the result that extra staff were employed to see that the table was cleared with dispatch between the fish course—including a lemon sole with ground almonds, a raised giblet pie, and a fricando of veal—and the second course, during which the cook presented his own masterpiece, a roast haunch of venison with new potatoes and glazed carrots.

Conversation throughout dinner was somewhat strained, no one daring to raise any topic which might inadvertently exacerbate the antagonism between the families. Yet, since no one was precisely sure what topics might result in heated words, even neutral subjects such as the weather or the price of wool were broached gingerly.

Even so, Sabina had the impression that all the Bromleys were making a special effort to maintain the civilities and wondered if they had made a united decision to do so. They would only be carrying out the late earl's unspoken request for them to resolve The Quarrel, of course, but Sabina was divided between admiration for her family, chagrin at her own past behavior, and confusion as to Robert's motives in appearing here, as if by sleight-of-hand, when he should have been in London. She made an extra effort to smile at Lord and Lady Kimborough, if not actually speak to them, attempting to distract herself by this means from speculation as to Robert's intentions.

Only Georgina managed to inject some enthusiasm into the conversation while avoiding or, if possible, deftly dismissing any sensitive topic.

"Try as I may, I *cannot* persuade my papa to take an interest in riding, or indeed in any country matter," Georgina said, appealing with her expressive eyes to Lady Kimborough's elusive sympathy. "It is very well to be bookish, I tell him, but if he is going to bury himself in his library, the library may as well be in the country, where at least the air is fresh and does not deposit soot on the books. Do you have a library at the Abbey, Lord Kimborough?"

Richard, considerably taken by this vivacious girl, the likes of whom he did not recall ever seeing in his part of the country before, replied that he did.

"Quite an excellent one, I am given to understand," he replied, "although I must confess that I am not particularly bookish myself. Would you care to see our library at the Abbey, Miss Campion? I should be pleased to show you around myself any day you care to come."

Georgina, catching Lady Kimborough's baleful eye on her husband, even if he was too dazzled to notice it himself, said, "Why, I thank you, sir—if Lady Kimborough does not object, I should be pleased to call."

The countess murmured her less than heartfelt consent, and Robert joined in to counteract the damper he had feared Lavinia might put on the entire evening if she were not kept in line—discreetly, of course, as Richard had requested before they set out for the evening's entertainment.

"Do you not read Lord Byron, Miss Campion?" Robert asked. "I thought all young ladies swooned over his lordship's poetry."

"I confess to having read *Childe Harold*," Georgina said,

turning toward him, "and even enjoying it. But *swoon* I will not. I hope I have more sense."

"Our Georgina is awake on all suits," Henry offered, at which Georgina pulled a face behind her napkin.

Randolph then treated the company to a rude, but amusing, literary review of *Glenarvon*, which had rapidly made the rounds of the family. This opened the way for Lady Kimborough to expound her views on the entire Devonshire dynasty, as well as their extensive legitimate and less than legal connections, comparing them, as appeared to be her custom, to the paragons of virtue whom she herself could claim as ancestors.

"At least she is discreet enough to blacken the names only of people with whom no one here has any direct connection," Robert whispered to Sabina.

"How does she know none of us does?"

"Lavinia's principal amusement is to know anyone of any breeding or importance at all, or at least know *of* them. If you do come to see our library, you will find that books of genealogy dominate the collection."

"Your brother invited Georgina."

"I trust she would not come alone."

"Would she require a chaperone?"

"Certainly not. Richard finds your cousin delightful, I'm sure, but he is not stupid. He wishes to make peace, too, believe me."

"Why?"

"Why believe me? Some people do, you know."

"I meant, why does he wish to make peace?"

"Because I have asked him to make the attempt."

That silenced Sabina temporarily. She had intended to treat Robert as if she had lost her memory again—at least about their time together on the canal—and converse with him only as a passing acquaintance with whom she was obliged for the sake of the family to be civil. Such indifference was impossible to maintain, however, so she contrived instead to speak as little as possible.

But he was not to be put off. On his inquiring if she had quite recovered from her accident, she disclaimed any lingering effects other than an occasional headache—a fabrication that she hoped pettishly would make him feel his part in her distress more keenly. He appeared unabashed, however, and proceeded to inquire about her horse.

"He found his way home quite unharmed," she replied, aware that he was being ironic and wishing he would be candid with his criticisms; she was not very tolerant of subtlety of this sort. She was accustomed to it in Randolph, of course, but then he had never directed his barbs at her.

"Do you remember the lockkeeper's cottage?" he said then, under cover of a lively exchange between Lewis and Georgina about the relative merits of the assemblies at the local towns and those at Leicester.

"No," Sabina said bluntly.

"I expect it will come back to you," he replied amiably. "Bill and George have finished the repairs and they have all moved in—although Bill still sleeps on the boat in any but the foulest weather. He claims that he cannot reaccustom himself to sleeping under a roof. In Spain, you know, when we had a roof over our billet, it was as often as not full of cannon holes."

Sabina wished she could ask him more about his life in the army—indeed, all of his life before he met her. She still longed, much against her will, to know everything about him, yet she dared not ask any personal questions, lest he feel he had touched her in some way. He must know he had taken control of her heart, but she could not bring herself to acknowledge it, just as she was reluctant to acknowledge that it was only she who forced their conversation into such unnatural lines.

There was silence between them as the sweet dishes were passed, until, over an excellent syllabub, she asked, to break the silence but keep to neutral topics, "Did you fight at Badajoz? A cousin of ours wrote to us just after the siege and was most vivid in his description."

"Regrettably, I was not present, there being little use for the cavalry under the circumstances. At the time, we were still in the north, although we saw action soon enough at Fuentes de Oñoro."

She was reminded then of his friends whom she had seen at the Ashtonbury fete and nearly betrayed herself into asking after them. It seemed there was no way to avoid intimacy with him, short of refusing to speak with him at all.

Indeed, despite her determination to remain aloof and not even meet his eyes, his mere presence beside her overwhelmed her senses. When he moved slightly, she caught a whiff of the same soap he had used on the canal. When she reached for her wineglass, her arm brushed his sleeve. He was far too lively a presence for comfort, and she breathed a sigh of relief when, seemingly hours later, Alicia signaled for the ladies to rise and leave the gentlemen to their brandy. At least she would have a few minutes' respite.

She looked back at him as she left the room. He had risen upon the departure of the ladies, as had the other gentlemen, and she could not help admiring the graceful way he moved and the breadth of his shoulders beneath his well-tailored coat. For the first time it occurred to her how naturally he seemed to fit, except for his fair hair, into a group consisting principally of her tall, handsome brothers.

Somehow, this notion was even more unsettling than the attraction she still felt for him.

Chapter 15

Sabina was astonished to learn afterward that the atmosphere in the dining room after the ladies had departed was even more charged with unspoken animosity than the area immediately surrounding her chair during the meal. Indeed, although conversation among the ladies had been desultory, Lady Kimborough offering monosyllabic contributions only when directly addressed, among the gentlemen not all the recriminations remained unspoken.

Robert had the impression that Earl Bromleigh wished for a private word with him but was constrained from achieving it by the necessity of keeping a tight rein on everyone else's temper. Indeed, Fletcher had just moved himself to the chair beside Robert's when Richard remarked on the fine quality of the Bromleys' brandy.

"Is it by any chance smuggled?" he asked offhandedly, holding his glass up to the light. "I should like to know how to contact your supplier."

Four Bromley heads turned toward Richard, whom his brother had to admire for his temerity. It was unlikely that any remark of his would precipitate a bout of fisticuffs among this company, but he was outnumbered four to one. He certainly could not count on his brother's support if he took a sudden turn to the obstreperous. Robert made up his mind at that moment to maintain a strict neutrality.

"The war is over, Richard," he remarked mildly. "There is no longer any need for anyone to resort to contraband spirits, however appealing they may once have been as a slap in Bonaparte's face."

Richard admired the color of the wine in his glass, then

sipped it appreciatively. "Why no, there is no necessity any longer, but one keeps wine in one's cellar for years sometimes. Just as one protects any other family treasure."

"If there is something you wish to accuse us of," Randolph said testily, "be so good as to come out with it so that we may show you the error of your thinking and proceed to a more amiable topic of conversation. You did come here to be amiable, did you not?"

Richard smiled. He had a charming smile when he chose to use it, Robert noticed, wondering if Lavinia had put him up to this. "I meant nothing by my remark, I assure you. I beg your pardon if my phraseology was—er, awkward."

Fletcher had by this time risen and quietly removed himself to a seat between Richard and Randolph.

"Will you be riding with the local hunt this autumn or organizing your own?" Fletcher asked his guest, as if hunting had been the topic of conversation all along. "We might perhaps join forces at some point."

"And hope there may be safety in numbers," Henry murmured. As he was seated directly opposite, Robert reached out one long leg and kicked him in the shin to silence him. Henry, surprised, looked at Robert, then shrugged and smiled, accepting the rebuke.

Fletcher contrived to keep the conversation on hunting for several minutes, during which the tension in the room eased somewhat and talk became more general. When pressed, Randolph offered his opinion of the hunting to be had around Stonehaven as compared to Melton Mowbray and others of the more celebrated hunts. Even Robert ventured a remark or two, although Henry confined himself to nods of agreement and the occasional "quite right" or "hear, hear."

It was only when Fletcher suggested that they rejoin the ladies that tempers suddenly flared again. Henry, attempting to catch Randolph's attention as they moved toward the door, chanced to jostle Richard, who stepped out of the way but refrained from expressing any verbal reproach to Henry, who finally said, curtly, "Beg your pardon."

"And how is your wife keeping?" Richard asked, continuing to glare. "She is well, I trust?"

"Very well," Henry replied, glaring back. "Thriving, in fact."

"So I observed over dinner. She must be a great satisfaction to you."

"As Lady Kimborough is no doubt to you," Henry returned.

"What do you mean by that, sir?"

"Why, what should I mean? Did you not refer to the fact that I am happy in my marriage? I only hoped that you enjoy the same happy situation."

Richard had got himself in over his head, Robert saw. His brother had never been subtle in the way of verbal expression, preferring even as a boy to get his way by pulling rank. Or putting up his fists. He stepped forward to interrupt any possible outbreak of either, but was forestalled by Lewis, who deftly wheeled his chair between Richard and Henry and looked up at them like a second in a duel determined to effect a last-minute reconciliation.

"Gentlemen, gentlemen," he remonstrated gently. "The ladies will hear you."

Indeed, the footman who had opened the door for their departure stood holding it, fascinated by this scene, and feminine voices could be heard down the hall.

"I venture a guess that my esteemed sister-in-law is preparing to conduct a tour of the picture gallery," Lewis went on. "She always does, given the least occasion for it. Perhaps we ought to join in."

He had pushed Henry slightly aside by judicious use of his chair, and Henry, again taking the rebuke graciously, fell back, out of Richard's view. Lewis continued to gaze pacifically at Richard until he, too, relented.

"Very well, then, let us get on with it."

Breathing a sigh of relief, Fletcher held Robert back for a moment before they proceeded out of the room.

"I thank you for your consciousness of the situation this evening, Captain Ashton, and for your efforts to ensure a congenial gathering."

"There is no need to say so, Lord Bromleigh. You must know that peace between our families is my chief concern—other than one other, of course, which I am sure you can guess."

"Indeed. It is of that I wished to speak with you. There are some new developments—well, never mind, this is not the time. Perhaps tomorrow?"

"Send word to me when would be convenient for me to request your permission—somewhat belatedly, to be sure—to court your sister."

Fletcher stared, as if he had not expected this answer. He would not, of course, if Sabina had reported their last meeting to him, as Robert now saw she had done.

"How will I contact you?" Fletcher said, after a moment's hesitation.

Robert smiled. "Consult your brother's wife, my lord. Lady Henry will know."

With that, he left the room, leaving Fletcher even more nonplussed and wondering what else he did not know.

The ladies came out of the drawing room just as the gentlemen emerged from the dining room and met them in the hall. Alicia, accustomed to guiding visitors around the grounds on public days, put her hand on Richard's arm and drew him along with her to the front of the tour group entering the long gallery by way of the public rooms. These, Sabina noted, had been made more impressive by the addition of various valuable pieces of furniture and bric-a-brac culled from other parts of the house.

"There are some fine views of the country hereabouts, Lord Kimborough, which I am sure you will recognize and admire. Many of the artists are local as well. Perhaps you will be acquainted with some of them."

Richard professed himself ignorant about the fine points of art, but declared a partiality for a good picture of a horse, and Alicia was able to say they had a very fine Stubbs which he would be bound to appreciate.

Sabina supposed that the family portraits had previously been inspected for possible black sheep or common ancestors, although she was not prepared to admit that there were any of the latter. She did recall her father describing some of the family scandals, which she would not dream of repeating, but the memory brought a smile to her lips just the same.

She wiped it away, however, when Robert Ashton caught up with her and detained her just long enough to ensure their position at the rear of the line of march. He took her arm and, despite her fulminating look, did not release it.

"Will you not walk on the terrace with me?" he whispered. "I should like to speak with you privately."

"I cannot imagine anything you may have to say which cannot be said in public," she replied. She sounded overly petulant, even to her own ears, and would have apologized had she thought he would then let her join the others.

In truth, she did not wish to be alone with him because she could not control what she said or how she behaved with him, and she was beginning to despise the person who said and did the things she had done because of him. She did not care to be reminded of that unpleasant female. If only he would give her an opening, she might summon the courage to take it in order to begin again with him—or at the least, take back those unjust accusations she now wished she had never voiced.

"Very well," he said, when she said nothing more. "I wished only to tell you that I will be away from home for a few days, so you need not fear encountering me when you venture out-of-doors. I give you back your freedom of movement."

She felt a sudden oppression over her heart, as if a weight had been laid on it, rather than lifted from it. He was going away again. She would not see him again for days. That must be a good thing. Yet somehow, the future looked even less appealing without the possibility of encountering him unexpectedly on the road or in the village. Certainly the past weeks, since she had learned from Edina where he had disappeared to, had been far from comfortable as she imagined what he might be doing in London.

She had never used to be so given to self-recrimination.

"I assure you, your presence in the neighborhood has

never stood in the way of my freedom." She pronounced this lie even as she watched herself, as if from outside herself, and was astonished at the cool way she still spoke to him. Why could she not simply ask him to stay, to help her begin anew with him?

"I was under the impression that you had just returned from London," she went on, unable to stop herself. "Are its attractions such that you must return so soon? I suppose we must be flattered that you came home to honor us with your presence tonight."

He smiled—condescendingly, she thought, no doubt unjustly—and said, "My dear Sabina, I cannot think where to begin to point out all the misconceptions you reveal by that remark. I am not, however, returning to London. I was feted to within an inch of my life there, but I couldn't stand the place. All the rooms have low ceilings."

She suppressed an answering smile at that, turning her head to hide it. She remembered feeling the same way when she spent three months with one of her aunts in Leicester in lieu of a London season. She too had felt closed in, but she bit her lip and did not tell him about it.

He did not seem to notice her hesitation, however, and said then, "The fact is, I am going to a wedding in Devon."

That surprised her into looking quickly up at him, but she saw only a mischievous smile in his eyes. "I don't suppose you would care to come with me—see how it's done, and meet the bride? You'd like Jane, I think, even if she is marrying a Frenchman. Or rather, remarrying him."

"What?" The inelegant question was startled out of her.

He gave her a thoughtful look. "Ah, another misconception, I perceive," he observed mildly.

"I'm sure I don't know what you mean."

"Yes, you do, but I won't point it out to you."

He was as good as his word and did not pursue the subject, although Sabina's mind raced with speculation, and she was having an increasingly difficult time maintaining her cool demeanor. How could Edina have mistaken Robert's relationship with this Jane? How could she have believed what Edina said rather than what her heart told her?

They strolled for a few minutes behind the others, making inconsequential remarks about a rustic landscape by Morland here, a Kneller portrait there, and at last she felt her breathing become more regular. She suspected that he was deliberately allowing her to compose herself before presenting her with some fresh shock.

She tensed slightly when they paused in front of a portrait of a striking-looking cavalier in blue silk and profusions of lace. He stood for the artist with one hand on his hip and the other on the head of a huge dog.

"At the risk of offending a Bromley," Robert said, grinning, "this fellow reminds me forcefully of Viscount Markham."

Sabina could not help seeing the resemblance as well. "I will not renounce any connection we may have with the Markhams out of hand."

"I am glad to hear it. Nicky said he might visit here again when he returns from Wales."

"I should be pleased to meet him."

They continued along the gallery, whose polished parquet floor echoed back the swish of Sabina's skirts. Alicia's musical voice was lost to them as she and Richard turned into another room. Walking just ahead of them, Henry had his arm around Dulcie's waist and was whispering something in her ear. Sabina tried not to look at them. She knew her defenses were crumbling, and the forced contemplation of another couple, happy in their love, the storm of their initial difficulties long gone, might undo her totally. She wondered where Georgina and Lewis had gone. Somewhere they could be alone together, she did not doubt.

"There is something I must ask you," Robert said, detaining her when Henry and Dulcie had also moved out of their sight.

"What is it?" She wished he were not so near. She wished she were not alone with him—it was too disturbing. Yet so comforting. She tried to move more quickly, to catch up with the others, but his hand on her arm detained her.

"Why do you despise my family so, Sabina?" he asked impersonally, as if inquiring whether she liked tea or coffee with her breakfast. "What have we ever done to deserve your scorn?"

Her anger flared again, briefly. "What have you done—"

He waved his hand impatiently, silencing her. "I do not mean all this nonsense about rights of way and stolen manuscripts and so on."

"It is not nonsense!"

"It involves only *things*, Sabina, not people. Like these portraits—they seem like people, but they are only paint and canvas. We Ashtons have never done anything to try to destroy the Bromleys as a family. Indeed, it could be argued that in the case of Lady Henry, we contributed to your family happiness—at our expense."

"It does not seem to me that your brother is nurturing a broken heart."

"No, I trust he is not. Even if he were, I will not be drawn into another quarrel about it. I have some family pride too, you know."

He stopped before a still life and turned her toward him. "Surely we can resolve our difference over things, over rights and possessions, easily enough if we just talk to one another. It need have nothing to do with the relationship between us two. If you wish, that subject need never be raised again. I ask you only to think about this, my dear, while I am away. I should not like to see my nephews inherit this absurd difference between neighbors which ought never to have begun. And somehow I cannot believe that you wish to inflict it on your niece and nephews any more than I do."

His words were so sensible, his request so simple, that she could not dispute them. Neither could she think about them. Only his suggestion that they never speak again about their relationship echoed in her mind, and the knowledge that he was going away gave her no joy and no relief. She should accept his offer to never again speak to her of love and be glad that she need never again be reluctant to meet him for the fear he would reawaken her love for him.

But no. She did not love *him*. It had been James Owen she loved, and he was gone as surely as if he had died beside Peter Ogilvey in the war.

It seemed she was to spend more time mourning lost love than enjoying its pleasures. She would never fall in love again; that was the only solution. She was doing right in removing to Carling. She would become a hermit if need be.

It was too painful to depend on someone else for her happiness.

If only she never felt this crushing hurt again.

He delivered the final blow to her pride then, when he leaned close to her ear and whispered, "Am I wearing you down yet, Miranda?"

She could not prevent a sob from welling up and nearly undoing her. She jerked herself out of his arms, but he would not give her an inch this time and brought her back to him, raising her chin so that he could look into her tearfilled eyes. Through the mist, she thought she saw James Owen—or at least a look in Robert's eyes that she remembered seeing in James Owen's eyes—and threw her arms around him, heaving a sigh of despair.

He showed what little sympathy he had with her wounded pride by chuckling and saying, "Sabina, what has come over you? Much of what I love about you is your lively spirit, and something has thoroughly dampened that. I sincerely hope it was not I who made you into such a shadow of yourself."

"Oh, no," she said, sniffling and searching in her sleeve for a handkerchief. She finally accepted his and blew her nose. "It is all my fault, Robert. I have been so foolish—indeed, I can no longer remember what I was being so stubborn about."

He smiled. "I shall not remind you then." He looked at her more somberly and said, "And I promise never to mention it again, if you will forget it."

"But—can you possibly forgive me? I cannot forget—and I cannot ask you to love me still, but—"

"Of course you can ask me anything. I forgive you. I love you. I agree with any foolish confession you wish to make, only do stop behaving like a watering pot." He stroked her hair lightly with his hand, making her scalp tingle with the whisper of his touch. "After all," he said then, so softly that she almost missed the words, "I cannot have a wife who weeps all day. What will the servants think?"

She looked up at that. "Wife . . ."

He took advantage of the opening she offered by raising her chin and capturing her mouth with his. His touch paralyzed her for a moment, but then she put her arms around him more tightly and pulled the kiss out of him, giving it back a moment later in double measure.

"Sabina, Sabina," he murmured into her hair. "I can think of no greater happiness than to be married to you."

She gazed up at him wonderingly, drinking in his loving words while at the same time fearfully anticipating the next shock, the next revelation or lie or hurt that would separate them again and prove that this moment was too perfect to last.

It came from an unexpected quarter.

"I tell you, that is Lady Seraphina!" came Lady Kimborough's voice, stridently, from the next gallery.

Sabina frowned, not sure what was happening, so caught up was she in her own confusion, but Robert muttered, "Damn and blast!" He took her arm, saying, "Come. Something has happened to cause a fresh outbreak of hostilities."

They hurried into the gallery to find everyone but Lavinia bending over a glass display case. Lady Kimborough was standing furiously erect, pointing an accusing finger at the case, in an attitude worthy of Miss Siddons at her histrionic best.

"That miniature is of my husband's ancestress. It ought by rights to be displayed in Ashtonbury Abbey. I cannot think how it came to be here!"

"Lady Kimborough," said Alicia soothingly, picking up the miniature to examine it, "please do not upset yourself. You see, there is no positive identification on the reverse. It says only 'Lady S.' Are you quite sure you recognize the portrait?"

Lady Kimborough reached for the miniature, but Alicia contrived to hold it out of her grasp without appearing to snatch it away. "Of course I am sure! There is a matching portrait in our own gallery, the other half of the pair, which is most assuredly ours. Do you doubt me?"

"No, no. I daresay you truly believe—oh dear." Even the ever tactful Alicia found herself at a standstill and appealed to her husband in frustration.

"We will be glad to have the portrait reappraised, Lady Kimborough, and its provenance confirmed," Fletcher said, although his tone told everyone he had no doubt that Bromley ownership would be proved. Nonetheless, he added soothingly, "By an expert of your choosing, of course."

When Lavinia looked as if she would accept no less than instant return of the miniature to its rightful owner, Richard spoke up at last. "You are most kind, Lord Bromleigh. We accept your offer. I am sure you will choose an appropriate person to examine the miniature. In the meantime, we will happily leave it in your care."

He took his wife's arm and said, "Come, Lavinia, perhaps it is time to go home."

Lady Kimborough sniffed, but with her husband propelling her firmly toward the door, she said no more. Fletcher and Alicia hurried after their guests to see them out, and Robert made a move to follow.

"Wait!" Sabina cried, not sure what she wanted him to wait for. He did so, obligingly, while she caught up with him, then searched for words.

"Good-bye," she said finally, inadequately. He smiled and kissed her hand.

"Good night, Sabina, not good-bye." He whispered in her ear, "Meet me tomorrow at noon, on the hill by the canal. You remember."

When she said nothing, he squeezed her hand reassuringly. "Trust me, my love."

She watched him disappear down the hall and sighed, unsure whether to fling herself from the second-story window or burst into tears of happiness. She was unsure, even, of what had just happened to her. Had they really been reconciled? Had she finally allowed herself to give in? Or had he simply been too kind, too loving, to resist?

The rest of her family, however, seemed to be unaware of her dilemma and stood looking at the miniature which Henry now held, scrutinizing the image as if the lady would identify herself to him and thus solve the question.

"She *would* pick the most valuable one in the collection," Randolph remarked acidly.

"And the most ancient," said Dulcie.

That caught Sabina's ear and she went to look also. "Why, that's"—she stopped—"my favorite."

The mysterious "Lady S" had indeed fascinated her since childhood, when she liked to imagine that the portrait was of another Lady Sabina, one who had lived during Elizabeth's reign and been a part of the great court of the Virgin Queen. She took the gold case from Henry's hand and caressed the polished surface of the portrait lovingly.

"Does anyone know of its being one of a pair?" Dulcie asked, to no response.

"To my eye, she does not look like any of us," Henry admitted, "but whether she is an Ashton is certainly open to debate."

A minor debate promptly ensued, Randolph contending that since neither family had risen beyond a baronetage in Elizabeth's time and neither resided then on their present estates, the portrait could have been acquired by anyone from anywhere in the course of the eighteenth century. Lewis suggested that it could have been stolen, or part of a pirate's booty, for all they knew. Everyone agreed that it would have to be reappraised but that careful investigation would doubtless confirm the Bromleys' possession.

Sabina took no part in this discussion and Dulcie, observing her sister-in-law's listlessness, put her arm comfortingly around her waist as they left the gallery.

"Well," she said, "God commands us to love our neighbors. Your father asked only that we tolerate them, but even that seems beyond our capability."

"I *was* asked to love one of them," Sabina reminded her.

"I know, my dear," Dulcie said sympathetically, "and I cannot help feeling this is all my fault. I wanted to do too much too soon. I so hoped that this evening would be the beginning of a new closeness between the families, and perhaps even a new opportunity for you."

"You did what you thought was right," Sabina said. "At least you *did* something. I should never have had the courage again—that is, ever—to take any sort of bold action. And—well, perhaps it was a new beginning. Do not regret your effort, Dulcie. I know it was done out of love."

Sabina hesitated, not sure what she wanted to say. Dulcie frowned, but did not press her, for which Sabina was grateful. She wanted to tell Dulcie that everything would be well, but she dared not. She still feared that her conversation with Robert had taken place only in her imagination, that his kisses had been only wishful thinking on her part. She felt his lips with her fingertips. No, that must have been real.

"I shall call on the Ashtons," Dulcie said, "and attempt to make peace. After all, I was almost one of them once." She stopped and hugged Sabina. "But then I would not have been *your* sister, Sabina dear."

Sabina looked at her with new eyes. "And *you* breached the gap between us in the other direction, by marrying Henry, didn't you? I know I am biased toward the Bromleys, but I'm sure I'm right that we all tried to help this evening—except me. I always seem to expect everyone else to make an effort for me."

Dulcie put a comforting arm around her sister-in-law. "Please don't fret, Sabina. I know everything will work out for the best."

Sabina sighed. "You and Henry are so fortunate. You saw each other, and fell in love, and there was never any question but that you would live happy ever after."

Dulcie smiled at her but said nothing.

Chapter 16

Sabina was too impatient to wait and arrived at the place Robert had asked her to meet him well ahead of their appointed rendezvous. She dismounted, setting her horse free to crop the grass on the hill, and looked out over the landscape. Robert was nowhere in sight yet, so she sat down under the oak tree and concentrated on remembering the view as she had seen it on the day they were last here.

It had been a day much like this, warm and sunny, with a slight breeze ruffling the velvety grass, and the distant canal sparkling with light. The level of water in the canal seemed to be slightly higher since the last rain, and tree branches dipped down toward it, as if to drink from the canal.

What had they talked about then? She could not recall anything except the warm, free feeling she had in his arms. That was odd, her feeling free in his embrace.

She remembered then what they had said—some non-sense about their previous lives as star-crossed lovers, kept apart by their families. She realized now that she must have been voicing her unconscious fears about their own families.

She smiled, remembering that he had promised to carry her off and slay dragons for her sake. He had certainly done his best. It was she who had conjured up the dragons, she who had proved as stubborn as either of their families.

She hoped she had not repented too late.

Her mind occupied with these still troublesome thoughts, she did not immediately see Robert approach, until something made her turn her head, and there he was—coming up the hill from the direction of the lock, carrying a picnic basket.

For a moment, Sabina thought she must have traveled back in time, and everything that had happened since that day was only a figment of her distressed imagination. Her heart was in her mouth as she rose to watch him come toward her.

He saw her and waved. Then something in her expression must have made him stop. He smiled, dropped the basket on the ground, and held out his arms to her.

She felt a rush of relief and happiness flood through her as she ran down the hill and into his arms.

He caught her and held her fast. Neither said anything for some time, and Sabina let the welcome sensations of being safe in Robert's love flow through her and wash away the doubts and fears that she had not been able to dispel alone. Now she knew that she would never be alone again.

After a few minutes, he whispered into her ear, "Are you happy now, Miranda?"

She put her head back to look up at him. "Yes—never so happy. I was so frightened that—"

He put his fingers on her lips. "There is nothing to be frightened of, not any longer."

She smiled. "I know that. I think I realize now that there never was anything—only my nonsensical notions—"

He stopped her with a kiss this time. When finally, a little shakily, he released her mouth, she sighed deeply but said nothing. "That's better," he said, smiling. The light in his blue eyes warmed her heart.

He picked up the picnic basket. "Look, Rose has packed us a nuncheon."

She laughed. "Dear Rose. She is always there when you need her and always knows what you need."

They walked slowly, hand in hand, up the hill to the oak tree, and did not speak for a few moments, while he spread out a blanket and she opened the basket. They ate in silence for a few moments, but neither had much appetite.

After a few minutes more, she said, "Robert, I—"

And at the same time, he said, "Do you remember—"

He laughed, but she brought his hand to her breast and clutched it with both of hers. "No, let me. I'm the one who must take the next step."

He raised one eyebrow questioningly.

"Rose told me so."

"Ah, I see."

"But she was right. Dearest, I don't want to remember anymore. I want to look forward and forget the past—or at least the past when I behaved so stupidly. I am ashamed to think of it. Please say you forgive me."

"It seems to me that I've already said that. I don't know what there is to forgive, for everything you have said and done was because you are you, and I cannot—despite the exasperation you have caused me—ever want to change you. But if you want to be pardoned, I forgive you freely."

She smiled and relaxed her grip on his hand. "Rose said something like that . . ." She frowned slightly, remembering. "She said I should not wait for someone else to assure me that I deserved to be happy, but that I should make up my own mind that I deserve it."

"And have you?"

"I . . . I think so. I still feel undeserving and a little apprehensive about allowing myself to be optimistic, but . . . I should not have begged your pardon, Robert. You were right too. You have already forgiven me in more ways than I can count."

"I only said you *need* not apologize, my love, not that I would not say anything you wanted me to say. None of it would be a lie. Nothing between us should ever be untrue."

"How can you be so generous? I cannot be like you, however much I would wish it."

"I'm no saint, Sabina. I have simply learned that there are some things in life which are useless to waste emotion on, particularly negative emotions that wear one down and leave no place for happiness—which generally comes in by unexpected windows—to enter."

She looked into his eyes. "It has come now, at last. I feel it when I am in your arms."

He pulled her toward him and would not let her speak again for several minutes, but she no longer wanted to. She wanted to make up for the time she had wasted, the time she had not been with him, in his arms. He tasted so good, felt so warm, that she wished they were married now. The thought of Robert making love to her intoxicated her.

He pulled away suddenly. Her disappointment must have shown on her face, for he laughed shakily.

"Sabina, you do not know what you are asking."

"Yes, I do," she said, moving the remains of their nuncheon aside to get closer to him. Then she felt herself begin to lose her balance where the hill began to fall away, and he had to catch her, holding her fast against him.

"Take care, or we shall become the next casualties of the canal. I would be even harder to haul out than Lewis was."

She moved back voluntarily at that. "That was *you*? Good heavens, I never guessed! I should have, of course, but I never really looked at you that day. Why did you not tell me who you were?"

"Your mind was naturally on your brother, and I did not care to volunteer information which would further upset you. Also, I did not want you to remember me as having anything at all to do with Lewis's misfortune. I was glad to see him well and happy at dinner last night, by the way."

"That was in large part due to Georgina's presence, I believe." She explained about Georgina's devotion to Lewis and their recent betrothal.

"I should have mentioned it to you last night, but I was so envious of their happiness that it would have been too painful a subject."

"I saw Fletcher this morning," he said, as he began packing things back into the picnic basket.

Surprised, she said, "When was this? I did not know you had come to the house yourself."

"I asked him to meet me in the village. I thought it was time I asked formally for your hand."

She laughed, envisioning the scene. "Was he pompous and did he make you feel suitably servile?"

"I would have tugged my forelock most obsequiously

had it been necessary, but it was not. He was perfectly civil and agreeable to terms—perhaps he was eager to be rid of you."

"I can believe that."

"At any rate, my own brother is something of the same sort, all too conscious of his role as head of the family. Left to his own devices, I think he could be softened up a little, but Lavinia keeps him in line with her constant reminders of our consequence."

They were silent for a moment, in mutual agreement that Lavinia would prove the hardest nut to crack in their continuing efforts to unite the two families.

"Fortunately, however, Richard is not influenced by her in any important way, and would not be swayed by her if she refused to receive you."

"Still, I should not like to be at daggers-drawn with her forever."

He put his arm around her shoulder and hugged her to him. "Thank you, Sabina. I confess I cannot be conciliatory when Lavinia raises my hackles, which she does all too frequently, but we will not be obliged to see her every day, and perhaps distance will allow us to be more tolerant."

She reached for his hand and they rose, as if by mutual consent, to begin walking back down the hill. The shadows were already beginning to lengthen, and the sun was lower in the afternoon sky. She wondered where the time had gone.

"Why did you go to London?" she asked. "And speaking of that—why are you not in Devon at this moment?"

"I wrote to Jane immediately after leaving you last night, begging off attending the wedding. I did not tell her why, since you and I had come to no agreement, but I think she will understand. As for London—well, I suppose I was becoming desperate. I went away to make you miss me."

"You did."

"Good," he said, unrepentant, but added, "I never meant to stay away. I could not have done so."

"It doesn't matter now. Perhaps you were right to be

angry and to wish to teach me a lesson. But do tell me about Jane. How did you meet?"

He explained the circumstances, and his description of their delight in setting the *ton* on its ear with their supposed infatuation with each other made her laugh, and she was able to dismiss the last vestiges of suspicion about his relationship with Jane Porter, if not quite all her envy of his warm friendship with her. What had he told Jane about her? She did not dare to ask. Not yet.

Instead, she looked up and smiled ruefully. "I hope I caused you a few sleepless nights as well."

"A few? My dear, I considered abducting you like a Roman carrying off a Sabine. Were I Ariel, I would have ruined the plot of the play by carrying Miranda off to a cave by the sea and keeping her there forever. Or at least long enough to compromise her reputation."

"I almost wish you had carried me off with you, instead of taking yourself to London all alone. Anyway, I was compromised that first night on the Theaks' boat. I knew perfectly well who and where I was, remember, if not who you were. I wanted to be compromised. I loved James Owen."

They were silent as, hand in hand, they reached the towpath and paused to watch a dignified mother swan and her three cygnets negotiating the slight currents stirred up in the canal by a pair of playful mallards. It was a moment before Sabina realized that Robert had been looking at her rather than the swans for some time. She gazed back at him, learning to read his thoughts in his eyes. She held her breath at what she thought she saw.

"Do you think you can bring yourself to marry Robert Ashton instead?" he said softly, as if half-afraid of the answer.

She looked at him, and he saw the real love in her eyes, unclouded by doubts or suspicion or old quarrels.

"They are both the man I love," she said, raising her hand to stroke his cheek lovingly. "If I marry one, I marry the other. I would not have one without the other. I love you enough for two."

"Then there may just be enough love to satisfy us both," he said, and pulled her to him to take its measure again.

"I have a proposition," he said when he let her go.

"A *what*?"

He smiled. "I beg your pardon—an unfortunate choice of words. An idea, then, about our wedding."

She sighed. "Oh, dear. I have been thinking ahead to being married and quite forgot the necessity for a wedding first. Will it be too tedious to wait and be married out of the village church? At least, that will be neutral ground."

"Actually, I was thinking of an even speedier route."

She looked at him, trying to read his thoughts, but he only smiled mischievously down at her. Then she realized what he must be thinking.

"Are you suggesting that we—*elope*?"

"Not precisely. It would certainly save a great deal of botheration if we had it done over the anvil in Scotland. But I know a bishop who might assist me to purchase a special license so that we could at least be married out of the church in Ashtonbury village—or in Market Harborough, if you like. We could spend our honeymoon on a narrowboat and be as far away from the world as if we had eloped."

She smiled. "I like that idea. Could Bill arrange it?"

"I'll speak to him before I leave. In any case, I must go away for a day to settle some—unfinished business before I will be free to stand before you at the altar, and at the same time I can procure the license."

"What business?"

He put his finger on her lips and smiled. "I'll tell you when I am successful."

She sighed. "I suppose you must have some secrets—until we are married. After that, my love, I shall expect you to confide your every thought. But I wish you did not have to go away again, Robert, even for a day. I daresay it is true that if we run to the border, we will be expected to marry in a more proper way later, so I suppose a special license would be the most agreeable option."

"At least we will be together and can do the proper at our leisure. Let our families quarrel about *that* if they will."

"Robert! I nearly forgot. *Where* are we to be together?"

He did not answer at once, gazing down at her thoughtfully. Then he smiled and said, "I don't suppose you would care to follow the drum?"

"Don't be absurd. Anyway, the war is over."

"So it is. A pity."

"Don't make jokes, love. It *is* a dilemma."

"I only meant that *I* do not care where we live, as long as we are together. So the choice is yours."

"We would not have to live at Ashtonbury Abbey?"

"Good heavens, no!"

"And I suppose Bromleigh Hall is already rather overcrowded with Bromleys . . ."

"It would be something of a squeeze, but if that is what you want—"

"No, I want us to have somewhere of our own." She held her breath for a moment, reluctant to hear his answer to her next suggestion.

"Would you dislike it terribly if we lived at Carling Manor?"

"Why should I dislike it?"

"Well, it is still a Bromley property, and—"

"A minor obstacle, I trust. How could it be if I asked Fletcher to sell it to me? Then it would be mine to give to you as a wedding present."

"Oh, yes! Oh, Robert, would you? I think Fletcher would agree. Indeed, I shall insist that he do so."

He laughed. "I doubt it will be necessary to threaten him physically, but I will speak to him as soon as . . . ah, no, I suppose it must wait until we return from our canal cruise, if he will not be angry with me then. Or I can leave him a note before we leave, apologizing beforehand for spiriting you away."

"We must both leave him word, I think. And for your brother. And Dulcie."

"It sounds as if we had better go home at once and begin our preparations before they develop into a greater rotomontade than posting the bans and receiving all those well-wishing—and curious—callers."

Suddenly conscious of the passing time, they quickly made a plan to meet the day after next at four o'clock. This would give Sabina time to pack and transport her belongings unobtrusively to Carling, where Robert would meet her for the drive to Market Harborough—and the start of their new life.

He saw her onto her horse, which had obligingly followed her down the hill. They parted as hastily as one more kiss, one last embrace, allowed, she to return home before her absence was noted and he to return to the lockkeeper's cottage to tell Rose the news and ask Bill to locate a narrowboat for them.

"Good-bye, my Miranda," he said, taking her outstretched hand in his. "Soon we shall set forth on our journey to Camelot and find only good things and kind people on our way."

She smiled. "Farewell, my knight errant. I wish I did not have to leave you, even for another day."

He kissed her hand and smiled up at her. "This will be the last time, my love. After tomorrow, nothing will keep us apart again."

Sabina waved as he turned back toward the lock, then reluctantly set her mount toward home—toward Bromleigh Hall, gazing at the countryside she rode over as if she would never see it again. That was nonsense, of course; they would be home again within the week, and nothing would have changed here. But this was the last time she would see it as Sabina Bromley.

Sabina Ashton. Robert's wife. It had a lovely, simple sound to it. People would continue to call her by her title, of course, but somehow she no longer cared about that. She felt like a butterfly emerging from a chrysalis. Lady Sabina Bromley was no more; Sabina Ashton would be a different creature altogether.

She did not know how she would get through the next day.

Chapter 17

After leaving Robert, Sabina was scarcely able to get through dinner with her family without revealing the unsettling mixture of sadness and joy that bubbled inside her. Later, she was too intoxicated with the memory of her meeting with Robert, and too full of the secret she could not yet reveal, to be able to sleep.

She had thus stayed up, choosing what clothing she would take with her on their honeymoon and then hiding it away where Emily would not notice. Early the next morning, she had taken those things to Carling, secreted among several small items of furniture and books. She had also written a note to Fletcher to place, as her last act before leaving her old home, in the box of cigars which he broached only after dinner. He would not find it until she and Robert were married and gone.

Yesterday, when they had made their plans, a day had seemed not nearly enough time to prepare, but now that same day seemed endless. It was an eternity until bedtime, and Sabina spent the day busying herself at Carling, as any good housekeeper would in preparation to welcome a new bride to the house. The fact that the bride would be herself only made the work more important—and exhausting enough to allow her, thankfully, to sleep that night through. The next morning, she would have one last task with which to occupy herself.

Sabina sat on the edge of the settee in the parlor into which the butler had shown her. He had betrayed no emotion on hearing her name and had certainly given her no hint as to how she would be received.

She had never been in Ashtonbury Abbey. She looked around her, consciously comparing this room, this house, unfavorably with Bromleigh Hall. She knew she ought not to think such uncharitable thoughts. She had come to put all that behind her so that she could go to Robert with no more of the baggage of the past than she needed to retain her identity.

It was also up to her, she had at last come to understand, to make friends with the Ashtons, and she was perfectly willing to do so now. The pride that had once ruled her was part of that unnecessary baggage which had weighed her down, and she felt lighter and happier for being able to discard it.

Still, the Ashtons could not know what she was thinking unless she put voice to her criticisms. She remembered her father once telling her that it was easier for one to act positively than to think positively, but if one acted in a charitable way long enough, one's inner self might eventually come around to charity as well. She hoped so. She feared her feelings had a long distance to come.

She glanced around the room again, looking for something she could comment positively on. The furnishings were massive but costly, of the sort that Randolph would have dismissed as attractive only to those "who wish to parade their wealth but have no notion of taste." The sofa and chairs were mainly of carved oak, with a minimum of padding beneath the upholstery, as Sabina was beginning to discover.

She shifted her weight slightly and studied the ceiling. It was, she thought, overly ornate, and she did not think she could praise it with a clear conscience.

The Turkey carpet beneath her feet, on the other hand, was new and its colors still bright. Sabina thought she preferred the slightly worn but elegant Oriental rugs scattered around Bromleigh Hall, but she thought she could honestly praise the carpet, although she did not think she could live with it.

Fortunately, she would not have to. Or . . . could Robert have disclaimed any desire to live at the Abbey solely for her sake? It was his boyhood home, after all, the only one he had ever known, and he had come back to it after being abroad for so many years, so it must exert some pull on him.

She wished she did not lose the self-confidence she had always commanded before whenever she was parted from Robert. It was very well to consider other points of view, but one must not lose one's own in the process.

Yet, Robert had given no impression of being fond of the Abbey, and it was his brother's home, not his. Perhaps Robert had some other house at his disposal. She must ask him while it was still not too late to change their plans for Carling Manor.

She entertained herself with this thought for several minutes, until at last the door opened and Lady Kimborough entered the room. She was dressed severely in a high-necked, wine-colored afternoon dress and gazed at Sabina's black bombazine as if she disapproved of anyone's coming to her house attired in a more sober mode than she chose to adopt.

In fact, Sabina had donned her gown this morning with the conscious thought that it would be the last time she would wear it. It was the last day before her new life began. Perhaps, when she removed it, she would leave the old, proud Sabina in her old clothes. She smiled to herself. She would buy a whole new wardrobe to dress a new Sabina.

The thought brought a smile to her lips, so that when she stood up and faced the countess, she knew she looked as approachable as she had intended to be when she came here. But when the other woman said nothing, she realized that she would not be met halfway. She moved forward, her hand outstretched. She was taller than the countess by several inches and tried to make herself shorter by leaning slightly forward, but the other woman seemed to regard this as an unwanted advance and stepped backward. Sabina had to take an awkward step to avoid stumbling and found herself becoming annoyed despite her good intentions.

"Lady Kimborough, it was good of you to see me," she said, forcing some measure of warmth into her voice.

Lavinia took her hand and shook it briefly, but did not ask Sabina to sit down again. She too remained standing, rigidly erect, apparently attempting to overcome her disadvantage of height by sternness of manner.

"What brings you to Ashtonbury Abbey, Lady Sabina?" she inquired haughtily.

"I wished to—to apologize for any offense I may have given on the occasion of our last meeting."

"The apology is somewhat belated," Lavinia said, "and it is not yours to make. I do not see your brother coming to call."

Sabina was rapidly losing the resolution she had willed herself to maintain. She bit back a retort and reminded herself that she had intended to display a positive attitude.

"I'm sure he will wish to call shortly. Now that I see the Abbey, I am sorry I have delayed so long myself. It is an . . . impressive home. You must be very proud of it."

Lady Kimborough nodded, but did not unbend.

"Did you choose the furnishings yourself? I imagine most of them must be family heirlooms, but this carpet, for example, is wonderfully bright and modern."

"Richard chose that," Lavinia said, looking down at the object of her scorn.

"Oh." Sabina thought she had best continue with her prepared speech. Her extemporaneous remarks were apparently doomed to be received with displeasure.

"I wished also to give you—that is, to return something you believe—something that may have mistakenly found its way to Bromleigh Hall," she said.

She drew from her pocket a velvet case and opened it. Inside was the miniature of "Lady S."

Lavinia stared at it, and it was a moment before she said, with no noticeable diminution of hauteur, "I do not understand—are you saying it is ours, after all?"

"I am prepared to admit there may have been an error made in the past, and I wish to make amends. Even if its provenance is never proved, I should like you to have it as a token of—as a peace offering, if you will. I assure you, my brother shares my sentiments. We both hope that we may even begin to think of the lady as belonging to both families, in a way."

Sabina's words sounded resentful to her own newly sensitized ears, as if she were making this gesture under protest. She had not intended to appear so, and despite her insinuation that Fletcher had given his blessing to her mission, no one knew she had come but Dulcie, in whom she had confided and who had told her she was sure it would be all right with the family if she gave the miniature to the Ashtons. It had been entirely Sabina's idea to come. Still, Lady Kimborough's disinclination to be receptive was making it difficult in the extreme to finish what she had come to say.

She was given a reprieve, and then a reward—as she saw it later, thanking providence that her efforts to be good had been recognized—when just then Lord Kimborough banged his walking stick against the half-opened door and put his head into the room.

"Lavinia, what are you doing—oh, Lady Sabina! I beg your pardon. No one told me you were here."

He shot a mildly accusatory glance at his wife, who shrugged. "I thought you were still at the stables," she offered halfheartedly.

"Haven't you sent for some refreshment for our guest? Why are both you ladies standing? Dear me, this will not do!" He came into the room, laying his stick against the wall and hastily removing his hat to reveal fair hair in some disarray. "Lady Sabina, please do sit down—no, not there, this armchair is more comfortable."

Sabina sank gratefully onto the chair he held for her. Lady Kimborough remained standing for a moment more, then appeared to come to a decision and said, "I shall see about some tea and cakes."

As she reached the door, her husband called out, "In twenty minutes, my dear, if that is satisfactory. I should like to chat with our guest for a little."

He patted Sabina's shoulder and then sat down himself

in another chair. Sabina thought she would have found his behavior annoyingly condescending at any other time, but compared to the countess, the earl was the model of a gracious host.

"Did you come to see Robert, my dear? I am sorry he is not at home, as I suppose Lavinia has told you."

Sabina tried not to smile. "I knew he was away from home," she said, explaining no more than that. Not wishing to complain of any lack of forthrightness in his wife's reception, she told Richard that she had stopped by unannounced.

"I came only to return something to Lady Kimborough which was—misplaced."

She glanced at the table where the countess had laid the miniature, and the earl's eyes followed hers.

"By Jove, that's—yes, it is. The infamous miniature! Really, Lady Sabina, it is too good of you. We have no proof that it is ours, you know, despite Lav—our wish that it may prove to be. It was not necessary to—"

"Lady Kimborough wished to have it, and we—I wish to try somehow to resolve that old, and possibly senseless, quarrel. My father desired it also, you know, and I have always tried to carry out his wishes. I would not like to think I had failed in this last request of his."

"I see." Richard gazed at her thoughtfully for a moment but then said only, "Well, what do you think of Ashtonbury Abbey, Lady Sabina? I believe you have not visited here before."

"It is very—stately."

He laughed at that. "Yes, you and Robert must agree on many things, for you certainly do on that head. He finds the old pile oppressive."

"Does he?"

"Indeed. Oh, Robin liked the place well enough when he was a boy, as did I. There is no fun like hiding in suits of armor, you know, or skulking about in the minstrel's gallery in the dead of night hoping to surprise an ancestral ghost. But I suspect Robin was secretly relieved that I was the eldest and would have to live here forever. After he came out of the army, especially, he felt confined here. He would sleep outdoors if he could, and in the stables, I daresay, in winter, and he is rarely inside on fine days such as this. But I think it more likely he will build his own home someday. Something like your father's estate at Carling, perhaps—cozy and a great many windows."

Sabina stared at him. How did he know about Carling? He was either much more perceptive than she had thought or he had made a lucky guess.

At that moment the tea things arrived. The countess did not return, however, and Sabina began to think she would have to put off convincing Lavinia to relax her hostility, which would doubtless increase when she learned about the elopement. Perhaps the earl would prove an ally in that regard.

He rambled cheerily while they drank their tea, dredging up stories from his and his brother's boyhood to put her at ease, and he did succeed in making her feel more comfortable. "Robin would not thank me for repeating any of this to you," he confided, "so do me the kindness not to tell him I did."

Sabina was searching for some response that would not give away their secret, when he put down his cup, clapped his hands on his knees, and said heartily, "Well, what do you say, my dear Lady Sabina—may I take you on a tour of the Abbey? Although it is not as elegant and modern a house as Bromleigh Hall, it too has its charms."

Since the earl had obligingly undergone a similar tour of her own home, Sabina could scarcely refuse and smilingly accepted. In any case, she would be interested to see more of the place where Robert had grown up—practically under her nose, so to speak, although she had not known him when they were children. She was beginning to think that a great loss.

He escorted her first into the great hall, by which she had entered the house, and paused to direct her attention to the dome, which she had not earlier noticed.

"I am told that it is a very fine example of baroque architecture," he informed her, "but as I told your esteemed sis-

ter-in-law, I am a poor judge of artistic merit from any period. I like it because the style and color of paint makes it
seem very much as if one is looking right through the ceiling to the sky. Don't you agree?"

Sabina gazed upward and thought that indeed, were it not
for the cherubs peeking mischievously from around the
perimeter of the dome, the clouds and sky were quite realis-
tic. She smiled and said she saw what he meant.

"Our old nurse fancied the second cherub to the left of
the pinkest cloud to be the image of Robin as a babe,"
Richard went on. "As for myself, I remember him only as
very red in the face—possibly because I was four years
older and thought him an intrusive little brat when he entered what had been my well-ordered personal domain."

Sabina laughed at that and said that doubtless her brothers had thought the same of her unexpected arrival in the
family, long after the last of them had joined it, particularly
since they had no notion that she would turn out to be a female, a species with which they had had little contact and
no experience.

"You understand how it was, then. I am glad to say that I
see less of a gap between my own sons—have you met
Robin's nephews, by the way?—but they are only two
years apart in age and appear to be great friends. David is
the more intrepid of the two, but I believe that is because he
feels himself safe in Geoffrey's protection."

Sabina said she regretted not yet having met the earl's
sons and wondered if she might suggest some way to bring
the younger generation of both families together. That was
something she and Robert must do when they were married. It was surprising to her to contemplate how full her
life would be when she was married. Why had she not
thought of these things before? Why had she not realized
that marriage would free her, not bind her?

It was not long before it became clear that there was a
theme to the earl's route through his home—he was showing it to her as a part of Robert's life that she knew nothing
about. They went up to the large room under the eaves
which had been their nursery, then to the miniature library

where they had been given their lessons by a series of tutors, all of whom, according to Richard, had favored his brother.

"How vexatious for you," Sabina said.

"It quite often was," he admitted. "But at those times, I reminded myself—and Robin as well, often in not the most cordial terms—that I was the heir and it did not matter whether I knew the properties of the most common metals or was on intimate terms with all the Roman emperors, for I would always be the eldest son and therefore always the next earl—although he did not hesitate to point out, when he was old enough to understand the distinction, that I was only the heir *apparent*."

Sabina smiled and studied Lord Kimborough more carefully. He was a handsome man, although a little less tall and a little less fair than his younger brother; his manner was more reserved, even aloof, yet she could scarcely accuse him of being unfriendly, particularly in contrast to his wife.

Had she met him under other circumstances, she might not have supposed him to be Robert's brother, and she had not given him much thought as a possible friend either. He was cordial, although not gregarious, and she had the impression that although he wished her to like him, he would unbend only so far to earn her regard. She would have to take him on his own terms, and she found herself unexpectedly willing, even eager, to do so.

It even occurred to her, a little surprisingly, that he might turn out to be the confidant she had been wishing for, someone to whom she could turn when she was puzzled or troubled about her relationship with Robert. She was not yet ready to confide completely in him, but this oddly biographical tour of Ashtonbury Abbey seemed to indicate that the possibility existed for the future.

Perhaps, for now, she could at least tell him what she had not said to the countess, the last words of her speech which she had been unable to utter. As they gazed at the view from the room in one of the remoter wings, where Robert had preferred to stay on his early leaves from the army, she broached the subject.

"Lord Kimborough, there is something—"

"Oh, please call me Richard, my dear. If we are to be related, we must not stand upon such formal terms."

She stared at him, astonished. "Related?"

He smiled. "Forgive me. I am always blundering in where angels fear to tread, but I do know something of the case between you and Robin, and I assure you, there is nothing I would like more than to see him happy. And I am certain, now that I have come to know you a little better, that you will make him happy."

She blushed despite herself. Robert had apparently not revealed their engagement, but had everyone but herself been so certain all along that it would come about?

"Well, then—Richard. There is something else I wish to say about the miniature."

She paused for a moment, looking down at her hands.

"Yes?" he prompted.

"I told Lady Kimborough that I hoped the lady in the miniature might belong in some measure to both our families—as my sister-in-law Dulcie does."

His smile faded slightly at that, but he said nothing, so she went on, "And as I hope I shall be—one day. Indeed, I shall—should be honored to be a part of your family."

His smile returned. "The honor, my dear, would be entirely ours."

He kissed her cheek then and, in perfect accord, they returned to the hall, where Sabina was just taking her leave, when Lady Kimborough made a sudden reappearance.

Both Sabina and the earl turned toward her in astonishment, for there was a look of undisguised fury on her face that imagination balked at interpreting.

"My dear," Richard said soothingly, "whatever is the matter? I had hoped you would come to bid our guest good day—"

"I most certainly will say not good day, but good-bye!" the countess declared, scarcely able to rein in her anger. "I trust she will never call here again. I will certainly not open my door to her ever again!"

"Lavinia!" the earl exclaimed, appalled.

Sabina stepped forward to face whatever accusation Lady Kimborough wished to hurl at her, but she was not prepared for what she heard.

"Lady Kimborough," Sabina began, surprised to find her voice level and her own temper in check, "whatever it is, I'm sure you must be mistaken. What have I done to upset you?"

"The miniature is missing!" the countess exclaimed, getting to the point without troubling to answer Sabina's question, which she apparently considered to be rhetorical.

Sabina was speechless, and Lord Kimborough stated the obvious. "But Lavinia, did Lady Sabina not give it to you only an hour ago?"

"Not *that* miniature, dolt," Lady Kimborough retorted intemperately. "The matching portrait. The one which proves that the set belongs to the Ashtons!"

Chapter 18

Now it was the earl whose temper was unraveling.

"Lavinia, are you accusing Lady Sabina of theft?" He addressed his wife in an icy voice.

Lady Kimborough's angry gaze faltered momentarily, but then she lifted her chin determinedly. "It seems to me a very peculiar coincidence that the miniature should disappear just when she has entered the house," she pronounced.

"Sabina had been in your company or mine since she arrived," Richard pointed out. "Do you know for a certainty that the portrait was not missing prior to her arrival?"

Sabina, still astounded at this turn of events and unable to believe that this scene was taking place, found herself yet farther outside the conversation as Lord and Lady Kimborough confronted each other, apparently having forgotten her existence.

"Lord Kimborough," she began, tentatively touching his arm to catch his attention. He started, then turned to her and quickly assumed the more genial expression he had greeted her with earlier. She could not be entirely sure, however, that his heart was in it this time. If it was not, had he been quite as sympathetic as she had imagined earlier? She felt not only confused, but uncertain of her ability to understand anyone's motives anymore.

"My dear Lady Sabina," Richard said, raising her hand to kiss it, "I cannot apologize enough. I am certain this will all prove an unnecessary and unfortunate obstacle to our friendship, and only a temporary one. Nonetheless, perhaps you would be good enough to leave and allow me to get to the bottom of the matter? I will call on you as soon as it is resolved, I assure you."

"Thank you, Lord Kimborough," Sabina replied, holding on to her dignity as her last measure of self-respect. "I am certain you are as good as your word."

His smile reassured her to some extent, but when Sabina turned to say good-bye to the countess, that lady refused again to take her offered hand. Instead, she turned wordlessly and went through the nearest door, closing it firmly behind her.

A moment later, Sabina found herself on the other side of the front door of Ashtonbury Abbey, struggling to control her tears of frustration and disappointment. She wiped the back of her hand over her eyes before donning her riding gloves and mounting her horse, which a groom held for her while he averted his eyes and contained his curiosity with difficulty.

She rode to Carling alone, refusing the groom's company since she could not chance his report of her behavior reaching Bromleigh Hall before she and Robert were on their way.

Oh, where *was* Robert? She had no idea of the time, but it could not be past noon. He had said he would meet her at four o'clock, but she had an overwhelming desire to seek immediate comfort in his arms.

What had she done wrong? She had set out this morning with the best of intentions, and now The Quarrel, which she had tried with a whole heart to end, had only been resuscitated. Robert would be at the least disappointed in her, at worst . . .

She refused to think of the worst that could happen, and soon, reason and something like her old assurance reasserted themselves. She had done nothing wrong. She had no idea what had happened to the Ashtons' miniature, but she had not taken it, and she knew that no one connected with the Bromleys had even seen it, much less stolen it. For all she knew, the miniature had never existed, and Lady Kimborough was using its purported disappearance to fuel her animosity toward Sabina's family.

And when she and Robert were married, would she still refuse to receive Sabina—and therefore Robert? Had she succeeded today only in separating him irrevocably from his family?

It was in this mood of uncertainty that she arrived at Carling Manor, composed but apprehensive. All she could do now, she supposed, was wait for Robert and discuss the matter with him. She could not think about it any longer without confiding in him or she would drive herself mad.

It was a moment before she noticed Fletcher's traveling coach standing in her drive, and another moment before she realized its significance.

"Good heavens! Edina!"

Sabina came to a halt, staring at the coach as a mountain of luggage was being taken down from it and carried into the house. A moment later, a very thin, very white-haired lady of indeterminate age, with bright brown eyes, stepped out of the front door and began directing the disposition of her belongings by waving a walking stick at the coachman and footman.

"Cousin Sabina!" this apparition exclaimed when she saw Sabina standing on the drive, nonplussed. "I knew I should not do wrong by coming to Carling first, rather than proceeding directly to Bromleigh Hall. After all, we are to stay in this lovely house together, are we not? We are, indeed, and so I thought it eminently sensible to have the coachman bring me here so that my luggage might be unloaded in its proper place. If I had not found you at home, to be sure, I should have gone on to the Hall, but here you are, just as I anticipated, and you do look lovely, Sabina dear, but where have you been?"

Sabina had found her voice sometime during the early part of this speech, but was unable to halt its course long enough to welcome her companion. She did have time to wonder, however, how she would inform Edina that she was unemployed already. How *could* she have forgotten about her?

"Oh, Edina, I'm so sorry," she said as she escorted her

cousin back into the house. "I must confess, it had completely slipped my mind that you were arriving today."

"But did you not receive my last letter, dear? Of course, you must have, for the carriage was there to take me up at just the right time yesterday, and here we are arrived an hour ahead of schedule, which was what made me think I should come to Carling first, as there was sufficient time for a little detour and I am not in the least fatigued after such a comfortable journey—this lovely coach all to myself, only fancy. Will you not invite me to step inside, Sabina dear?"

"Oh, goodness. Please—do come in, Edina. I don't know what I am thinking. Would you care for a cup of tea?"

Edina sailed gaily into the house, past the bemused footman, who had been on the point of departing for Bromleigh Hall himself on being given leave to do so by Lady Sabina before Miss Bromley's sudden descent. Instead he was now holding the door open as Edina and her luggage were carried in.

Sabina's erstwhile companion, it transpired, preferred ratafia to tea, and sherry to either, but as Sabina had not yet thought to stock the manor with spirits, Edina was forced to take tea, which she did with good humor but with the tacit understanding that she was making an exception to her usual practice.

"Why, you have done wonders with the house," she exclaimed, after taking herself on a whirlwind tour of the lower floor, teacup in hand. Sabina, glancing at the clock whenever she passed one, followed in her wake, her mind spinning in an attempt to keep up with her while worrying about what she would say to explain Edina when Robert arrived. She must get rid of her before four o'clock!

"I can see that you are not nearly finished," Edina was saying, "but now that I am here to assist you, the work will go so much faster. I must tell you, I am accounted a fair hand at interior decoration, but I do not only design, I am perfectly happy to perform the physical aspects of the work as well. Tell me, how many bedrooms have you, Sabina, and how many are ready for occupation?"

Sabina had quickly comprehended that the secret to her cousin's conversational skill was that she obligingly ended every oration with a question which she did not immediately answer herself, thereby giving those whom she addressed an opportunity to contribute their share of the exchange.

"I'm afraid there are only two bedrooms partially ready, Edina. I would be happy to show you to yours, but I fear you would not yet be comfortable there. Would you mind very much going to Bromleigh Hall after all and waiting for me there? I have no doubt that Alicia will be eager to welcome you, and—and we will meet at dinner, I daresay, after you have had a rest."

Edina waved her teacup merrily. "Dear me, no. I must tell you, Sabina dear, that unlike most wayfarers, travel invigorates me rather than the opposite, and I am perfectly willing to begin the duties of my employment today—instantly, if you like. In any case, the coachman has already returned to the Hall, I believe. Is this the library?"

She sailed into the room which, by the numbers of cartons of books scattered about the floor, she guessed rightly to be the library. Sabina stayed outside the door for a moment and sank back against the wall, closing her eyes, to compose herself and try to think what to do.

Where was Robert? What was she to do with Edina? Was the footman still about? Should she send a message to the Abbey? What if it passed Robert on the way?

She smiled wryly to herself. She was already picking up Edina's habit of composing questions for others to answer.

Just at that moment, she heard voices from below and, abandoning her visitor to her own devices, fled down the stairs, not daring to hope it was Robert already. She ran outside—only to see Henry pull his horses to a stop at her door. Dulcie sat on the perch beside him, looking very fetching in a white muslin day dress, but with an anxious expression on her face.

"Oh, Henry, not you now!"

Her brother got down from his curricle, looking very cool and much the country gentleman in his breeches and

Belcher handkerchief, handed the ribbons to his groom, and assisted his wife down. Then he approached his sister.

"Sabina, whatever is happening? The coachman has just reported leaving Edina off here. Why did she not come to the Hall first?"

Sabina took his arm to pull him toward the door. "Henry, dearest, I have no idea what possessed her to come here. Perhaps the journey fatigued her more than she realizes. Why do you not go inside and persuade her to go home with you—at once."

Behind Henry, Sabina saw Dulcie shake her head vigorously and, sensing that she had something important to say, Sabina pulled her brother into the house before he could protest. There Dulcie held back while Henry was taken into the parlor and left to be subjected to Edina's profuse exclamations of delight at seeing him.

As soon as Edina had drawn the bemused Henry into her voluble orbit, Sabina slipped back out into the hall, closing the door behind her and turning to her sister-in-law.

"Sabina," Dulcie spoke in an urgent whisper, "one of the maids noticed this morning that the miniature was missing, and fortunately came to me to report it. I did not know what you wanted me to say, so I insisted that Henry bring me along when he came here."

Sabina sighed and leaned back against the closed parlor door. "I suppose there is no need to conceal that I took it, and why. Unfortunately, my gesture achieved an unexpected result—it appears that the Ashtons' matching miniature has disappeared."

"Do you mean, there actually was another one?" Dulcie exclaimed.

"I suspected that was just a ploy, and I am still not sure it was not, but in any case, Lady Kimborough has as good as accused me of theft."

"But that's absurd!"

"It is, if only because I was in her company or the earl's the entire time I was at the Abbey, but she is nonetheless convinced that the Bromleys had something to do with it."

Now it was Dulcie who sighed. "Oh, dear. What next?"

Unfortunately, this remark appeared to be prophetic in a way neither lady expected. They agreed to discuss the matter properly after persuading Edina to accept Henry's escort to Bromleigh Hall so that she might be welcomed by the rest of the family and take dinner with them. They then repaired to the parlor to rescue Henry from Edina's effusiveness.

He looked both relieved to see them and exasperated at them for leaving him alone with his cousin. But after his wife and sister had exercised their considerable social skills to draw Edina's attention to themselves and Henry was able to sit back and draw breath for a few moments, it was not long before he was joining in their pleas for Edina to go with him to the Hall and even spend the night there before settling in properly at the Manor.

Indeed, Edina had scarcely departed to collect her overnight necessities when the sound of yet another carriage was heard from the drive. Sabina sat up, her head turned to the window, and whispered, "Robert!" Fortunately, only Dulcie heard her and gave her a quizzical look before rising to follow Henry into the hall to see who the new arrival might be.

A groom in Ashton livery stood on the threshold.

"The earl and countess wish to speak to Lady Sabina," this worthy announced. "Is she at home?"

Henry planted his feet in the doorway and crossed his arms, as if prepared to defend the castle from invaders. Sabina edged past him before he could say anything, however, and told the groom, "Please tell Lord and Lady Kimborough that I shall be pleased to receive them."

"Sabina, what is all this about?" Henry demanded. "Did you know they were coming?"

Dulcie interrupted to assure her husband that the visit was a complete surprise, but after their previous efforts at hospitality, they could scarcely now refuse to see the Ashtons, who were at that moment approaching the house. Richard removed his hat and bowed to the ladies; Henry returned the bow and raised Lady Kimborough's hand in a brief salute.

"It is good to see you again so soon, ma'am," he said, reverting to his normally courteous manner. Lady Kimborough did not unbend appreciably, but she did essay a tight smile. To Sabina, she said nothing. Sabina realized that she did not intend to speak until she must, so she led them both into the house where she hoped she might deign to do so— and met Edina descending the stairs.

"What is going on, Sabina dear?" asked Edina, reversing her normal style of conversation. "I was just admiring the wallpaper above the wainscoting in the library," she said. Apparently the question was rhetorical after all. "I see it is new and I daresay your doing. I cannot tell you how I look forward to assisting you—"

"Edina," Sabina dared to interrupt, "we have visitors whom you must meet."

The introductions were made, and Edina was apparently suitably enough impressed by Lady Kimborough to assure the countess that she was receiving the proper deference, and the party gathered in the by now somewhat crowded parlor. In the absence of servants, Edina offered to obtain some refreshment. She went off in the direction of the kitchen and could be heard talking to herself until she was out of earshot.

After a few moments of silence, Lord Kimborough announced, "My wife has something she wishes to say to you, Lady Sabina."

All eyes turned toward the countess, who looked as if she had hoped this meeting would be somewhat less widely publicized, but she went determinedly ahead with what soon revealed itself as a rehearsed speech, apparently insisted upon by her husband.

"That is correct," she said, meeting neither Sabina's nor anyone else's eyes. "I wish to apologize to you, Lady Sabina, for my rudeness earlier today. I realize that you could not possibly have had anything to do with the disappearance of our miniature, and it was unjust of me to accuse you. I hope—I trust you will forgive me."

Sabina found that she had been holding her breath again, but when it became obvious that for Lady Kimborough, this apology was a great concession, she let it go, smiled, and said, "Of course I do, Lady Kimborough. Please forget this incident, as I shall. And please, let us call on each other— as neighbors—more frequently in future."

The countess met her eyes finally and nodded. "Thank you, Sabina dear. I hope we may do so."

Henry felt it safe to inject a question at this point. "I beg your pardon, but do I understand you to mean that the *other* miniature has gone missing?"

Richard spoke up on his wife's behalf, thanking Sabina for bring the Bromleys' half of the set to the Abbey— which he realized, somewhat belatedly, was news to Henry, but both gentlemen glossed over their ignorance of facts that appeared to be plain to all the ladies.

"This prompted my wife to compare the two pieces," Richard went on, "but when she went to the cabinet in which ours was kept, it was missing. She was naturally distressed, and in her agitation, made remarks which she now regrets. But I beg your pardon, Lavinia, for putting words into your mouth. Is that what you wished to say?"

"Yes, thank you, Richard."

"Well, that is wonderful," Dulcie put in brightly. "I mean, it is a shame that the other miniature cannot be located, but if we put our heads together, perhaps we can organize a search, or simply ask among the servants—which I'm sure you will do at once, Lady Kimborough. I daresay someone simply took it away to clean or some such thing."

"It was some such thing," said a voice from the doorway.

Sabina, who had jumped up at every approach of a carriage in the hope that it meant Robert had returned, had entirely missed the sounds of the latest arrival at her doorstep. She rose quickly, but managed not to run into his arms when he shook his head slightly, then gave her a quick, reassuring smile.

"Robin!" his brother exclaimed. "Do you know something about this? Where have you been?"

Robert came fully into the room and took up a position before the fireplace as if he were prepared to address the gathering. All heads turned as one toward him, but he said nothing for a moment as he surveyed the assembled friends and relations. His eye lit on Edina.

"I believe we have not met, ma'am."

"Oh, I'm so sorry," Sabina exclaimed, stepping forward to perform the introductions. "Edina, this is my—my friend, Captain Ashton, Lord Kimborough's brother. Robert, I should like to present my cousin, Mrs. William Bromley, who has—ah, come to live with me here at Carling as my companion."

Robert not unnaturally raised his eyebrows at this piece of news, and Sabina attempted to convey with a look that such plans had yet to be altered. He smiled wryly and seemed to understand without words.

"I'm pleased to meet you, Mrs. Bromley," he said warmly, instantly enchanting Edina, who would have become immediately profusive had Robert not gone on. "I hope I may see you often at Carling in the future. For the moment, however, I fear we have a pressing matter to address, which I propose to do at once, since we are among friends." He glanced at his sister-in-law and added, "So to speak.

"I gathered from what I heard on my arrival that the miniature which resided in the Abbey's collection is thought to have disappeared. I assure you, it has not."

With that, he withdrew a small case from his pocket and opened it to display the miniature portrait of a young man in Elizabethan garb. Lavinia let out a gasp and rose to take the object from Robert, but he held it out of her reach.

"One moment, Lavinia, if you please.

"I spoke with Lord Bromleigh about the miniature which we all saw in the collection at the Hall the other day, and I was convinced by the documentation he showed me and by his personal recollections that the mysterious 'Lady S' does indeed belong to the Bromleys. However, he had no knowledge of a matching portrait.

"I therefore took the portrait in our collection to the dealer who had most recently appraised the Bromleys' piece. Fortunately, this gentleman, whose shop is in Leicester, later, out of personal curiosity only, researched the provenance of the miniature of 'Lady S' and discovered that there had been a matching portrait, also by Nicholas Hilliard, the well-known Elizabethan court artist, of the lady's husband. His—that is, the dealer's—intention was to seek out the second portrait and offer it to Lord Bromley. He had been unsuccessful until I presented the piece to him. He confirmed that it was the missing portrait, although he had not yet made the connection between the last known owner, at the time of William and Mary, and its present whereabouts.

"He also confirmed," Robert added for the countess's benefit, "that the miniature of 'Lady S' was legitimately purchased by the present Lord Bromleigh's great-grandfather and that it therefore belongs to the Bromleys."

"Not anymore," the earl said sardonically.

Robert looked at him. "I appear to have missed that part of the discussion. Would you care to explain, Richard?"

His brother explained that Lady Sabina had called on them that very morning to make them a gift of the miniature, at which revelation Robert looked admiringly at Sabina, who blushed and lowered her eyes. He then, to make his admiration perfectly clear, took her hand to kiss and leaned over to whisper in her ear, "That's my darling." Sabina blushed more deeply.

A general murmur of discussion broke out among the assembled Bromleys and Ashtons, but Robert stilled it long enough to say one more thing.

"In view of Sabina's generous gesture, I think the only thing I can do with this charming portrait"—he held it up to study it fondly—"is to present it to the Bromleys. Lady Henry, would you be so kind . . ."

Dulcie accepted the miniature, but before she could voice her thanks, Lavinia protested, "But that will break up the set!"

Robert smiled in Sabina's direction and said mildly, "I think not."

The countess sank back in her chair with a dismayed cry, sending Edina scurrying for restoratives, which were in lamentably short supply at the Manor. There being no hartshorn or sal volatile, she spent a fruitless ten minutes searching for a feather she could burn under Lady Kimborough's nose, by which time that lady had revived and was again insisting that the portrait of the gentleman belonged at the Abbey.

Henry interjected his opinion, saying that both miniatures should be kept in a neutral place, where members of both families could enjoy them whenever they wished. This naturally provoked a heated discussion about what places might qualify for this honor, which led to the suggestion that the portraits might reside in one house for six months each year and the other for the remainder of the year, which led in turn to a disagreement as to who should have the honor of providing a home for them first.

It was at this juncture that Robert, aware that he and Sabina had been forgotten in the general uproar, pulled her into the hall and drew her into an embrace that quickly eased her mind and warmed her body. When his lips parted from hers, she sighed and laid her head on his shoulder.

"Poor Miranda," he said. "You must have had the devil of a day."

She had to laugh. "Why is it that the family I once thought so eager to be rid of me is now so determined never to let me escape them?" she asked of his laughing eyes. "It's too absurd! One would think they had planned all this deliberately!"

"Personally," he said, "I know exactly where the two miniatures should reside."

"I did think of that as soon as Henry made the suggestion," she said, "but how could I say anything?"

"I expect we can convince them of the wisdom of displaying them prominently somewhere in this house when we return. By that time they should have exhausted their discussion of the alternatives. This is a lovely place, by the way. I should have asked you long before this to show me around."

"I can do so now, if you wish."

"I certainly do *not* wish. Do you realize, my darling, that had we known all this about the two portraits to begin with, we should have been married for years by now?"

She smiled. "It does seem a waste, doesn't it?"

"Well, I for one do not wish to waste any more time. Where is your luggage?"

She was puzzled for a moment. "What luggage?"

"The things you were going to pack to take on your honeymoon, my sweet simpleton."

"Oh!" She laughed at her own idiocy. "They are—oh, dear, my mind is in such a muddle, I can't think—oh, yes, in the hall outside my bedroom."

"Which is where?"

"The second door to the right at the top of the stairs—the back stairs."

He grinned. "Good girl. I'll send Foster up to collect it while I get my carriage. Ah—I don't suppose you could change quickly into something a little more—cheerful?"

She looked down at the black bombazine, which she had almost forgotten, and grimaced. "I can certainly do better than this, even without Emily. I will meet you in five minutes."

As good as her word—if slightly disheveled from tearing off one dress and throwing another on with a minimum of closed fastenings—she descended to the hall again and heard that the level of voices in the parlor had scarcely abated. She had just reached the door when Dulcie came out into the hall and saw her.

"Sabina! Where are you going?"

Sabina signaled her to close the parlor door, then whispered, "There is a letter for you in your jewelry box, Dulcie. Please don't say anything to anyone until you read it, I beg you."

Robert opened the front door just then, and understanding dawned in Dulcie's eyes.

"Sabina!" she whispered delightedly. "You're eloping!"

Robert laughed, kissed her on the cheek, and said, "Don't you dare try to stop us, Dulcie—you did it long before we thought of it."

Dulcie smiled and conceded the point. "Well, don't just stand there, you two. Hurry!"

Wasting no more time, they hastened out of the house. Robert helped Sabina up into his light traveling carriage, then mounted the perch and took up the reins.

Before he set the horses in motion, however, he turned to her. "Do you have everything, Miranda?"

She smiled and snuggled more closely beside him. She did not care if she had nothing left to call her own—except him.

"Everything in the world!" she assured him.